Also by Camille Mariani
Lucille's Lie
Aletha's Will
Pandora's Hope
Links To Death
Prelude To Murder
Invitation To Die
Astrid's Place
Abram's Puzzle
Aura Of Peril

JUSTICE, RIGHT or WRONG

FOURTH IN THE ASTRID AND ABRAM SERIES

CAMILLE MARIANI

iUniverse LLC
Bloomington

JUSTICE, RIGHT OR WRONG

iUniverse books may be ordered through booksellers or by contacting:

iUniverse LLC
1663 Liberty Drive
Bloomington, IN 47403
www.iuniverse.com
1-800-Authors (1-800-288-4677)

ISBN: 978-1-4917-3241-0 (sc)
ISBN: 978-1-4917-3242-7 (e)

Printed in the United States of America.

iUniverse rev. date: 04/21/2014

DEDICATION

To Albert Mariani, my constant companion, my true friend, and my inspiration since our union in 2004. It couldn't be better, my love.

* * * *

ACKNOWLEDGMENTS

I wish to thank friends who have been supportive beyond measure since my arrival in Florida. In particular, Carolyn and Walter Wight; and Joan and Jim Weening.

To all my friends, old and new, I wish good health, happiness, and long life.

There is no such thing as justice--in or out of court.

Clarence Darrow

PROLOGUE

Wednesday, February 7, 1990

Should anyone ask, Judge Randolph Rutherford could recite countless names of offenders that he sentenced during his years on the New York bench. Over his desk hung a plaque marked simply **Justice.** He believed in justice, believed that criminals deserved maximum sentences, and he favored the death penalty. At the same time, he was aware that attorneys referred to him as the hanging judge, an epithet taken from the annals of 19th century Judge Isaac Parker. No amount of criticism shook his self-confidence, ever.

Yet one case alone did change his life, if not his heart. It was the case he could not bury along with dark secrets and dealings when he left the city 15 years ago.

In leaving New York, the judge sought anonymity, which he thought he could find in Fairchance, Maine, where he could teach law part-time at the local college. His wife Winona preferred volunteer work at the pre-school Day Care Center over the heartaches of her former Social Services work in New York. And their adopted daughter Holly, an above average student throughout her school years, now excelled in property sales work.

This morning the judge looked at the calendar and recalled 20 years ago when prison doors shut behind the man he never wanted to see again, Holly's biological father. Even if he had been paroled for good behavior, there was no reason to believe that he would come here. Randolph had tried to cover all the bases to keep their lives private. No one could possibly guess that the judge and his wife would move to a small city in the heart of Maine, where they cut all previous ties. They were safe here, or so he thought when he chose to call Fairchance home.

"Do you plan on going out today?"

The question barely penetrated the shroud of memories twisting about his brain.

"What? What did you say?"

Taking a pan of muffins from the oven, Winona gave him her disgusted look for not listening.

"I said, are you planning to go out today?"

"Oh," he said. "I hadn't thought about it. Why? Did you want me to take you somewhere?"

"Of course not. If I want to go somewhere, I'll drive myself." She put a hot muffin on a plate for him and poured coffee. "I'm going to spend some time at the sewing machine so's to get Holly's gown finished. If you're going out, I'd like to know."

"No, I'm not going out. If I decide to, I'll let you know."

"I can't hear a thing in that back room when I'm sewing. I should move to the front spare room where I can hear. Then I can see the street from the window, too. Out back is like a tomb."

"When you want me to start moving things, just say so."

She knew how to plead with a longing look and squeaky voice. A pout usually helped, too. But today, he wouldn't notice if she stood on her head.

"I wouldn't move to that front room without having it painted first. It's drab, that old green paint. I'd like to have it brightened up. Maybe a light rose or pale yellow would make a cheerful sewing room. What do you think?"

"That would be nice."

"And a white loveseat."

"Mmm. Fine."

He laid the newspaper on the table and picked up the muffin. He hadn't read a word of news, his thoughts were so occupied by that one case, the one that he vowed to put behind him 20 years ago.

"You seem distracted this morning," she said. "Anything wrong?"

"No. Nothing."

Nothing wrong except a sudden wash of worry. He still remembered the man's emotional outburst as guards led him from the courtroom, "You're sending an innocent man to prison. You'll pay for this, Judge Rutherford."

The fierce timbre of his voice unnerved Randolph. The killer was capable of anything, the prosecutor had said in court. Anything.

Here at the kitchen table, that moment of vulnerability flooded over him again, and he remembered the sudden doubt that crossed his mind, a first in his long career of handing down judgments. Randolph looked from side-to-side, in an involuntary search for possible danger, though he knew he was safe in his own home, off the beaten path in Maine.

"Why did you put on that stained shirt this morning? Look at that. A big spot right in front. What did you spill on it, anyway? I told you I would bleach it."

He looked down at the spot--a mere speck of tomato sauce. Of course, it did show up more on this white shirt than it would have on a dark color.

"I like this shirt."

Stop nagging me, woman. He would never say it out loud, but of late he'd become conscious of her constant harping.

He jumped at the sound of the front doorbell.

"My goodness, Randy. It's just the doorbell."

"You expecting anyone?" he said.

"No, but I'll go if you want."

"No. I'll get it."

Fighting apprehension, he told himself on the way to the front door that he needed to get out of the house. He hadn't been out in a week, and languishing like this must be the reason for disturbing memories. If he didn't shake himself out of it, he might become depressed, and he never allowed himself to do that.

At the door, he hesitated, tried to peer through the frosted glass, could make out only a shadow. The instant he opened the door, he attempted to shut it in reaction to the cannon-like gun pointing at him. The one who held it pushed in, and kicked the door shut. Randolph forgot to breathe. His heart stopped, jump-started, and he stumbled toward the sofa to steady himself. He knew guns well enough to recognize a silencer.

"What are *you* doing here?"

His voice should have been strong and commanding like in the old days, not raspy and weak.

"What should have been done long ago."

Randolph thought of lunging for control of the gun, but age and arthritis had slowed him too much.

"There's no need for violence here," Randolph said.

In a gesture of friendship, he took two steps toward the intruder, and held out his right hand, the one that had dropped the gavel on an infinite number of judgments. It was ignored.

"You can't escape justice forever, Judge. This is your judgment day."

"Now...now...don't get hasty."

Randolph's hand remained out there, turned upward, quivering. "Let's talk this out."

"You have something to say in your defense for sending a life to hell?"

"There was nothing I could do."

"Then there's no more to be said except guilty!"

The gun barrel rose. The shot felt like a blow to his chest. Randolph toppled to the floor, helpless. *I'm going to die,* he thought. He looked up and saw Winona at the archway, a domestic vision in blue coverall apron. Backlit by the morning sun, her white hair looked transparent. He opened his mouth to warn her but had no voice.

"What's going on?" she asked. "Oh my God. Randolph!"

Winona hurried toward her husband. A step away she, too, wilted.

Only a whisper disturbed the deadly silence that fell over the scene: "Justice, Judge Rutherford, right or wrong."

CHAPTER 1

Holly explained each of the purchase offer pages in detail until Astrid wanted to sweep them all into the wastebasket and say, "Enough, dammit. Just give us a bill of sale, and let us go." However, as impatient as she felt, she knew that, in an attempt to close legal loopholes, the law had gone way beyond a handshake in property sales to the point of being ridiculous. When they signed and initialed the last page, she got to her feet, ready to leave.

"Finally," she said. "When do you think we'll hear from the Wilsons?"

"I'll fax the papers today," Holly said. "They'll get them back to me immediately, so you should know if they agree to everything in about a week, I believe. Shall I call you at *The Bugle* office, Astrid?"

"Either there or at home, any time of day or night. I'm anxious to actually have the deed."

"I sort of thought that."

Holly had become such a good friend in the months Astrid had been in Fairchance that she invited her to the wedding a month ago. The transaction today was the third they had negotiated since Astrid arrived in the city including the Sears home she bought, the Wilsons' home that she and Abram were renting, and now the purchase offer to buy that same house.

While they were signing papers at the round table, a computer technician worked at Holly's desk to set up a new computer system. Astrid noticed that he appeared to study Holly for seconds at a time. At last, he broke his silence.

"All done, Miss Rutherford. Oh, sorry. Didn't mean to interrupt."

"It's okay, Chris. Please wait. I'll try it when my clients leave, but I'll need help, you know," she said with a laugh.

"No doubt. Glad to help."

Turning to Astrid, Holly said, "This is Chris Benning. He just installed a new computer, and now I have to learn the new program. It's all a big mystery to me."

"Nice to meet you, Chris. I'm Astrid Lincoln and this is my husband, Abram."

"Abram Lincoln. An honest name if ever I heard one."

Astrid appreciated his sense of humor, though Abram merely smiled. Chris appeared to be in his early 50s, wore dark gray cotton coordinates with the company's logo, Chip's Computers, on the back of the shirt. Even though the weather remained cold every day with snow at least once a week, Astrid thought that being inside in winter didn't make a person so pale or hair almost colorless like this man's.

Holly knew everyone in town and called them by their first names. Although Astrid had been in the electronics store, she'd never seen this Chris before. Must be a new man on the job. Then she remembered that there was a branch store in Greenboro. He could be from there.

At the door, Holly held out her hand to congratulate Astrid and Abram just as the phone rang at her desk. She hurried back to answer it and though Chris stood aside and motioned for her to sit, she remained on her feet.

While she talked, Abram pulled Astrid close to whisper in her ear.

"I have to go to the college now. I'll get lunch in the cafeteria. I guess I'm done here anyway."

"You'll be working tonight, right?"

"Yeah. I'll be late, so don't wait up for me."

"You know I will."

After a quick kiss, he buttoned his coat and made a hasty retreat to his truck. Watching him, Astrid felt her throat tighten. If it hadn't been for Sheriff Larry Knight he might not be enrolled this semester at Fairchance College. It was a hard grind, classes in the afternoon and working as dispatcher for the sheriff at night. But they had so much to be thankful for. She was still alive, they had agreed to buy their rented home rather than build a new one, and Abram was beginning studies in anticipation of becoming a sheriff's deputy.

She tried not to think that barely three weeks had passed since General Metcalf attempted to assassinate Maine's governor when he came to Fairchance during a speaking tour of the state. If Catherine Cotter had not taken the fake gun out of her bag and confronted the crazed terrorist, there was no telling how many he would have killed in that senseless rampage. The governor would surely be dead. She shuddered when she thought how she bent over poor Cat, then looked up at the weapon, certain that it was her final moment on planet Earth. She nearly collapsed when he didn't shoot her. That crazy man, the so-called General Metcalf, said, "Not you, not you," and in the extra couple of seconds he took to lower the gun, law officers fired round after round. It was a sickening experience. She wouldn't be here now except that Metcalf admired her, much to her secret embarrassment after he said as much to her.

Astrid still felt relief and happiness that life returned to normal with only an occasional mention of the tragedy, in part due to the disappearance of all the militia at The Kingdom, scattered to parts as yet unknown now that the deluded general was dead. And who in town wasn't glad to have television crews cleared out of Fairchance finally? Assignments at *The Bugle* were once again routine, sometimes bordering on dull, and on those days when all was quiet, she looked out her office window down Main Street, watched townspeople shopping, hustling to work, chatting with friends, just as she was doing now at the real estate office. Quiet was good, for a while.

The phone clicked, and Astrid turned around to speak to Holly and saw that she appeared to have turned into a helpless rag doll. She stumbled to her chair and dropped into it as if she'd lost all body muscle. Her sudden paleness contrasted to the green gabardine suit she wore. Holly always looked like a richly dressed mannequin in a store window, except that she was probably no more than five-two.

"Holly. What's wrong?"

"I can't …" She tried to stand, flopped back into her chair.

"Holly! Are you sick? What can I do? Water?"

Holly nodded.

Astrid looked at Chris, "Get water. Over there," and pointed to the cooler.

"Right."

He was at Holly's side quickly. He held out a hand after she took the cup, as if he would touch her shoulder. Instead, he stepped to the side and watched.

"Drink slowly," Astrid said.

"What happened?" Chris asked.

When she put down the cup, Holly looked first at Chris and then at Astrid. She tried to wipe away the persistent flow of tears.

At last, her voice shaking so badly that she was barely able to say the words, "My parents. They've been shot."

Astrid hoped she heard wrong. It couldn't be another shooting. And not Holly's family. Dear God, not her parents.

"Shot?"

Holly nodded.

"Tell me they're not dead."

"They are," she said in a whimper. "Dead."

"When did it happen? Are you sure? Who called?"

"Chief Raleigh. He said Mr. Jones, the neighbor across the street, saw a rusty old car drive away and noticed the front door to our house was wide open. He went over … and … and found both of them in the living room, on the floor."

She choked up again. Her sobs wrenched her whole body. She bent over the desk to hold her head in both hands.

"I'll help you, Holly. Don't worry. I'll help you get through this."

Astrid asked herself how she expected to do that. How could she help Holly? Anything she might think to do would be done by law enforcement officers. But maybe a sympathetic voice would give her some bit of hope.

"Thank you, Astrid."

Chris ran his fingers through his thick hair. He swayed from side-to-side apparently fighting a strong emotion that Astrid interpreted as desperation. She jumped when he took her arm in a powerful grip.

"Is there anything I can do?" he asked.

"I'm not sure."

She was with two pitiful people, a grief-stricken woman and a helpless, but deeply concerned, man. She placed her hand on Holly's back and rubbed gently.

"Right now, I need to--well, I don't know," Holly said. "I just don't know what I need to do. My boss will be in soon. She's out showing property. I can't leave now. But I can't remember what he said. He told me something about what I should do. I don't know."

"Who said?"

"Chief Raleigh."

Astrid picked up the telephone and dialed the police station, all the while focused on Holly to be sure she didn't faint or get sick.

"I'll find out. Don't worry," she said. "May I speak with Chief Raleigh," she said when an officer answered.

"He's busy right now."

"This is Astrid Lincoln. He knows me. I'm calling for Holly Rutherford. Her parents have been shot to death. She needs more information."

"Just a minute. I think I hear him talking in the hall. Yes. Here he comes."

Astrid heard them speak, and the chief came on line.

"Astrid? This is Jake. You're with Miss Rutherford?"

"Ya. She's so shaken up that she can't remember what you told her she needs to do. I'm calling to find out."

"Stay with her if you can. This is the worst shock of her life. It won't be easy for her to cope. Well, she needs to see the funeral director. That's Kinsley's Mortuary. You know it?"

"Ya. I know where it is."

"He'll give her specifics about the autopsies…you know, that's necessary in murder cases…and her options for services, burial, newspaper notices, and the like. In the meantime she shouldn't return to the house. It's a crime scene. And there's a lot of blood in the living room."

"I understand. She can stay with me."

"Good."

"Any idea who did this?" Astrid asked.

"Not yet. Sheriff Knight has a couple names of known offenders, but nothing definite. Don't quote me on that. Call him if you want to."

"Ya. Okay. Mr. Rutherford had been a judge, right?"

"That's right." The answer came from Holly.

"I heard," the chief said. "Yes. He was on the bench in New York, I understand, but he wasn't a judge here. He taught a class or two at the college. But Holly can give you those answers."

"Uh, huh. Did you know him at all?"

"No. I've heard that he was a bear in the classroom. One of his students came to work for us here and said he even marked papers on penmanship."

Astrid looked at Holly.

"I'll talk with you another time, Chief. Thanks for your help. Oh, did you talk with Charlie yet? Has he been out to get pictures?"

"Sheriff Knight called the newspaper first thing, and Charlie went to the house. We waited an hour before calling Holly, just to do the usual clearing away of the bodies and looking for any apparent clues. I guess we'll be seeing the TV trucks roll in again. Just when we thought we were rid of them. We're getting great PR for our community, I must say."

"Oh ya. Great. Maybe we could burn the town down. That might make it even better."

She heard the chuckle.

"I'll be here tomorrow morning, in case you need anything more."

"Ya. That works for me."

While she was talking, a woman of considerable girth, came through the door, beaming. Astrid heard only part of what she said, "…a sale, I think." When she noticed Holly's face, she stood square-footed in front of her, displaying no compassion, not moving toward Holly.

"Now what's wrong?" she asked.

Astrid finished her phone call and stood beside Holly in a protective gesture.

"What's your name?" Astrid said.

"I'm Letitia Udall, owner of this business. And who are you?"

"Astrid Lincoln. Holly needs to leave. She just received word that her parents have been shot to death."

"Good God, why didn't you say so? That Jew got him after all, did he?"

"No," Holly said. "He wouldn't."

"Well, it wouldn't surprise me. Anyway, you go. I'll hold the fort."

She turned to Chris.

"Are you with her?" she asked.

"No. I installed the new computer. I'll come back later sometime, when she can work again."

"You do that. All right. You need anything, Holly?"

"No. Astrid will take care of things. I'll call you when I know more. The papers on the desk need to be faxed to the Wilsons, you know. Will you do that, Letitia?"

"Don't worry. I'll take care of it."

Astrid steadied Holly through the door and to her own Jeep.

"I'll take you to the funeral home. I can call my office from there while you talk. And you can stay at my house for a while. We have plenty of room, as you know."

"Thanks, but I'd rather stay with my friend, Ginny. We're like sisters and her parents are like my own parents."

Astrid nodded. "It's best to be with someone close at a time like this."

She brooded over who had been so bold as to do this thing in broad daylight. Holly had never spoken of her parents, but if they were like her, they must have been good people. What possible motive would anyone have to murder them? She'd like to help capture the killer or killers. Obviously police wouldn't know if only one shooter was involved or if there were two or more. Forensics would likely be able to determine that. And why was the front door left open? Maybe the killer wanted the bodies to be found quickly. Maybe he didn't want Holly to go home after work and find them. Would a killer be that considerate? Was this cold-blooded murder an act of revenge or maybe simple hatred?

One thing could not be denied. General Metcalf had nothing to do with it, even though it smacked of his style. That was a strange thought. She should be over his death, but she couldn't deny that he continued to haunt her. His off-the-wall political views and Messiah Complex not only got him killed, but infiltrated the minds of others, as well. If he could have carried out his plans, he would have reigned over a large contingent of malcontents, incited revolution among small and large home-grown militias. Worst thought of all, as he envisioned, he might have pronounced himself another Hitler. All it would take was someone as delusional as he was to carry out such an agenda. Even planting seeds of revolution in a single mind could inspire a destructive robot as crazy as himself to bomb and kill.

Astrid shook her head, told herself to stop imagining the worst. Right here and now she was faced with trying to console Holly.

No one should have to get this kind of news.

CHAPTER 2

Sitting in his Chevy wagon, Chris watched as Astrid drove away with Holly. He was heartbroken for her, but couldn't honestly say he was sorry for the judge. The wife probably didn't deserve to die. He never met her, but he knew all about the judge. Prisoners could get any information they wanted about anyone, especially about lawyers and judges.

He drove away from the Fair Hills Realty parking lot having decided to end his work day and return to the Greenboro office. He had no heart for more work today. He'd call his next customers and tell them to contact the Fairchance office if they needed immediate help. He was ready to go home.

By chance, the Fairchance home office manager called needing help to install the new computer Holly Rutherford wanted at the real estate agency. When Chris heard the name, he said he would take care of it immediately.

Chris considered himself lucky to have had the opportunity to get instruction in computer science. He took to it readily and by reading all that he could find on the subject, he sharpened his skill to be competitive on the outside. He wondered if Judge Rutherford knew that some of those he condemned as worthless in society struggled on the inside to take a responsible position when they got out.

But now the question was who killed the judge? He mulled that question over and over, but he couldn't think of anyone, never heard of any plan to take revenge on the judge in the form of murder. Oh there were enough who said that they'd like to have five minutes alone with him, but that was all bluff and bluster. If anyone had just cause, it was himself. But he gave up his anger and lived for the day he could meet his grown-up daughter. He wouldn't barge into her life, wouldn't even tell her that he was her real dad. He just wanted to meet her; and today he did. She looked so much like her mother, a real beauty. His heart about broke to see her in all that pain. There was nothing he could do then, and nothing now. If he could, he'd find the killer and see that he paid for the murders.

"Not much chance of that," he mumbled.

At the office, he went to the manager behind the glass divider.

"What's up, Chris? Everything go all right in Fairchance?"

"Not exactly, Jerry. I need to take a day or two off. I'll call my customers and tell them."

"I'll do that. Just leave your book. Take all the time you need. You sick? Customer get upset?"

"No. Neither. Personal stuff. Watch the six o'clock news tonight. You'll see how my day went."

From downtown Greenboro, it took 15 minutes to drive to The Kingdom. He barely realized that he'd turned onto the bumpy road to the campground until he felt the hard jolt of tires hitting a pot hole.

"Damn. Hope I didn't break anything."

He parked in the guest spot when he arrived at the village. Living here was a temporary arrangement. He expected to find a permanent address by the weekend to give to his parole officer.

Released from prison the same day he was, Drew had asked where he was going, and Chris didn't really know. But having learned that Judge Rutherford moved his family to Fairchance, Maine, Chris thought he'd go there just to get a look at his daughter. He wouldn't bother the family.

Once he faced the fact that he himself tore his family apart with his drug dealing and drinking, he overcame his self-pity and depression, and gave up thoughts of settling the score with the judge. Learning computer skills almost certainly would lead to independence without lawless endeavors ever again, he had thought. He would make sure of it. But there were times when the loss of his wife and child, as well as years of incarceration, got to him. He couldn't overlook the emptiness in his gut, the desire for a female companion and family. At those times he could almost do what was done today to the judge.

No. I couldn't do that. I'm no killer.

Those words brought him back to reality. He was no killer. That alone should inflame his anger over being sent up for a crime he didn't commit. He didn't kill Luann. All the rest, though, was right. He was high when the police came. He was covered in his wife's blood. He had marijuana in his pocket.

He tried to tell the court that he'd been in a deep sleep in the bedroom when a noise woke him up. At first he didn't know what it was until he heard it again--a gunshot. Groggy, he stumbled to the kitchen and found his wife, shot, bleeding profusely. Not thinking of anything except that he needed to find out if she was alive, he leaned over to feel her neck pulse but fell onto her body, accounting for the blood on his clothing. His reaction was slow because he was too out of it and too stunned at first to know what he should do. His failure to call police immediately was a big strike against him. The evidence, presented forcefully by the district attorney, convinced the jury of his guilt. And the judge had no sympathy. He sentenced Chris to serve 20 to life.

Now the judge and his wife were dead. Chris felt the heartbreak that overwhelmed Holly, the daughter he held when she was a sweet, funny, cuddly toddler. He'd had the same heartbreak when he lost his beautiful wife and then the only ray of joy in his life afterward, his child.

After Chris gave up parental rights, Holly was adopted by the Rutherfords, called them Dad and Mom, no doubt. The irony of the murders was the similarity to his own tragic loss by an intruder.

Exactly the same.

"Hey, Chris. You okay?"

Drew had driven in behind Chris, walked over to the car, and tapped on the window. Chris opened the door.

"It's a long story. Let's get to the house and start a fire. Get your brother to come over and I'll tell you both together. You won't believe this."

Drew's brother, Lester Godfrey, had invited the two of them to come to The Kingdom and stay in one of the six empty duplexes. He said the owners might show up any time, so they shouldn't get too settled in.

Chris turned the thermostat up and started a blaze in the fireplace as soon as he entered the living room. The temperature seldom got above 20 degrees these days, and Chris always felt cold. He went to the kitchen and brought out two bottles of beer for his friends and a Coke for himself. Having gotten out of the habit of drinking, he didn't want to start again.

The brothers arrived, tossed their coats on the sofa and, like Chris, chose to sit in front of the fire.

Chris shook all over again just thinking of the panic he felt when Holly became almost hysterical.

"I don't think TV has had time yet to get it on the air, but there was a double homicide in Fairchance today. A man and his wife."

"Good God, Chris," Drew said. "In that small city?"

Drew had applied for work in one of the law firms there, and had previously commented that he wondered how the attorneys in three law offices managed to keep busy in a city of about 7,000.

"The victims were Judge Rutherford and his wife."

"You're kidding," Drew said. A slow smile crossed his face. "So he got what was coming to him."

Les remained silent, stared into the blazing flames, and gulped his beer.

"I don't know that he deserved to be killed. His wife certainly didn't," Chris said. "The one who's suffering is the daughter."

"*Your* daughter."

Chris stood up, ready for a fight if need be.

"That's for us to know, just the three of us, and no one else. Keep it that way. Okay?"

"Sure," Les said. "Why would we tell anyone? But you can't tell me that you don't feel damned smug about it. Huh? He took 20 years of your life away from you."

"You can look at it that way. You could say he gave me 20 years to get it together, and to live, for that matter. I might have died just like Luann did, in a pool of blood. I guess I'll never know who killed her or why. That's the worst I live with daily. Someone got away with murder. I hope whoever killed the Rutherfords doesn't get away with it."

"Probably will," Les said.

Chris eyed him with suspicion. Unlike his brother, Les was handsome with a self-assured, slick presence. His bland expression gave away no emotion. Prisoners often had that cold approach, and could as easily kill as eat a meal. Though he had been found guilty of murder, Drew never displayed a vicious temper as long as

Chris knew him. In his view, Les was the more likely candidate for prison. But he wasn't the only one in this compound who appeared untrustworthy.

There was something fishy about this place. Drew said the men and their wives built it from ground up and that it would be a special retirement place for all of them. Yet they met in secret, making sure he didn't attend. They had daily rifle practice, but didn't invite him. He had seen seditious and anti-Semitic reading material on tables in the library.

When Drew applied to work at one of the law offices, Chris thought he had the job at first. But when the brothers visited a couple of evenings later, Drew said he wouldn't be working at that office. Chris asked why not, got no answer from Drew, but Les was quick to explain.

"My brother's not about to work for a Jew."

His words felt like a slap in the face to Chris. Drew walked away, obviously not in agreement with the decision his brother made for him.

While Chris recalled that episode, he observed the brothers and once again was struck by the difference between them. He would have thought that Les, the wealthier one, was older, but he was younger. Chris had never heard how Les came by his money. His clothes, his BMW, his home furnishings all were top dollar.

They had been quiet for about five minutes, until Drew asked, "Will you tell her now, Chris? Will you let her know that she has a dad?"

He'd been so distracted, deep in thought about the brothers and what was going on here, that the words didn't register at first.

"Huh? Oh. No. She's had enough of a shock. I don't know. Maybe I'll go somewhere else after I'm sure she's okay."

Drew nodded. "I understand. Can't blame you."

"I'm going home now," Les said without preamble. That was his way--brief, detached, disinterested.

"Sure," Chris said. "See you later."

Drew watched his brother leave, and stood to go himself, hesitated.

"You have any idea who killed the judge, Chris?" he asked.

"Not a clue. He retired years ago, and I can't believe he would make enemies here like he did in New York. He wasn't on the bench any more."

"Maybe it was someone who'd served time. We found Fairchance. Maybe someone else did, too."

"Maybe."

Chris glanced at the fire sparking in a sudden burst of fury. He wanted answers to other things, too. In the past, he'd always hesitated to ask, but he was going for it today.

"Tell me something, Drew. What is this place? Something's going on. What is everyone doing here that's so secret? Except for you and Les, no one talks with me. I see men walking down the street with their guns, and I hear shooting in the woods. What's all the practice for?"

Drew sat down again and beckoned for Chris to do the same.

"I'm not supposed to talk about it to you but you and I shared a lot of tales in the big house. I guess you should know as much as I do."

He bowed his head and took off his glasses, rubbed his eyes with a knuckle. He pulled a handkerchief from a pocket and wiped the glasses before putting them back on. Obviously he was measuring how much to say, just like he used to in prison when he wanted to tell about his childhood or his marriage.

"Remember Watson, the guy who rattled on about how he was going to blow up the White House some day when he got out?"

"Yeah. I remember. A real kook."

"That's what we all thought. He was nutty as a fruit cake. He got in a fight with someone in the yard one day when that guy called him crazy. Nearly killed him. Remember? Well, maybe he wasn't as crazy as we all thought. Everyone here has about the same goal."

"No! They want to blow up the White House?"

"Not that in particular, but something big. This is a home-grown militia compound, associated with the underground Patriot movement around the country. You ever heard of it?"

"Can't say I have."

"They're mostly hate groups, white supremacists. Les has told me a few things about them. This one is unusual since everyone has dough, not like most of the militia types that are often made up of poor guys and women who blame big government for all their problems. But don't ever say they're rich here. They claim to be just common citizens who want to make the American way of life better, mainly by disrupting or destroying Washington politics. They had a leader who was killed just a few weeks ago right in Fairchance. General Metcalf. He called himself general, but he was dishonorably discharged from the Army, Les said. He just had a lot of money and a lot of hate, so he created his own reality. Said he would start a national revolution."

Chris looked at the fire again. A mini explosion sent a large, live spark to the carpet. He kicked it back.

"It's unbelievable. I don't think I want to stay here after what you're telling me. I served time, and I don't want anything to go wrong again. How about you? You plan to stay here?"

"Naw." Drew tugged at the small mustache he'd nurtured. "I'm going someplace else as soon as I can get a job. I may go back to Fairchance and try again for a spot in an attorney's office. I'm not sure Les would leave me alone, though. I could go southward. Maybe Portland or Boston, some place where I can start again,

17

just like you're doing. I passed my law exam and I'm qualified to practice. I think I like corporate law best. That doesn't go over big with Les."

He got to his feet, and Chris did the same, walking to the door with him.

"I'll go back to Fairchance tomorrow morning and find a rent," Chris said. "But I want to thank you for giving me housing when we came here. You're a good friend. You know, I'd think twice before cowing to your brother's demands. If you want to work for one of the Fairchance lawyers, go for it. Les isn't your keeper."

"I'll think it over," Drew said.

Alone, Chris mulled over the events of the day, the strange way Les said, "Probably will," to the observation that someone could escape capture just as they did when they murdered his wife. Did he actually know something in particular about the murder, or was he just making an attempt to act smarter than everyone else?

To think anything more sinister than that would be appalling. After all, Lester was Drew's brother. Brothers could be different from each other, but Chris hoped these two weren't so far apart. However, the militia and plans for widespread destruction were terrifying. Putting distance between this place and himself suited him just fine. His hope was that Drew would get over that submissive attitude. He didn't seem like that in prison. What was it with Les? How come he could call the shots and Drew felt helpless? Maybe Drew just felt intimidated by being out on his own. Maybe his brother was a crutch, so to speak, someone he knew he could go to for help. That would explain why he didn't want to go against his wishes.

Whatever it is, I have myself to think about right now. I'm not going to stay here and possibly be arrested for something these weirdoes do.

CHAPTER 3

A strid called *The Bugle* office from a side room while she waited
for Holly to talk with the funeral director in his office. Now
that Charlie Hart was editor, Astrid asked for him, though she
really wanted to talk with Dee. He was a capable editor, and Dee
seemed perfectly happy in the publisher's position. But Astrid
missed her. They had a special rapport that she had not experienced
before, even more so than with her own brother. As she waited,
Astrid thought about what drew her to Dee--that common sense
approach to life found in persons who had experienced much
harshness and overcome great obstacles.

"You've talked with Chief Raleigh?" she said when Charlie
came on the line.

"Right. He gave me what he could, and I took Will with me
to the house for photos. You have anything new to add?"

"No. Lots of TV vans are showing up here, so the six o'clock
news will have another lead story about Fairchance, I'm afraid.
Poor Holly is just about coping, but it's so hard for her, of course.
I'll stay with her until she's settled at her friend's house. She'll need
some protection from the vultures out there."

"It's a terrible shock for anyone," Charlie said. "I hate to ask
for a picture of her, but…"

"I'll get one, don't worry. We have a few days. Before the weekend I'll take a photo or get one from her. Have you talked with Sheriff Knight?"

"I had to leave a message, and he hasn't called back. Maybe you could drop in there after you get Holly settled."

"Ya. I'll do that. I expect he's still at the crime scene. You know Larry. He's meticulous. Anything else?"

"That's it for now."

Astrid called Abram next.

"You've heard?" she asked.

"Everyone was talking about it when I came to work. You must have still been with Holly when she got the news."

"I was. I'm with her now at the funeral home. I'll take her to her friend's house, and then I'll go see Larry."

"Be careful, Astrid. Remember, there's a killer abroad."

"Oh Abram! He's not after me."

"For a change, you mean?"

She gave him the raspberry and hung up just as Holly appeared at the door.

"I'm done here," Holly said. "Why don't you take me back to the office and I'll get my own car. I'm calmer now."

"No. You can get your car tomorrow. See those TV reporters and all the cameras out there? They'll follow you, and you won't be able to get away from them. I'll drive around to the side door. I doubt that they'll follow me. I'll pick you up and get you to Ginny's. What's her last name?"

"Siller. Her parents are Nigel and Eleanor Siller. They live in the Maple Ridge development. Do you know it?"

"No."

"I'll show you."

"Just wait at this entrance."

Astrid told the funeral director not to let anyone in when she went out and he agreed. No one paid attention to her outside. She walked slowly as if in mourning, got in her Jeep and drove with caution around the building to the other side, where Holly waited. Astrid looked back in her mirror as they moved calmly along the street without anyone's notice.

"Ha. Fooled them."

Astrid had not seen the Maple Ridge development here in the northeast corner of Fairchance before. Set among maple trees, the houses were built on a gentle hillside of white birch trees with a scattering of firs. Each house had a front porch, high pitched roof, and attached garage. The homes were all white, individual tastes apparent in trim colors--predominantly red, black, and green. Like all places with altitude around Fairchance, each house obviously was built to take advantage of a lake view.

"This is a lovely neighborhood," she said. "I had no idea it was here. I don't get to this east side of the city very much."

"It was finished five years ago," Holly said. "Peaceful. I'll move here some day."

Ya, Astrid thought, *find the most peaceful place you can. You'll need it.*

"It's not all houses." Holly's tone was flat. "There's a small shopping plaza where people can buy some food, have a pizza, get their hair done. Probably the best music store in Fairchance is here, too."

Astrid slowed the Jeep, waiting for instruction where she should drive.

When Holly realized this, she said, "Oh, two streets over and turn right."

On Blue Jay Street, Holly pointed to a white house with black trim.

"There. I'll just pop out. They're expecting me."

"You called ahead?"

Holly nodded. "At the funeral home. Ginny came home. She works at the beauty salon in the plaza. That's her car."

She indicated the copper tone Volkswagen in front of the garage doors.

"Sure you don't want me to come in with you?"

"No. It's okay now."

"Holly. Listen to me. If you need me any time, day or night, just call. Here's my card with both office and home numbers. Call me. I mean it."

"Thanks. I will. I'll let you know when your papers are back."

She wiped tears from her eyes and squared her shoulders as she walked toward the house, and the front door opened. By the greeting and hugs she got from the three who came out, Astrid knew she was in safe hands, and drove away. But she didn't go directly out of the development. She toured the various streets to get a good look at all of it. She determined that this was a community designed for the upper middle class. She saw no old cars, no driveways unplowed, no garbage cans outside the garages. Though snow had not melted a great deal yet, making it hard to see everything, three seasons must be gorgeous here, with well manicured lawns, ample flowering gardens, and the beautiful maple trees. Finally, she was back on the entrance/exit road, and she drove the three miles to town thinklng of those she might interview, those who could shed some light on why the couple was murdered, execution style.

Execution style.

Could it be? Was the judge targeted by some gang for execution? Incredible thought. No one could say that Fairchance hadn't had its share of unusual crimes of late, but an execution style shooting? The more she thought about it, the more she felt the urge to find out. Sheriff Larry Knight would be the likely one to discuss it with her, either he or Sheriff's Detective Green.

Other than General Metcalf with his militia group, now gone from Greenboro as far as she knew, there had never been a local gang here. That's why she needed to find out if she was right or wrong in that judgment. Maybe there was a young gang, maybe college kids, who hated the judge for his strictness in class. She never saw that much hatred among students, although she had seen some that were furious with a professor. But to be so horribly callous as to shoot two in cold blood was unthinkable ... except that she was thinking it.

"That can't be what happened. This is something bigger than a disgruntled school kid. Has to be."

The logical person to ask about the judge was Holly, and that was out of the question for now. The poor girl could hardly keep her balance walking to Ginny's house. She had wept intermittently ever since the news, trying to compose herself, but losing the struggle each time she remembered her loss.

Astrid now approached Court Street, where she turned and drove to the Sheriff's Office parking lot. If the sheriff wasn't back yet, she'd go to the Rutherford house, talk with him and with some of the neighbors, and later talk with Holly when she was ready. The Fairchance College president would be another good source of information.

What are you thinking? You're not an officer. It's not your place to solve crime. Let the authorities do their job and keep out of it.

She knew what Abram would say to her, "Keep your nose out of it, Astrid. All you'll succeed in doing is making a mess of things."

He was right, too. *Pay attention to him, dammit.*

Before she went to the sheriff's door, she stopped at the dispatch office to see Abram. He said, "Hi," and as soon as he was free, "How's Holly?"

"All broken up. I left her with her friend. Apparently they're like sisters. She's lucky to have someone to turn to. I don't know if she has any other family."

"I'd like to chat, dear, but as you can see, I'm real busy. I heard Larry talking in the hallway, so he's back now."

Before saying, "See you later," she gave her husband a warm kiss, then ran down the hallway and found Larry's door closed. She knocked. No surprise, Police Chief Raleigh opened it.

"Astrid," he said, hesitating before opening the door wide.

"Come in, Astrid," Larry called. "You might as well sit in on this meeting. I'll tell you what we know so far."

"Good. I hope you can tell me you've found the killer."

"Not yet. Wish we could."

"You can't tell me yet because you don't know, or because you just don't want to release it?"

The lawmen exchanged glances. She understood--the press, always pushing for more than you have.

"We don't know," the chief said. "As far as we can find out at this early stage, the judge had no enemies. He was well liked in town, and respected at the college. And you may quote me on that."

Two others were with the lawmen, Sheriff's Detective Paul Green, and a police officer she had not met.

Before sitting down, Astrid went to the two and shook hands, stopping at the one she didn't know.

"Hi," she said, "I'm Astrid Lincoln. Don't think we've met."

"Glad to meet you, Astrid. I'm Police Sergeant Lewis Lenfest."

She nodded, went back to the one empty chair, and sat next to Detective Green.

After Larry revealed that there were no fingerprints, no footprints, and no other clues to go by in the Rutherford house, he explained the contacts each one needed to make ... friends of

24

the family, neighbors, college professors that he associated with, church friends, and his barber.

"Barbers are notorious for their knowledge about everyone who comes to them for haircuts. Maybe Rutherford dropped something of interest to his."

"Just like hairdressers," Astrid said. "I can do that, Larry. If you want me to I'll see Mrs. Rutherford's hairdresser."

The frown and pained look Larry gave her said volumes. If he didn't want her suggestions, he could have saved himself embarrassment by not inviting her to sit in on the discussion. Naturally she thought she was included in the investigation to a certain extent.

"I'm not going to deputize you, Astrid." All he needed to add in that tone was, 'Are you an idiot?'

Damn.

"Well, you won't mind if I do some digging for my story, will you?"

"Just as long as you share with us anything that you find pertinent to solving the murders. I don't want to read in next week's story a vital piece of evidence that you've unearthed."

He tamped a pencil on the desk, like a teacher telling a pupil that the next time he goofed off he'd be expelled.

"And how will I know what you have and don't have?"

His voice lowered. "If you have a question, call me."

She studied his tight lips, his intense blue eyes, moving jaw. This anger gave her an uneasy feeling that more was going on than just a bit of pique over her getting involved with the case. She nearly blurted that he should tell her if she'd done something wrong. However, that wouldn't help.

"Sure," she said.

They'd never had a problem before when she got involved. But then, previous involvement could be the reason for his coolness now, considering all the situations. Still, she had actually helped in each of those cases. For now, it would be best to ignore what appeared to be a reprimand.

"I don't have any background on the family," she said. "Do you know how long they've lived here?"

"Not sure. His adopted daughter went through the schools here, so maybe 20 years. Don't quote me."

"Adopted? I didn't know that." Astrid was genuinely surprised.

"They never tried to hide it. My sister runs a consignment shop and takes unsold clothing over for the Baptist Church sale. She heard Mrs. Rutherford say they adopted Holly when she was a toddler."

"Is that The Top Shelf consignment shop?"

"You know it?"

"I shop there some."

She almost added her intention of going to talk with his sister, but given his attitude today, she held her tongue.

"I see."

He did seem distracted as well as upset. This wasn't like Larry Knight. She had worked with him enough now to know that even in the worst situations he remained level-headed and calm.

"Okay. Now, any suggestions from any of you?" Larry said.

They talked about tracing the ammo. That should give them the make of weapon used and from there they could find the seller. With any luck it could lead to the killer. At this point, they agreed that it appeared to be only one killer. Astrid barely listened to all of this. She was thinking of words that Holly whispered just after taking that dreadful phone call, "It couldn't be him." Now that she thought about it, Astrid had to believe that Holly suspected someone. Odd that she didn't mention it to the police, presuming that she didn't.

"Are you planning to interview Holly?" she asked.

"We will do that. I thought it wise to let her have a night to get over the initial shock," Larry said.

Astrid had thought the same thing. Now she decided she would need to wait and let the lawmen do their thing first.

CHAPTER 4

Given the limits she now felt by the sheriff's warning to back off, Astrid did little interviewing other than for the sidebar to Charlie's lead story for page one. She focused on the Rutherford family in the community, their college and church volunteer work, and Holly's local education. As she talked with individuals, she made discreet allusions to whether they could think of possible reasons for the attack, but came up empty-handed. No one could cite even a minor dispute that the couple engaged in with anyone.

"Something wrong, Astrid?" Charlie said. He laid his heavy glasses on the desk and rubbed the narrow pinched area across his nose.

She jerked to attention, unaware that she'd been idle for five minutes while her mind turned over everything she'd seen and heard today.

"Aside from the murder of my friend's parents, you mean? I guess it's Larry Knight. First he invites me to sit in on his meeting, then he acts like I shouldn't poke in where I don't belong."

"And that bothers you?" Charlie could be snide.

"Ya. That bothers me."

"What bothers you? Isn't he always lofty?"

"No. Well, maybe."

She had noticed a more stand-offish way about him with some of his officers lately. Almost certainly it was brought on by the death of Police Chief Nolan, his good friend and often fellow investigator.

"He never has been that way with me. He was cooperative about getting Abram into the classes this semester. But, since General Metcalf's attack, he seems somehow different toward me. I wonder …"

Charlie's eyebrows rose as high as they could go.

"What? You wonder what?"

"Oh nothing. Just thinking out loud. It's nothing."

She started typing furiously, to keep from answering any more questions. Yes, she wondered if Larry saw the general's hesitation that Sunday, the way he lowered the gun instead of shooting her after felling Cat Cotter. Maybe he even heard what the general said. Could he possibly think she had something going with that crazy man? Damn. She hoped that wasn't what he thought.

When she had almost finished the sidebar, Astrid looked over at Will, wearing his usual well-kept but shabby wool trousers, pullover turtle neck sweater, and shoes with cracked leather uppers. He worked on a basketball story now after finishing captions for photos he'd taken today. He wasn't directly involved in news gathering for this murder story. Astrid knew how it was to be new on the job and to want to be part of the current scene. One thing she liked about Will--he didn't complain. Nothing had stirred his outward emotion since she'd known him.

"What I think we have here is the murder of two saints," she said. Realizing the callousness of that statement, she added, "It appears that I'm not joking. People say they were well-liked by everyone in the community."

Charlie pushed away from the computer. He leaned back in his chair, stretched and moved his head in circles to limber the neck. It had been a long, hard day for him, going from one place to another for interviews.

"You're right, Astrid," he said. "I found the same thing. Folks thought they were both upright citizens, the last people in the world to be murdered in their home."

Since coming to *The Bugle* last month, Charlie had proved to be a sharp editor. When Dee said she was hiring him and that he was moving here from Twin Ports, Astrid was skeptical, especially when she first met him. He wore good enough sports outfits, but unlike Will, always looked like he'd just showered, threw on clothing, and left the house without combing his collar-length graying hair. But she soon learned that he was every bit as capable in the chief editor's chair as Dee was.

"I'd say they had a 99 percent approval rating," Will said.

Astrid laughed for the first time today.

"You spent too many hours covering the last election, Will."

"I can't dispute that."

"So you like political stuff?" she said.

"You bet. Maybe I'll run for a state office one day when I'm a little older and know the ropes better. I figure if I don't like the way things are run I should jump in and help run them better."

"Commendable," Charlie said. "It takes a lot of money to run for office, to say nothing of elephant skin and skillful use of buzz words."

Will didn't reply.

"You don't like the way things are run in Augusta, Will?" Astrid couldn't resist asking.

"If I thought that was a serious question, I'd do my half hour monolog on *What's Wrong in the Legislature*. But I know it's not, so I'll reserve my soap box spin for another time."

"Thanks ever so."

Aside from the occasional story required for a political event, Astrid had no love for politics nor for the lies some politicians told.

It was soon time to go home for the night, but Astrid felt like talking with Dee, who was a calming influence for her after a particularly stressful day. This day qualified. She put away notes and pens, aligned the thesaurus and dictionary on her desk, and was ready to leave. Almost at the door, she heard her telephone ring and returned, muttering, "Now what."

On answering she heard a whimper, as if the caller were crying.

"Is someone there?" she said.

"Yes, Astrid. It's me. Holly. Sorry. I can't seem to stop this crying."

"It's all right. Do you want something?"

"Yes. I need you to do something for me. Can we talk? Will you pick me up? I still don't have my car. You could drive me over to the agency, and I'll tell you what I need. I can drive myself back now."

"Are you sure? You still sound rocky."

"I'm sure. Besides, what I'm going to ask you is important--to me, anyway--and I want to talk in private."

"Of course. I was just leaving the office. I'll be right over."

· · · ·

On the route to pick her up, Astrid thought of Holly's reaction after the call about the murders, when she folded into the chair unable to speak. It heightened Astrid's own sadness. She remembered how hollow she felt when she thought Abram had perished in the explosion at her home. To cope with death was never easy, but so much more devastating to lose a loved one suddenly in a violent act for no apparent reason. Yet there must be a reason. Someone hated her parents enough to shoot them. Plain to see that. The more she thought about it, the more she thought that maybe the sheriff's short temper was merely due to the pressure of the murder and nothing to do with her. Abram would say, 'Don't internalize everything.' He was right. It wasn't about her, and just maybe it was something she shouldn't be concerned about.

Holly out the door as soon as Astrid turned the corner. She climbed into the Jeep, snapped the seat belt into place and laid her head back on the leather seat.

"Thank you, Astrid," she said with her eyes closed. "You said you would help me if I needed it."

"Of course. What can I do?"

"I just hate to ask you to do something so--well, sneaky, really."

"Sneaky?"

"I don't know how to say this. My goodness. I've been going with Danny for a year."

Astrid waited. She didn't know Danny and had no idea how he was relevant, unless Holly wanted him to be notified and didn't feel that she could do it herself.

"Yes? So what …?"

"Oh dear. I hate to say this. But I think he may be the killer, Astrid. The man I want to marry, and I think he may have killed my parents."

That started a fresh flow of sobs. She took a Kleenex from her bag, wiped her eyes, blew her nose, and sighed.

"Danny and my parents didn't exactly like each other. My dad thought he wasn't good enough for me. He is, Astrid. He's a wonderful person, but you have to get to know him. He's sweet, caring. But they objected to his background."

"And that's why your dad didn't like him?"

"Partly. He'd like, or rather he wanted, me to marry a doctor, or an attorney, or even a college professor. In other words, someone with position in society."

"What does he do? Danny."

"He works with animals at the SPCA. He's still studying at Fairchance College in animal science. He loves animals."

"I see. That sounds good and responsible to me. He may become a vet himself. Odd your father didn't approve."

"That's not all. His parents live on a farm."

"I lived on a farm," Astrid said. "Nothing wrong with that."

"Yeah, but look at you. You have a fortune from it, don't you?"

"I inherited money from my grandfather because of his agricultural enterprise, ya."

Astrid had stopped the Jeep at the agency parking lot, next to Holly's Buick. It was too cold to turn off the ignition while they talked.

"So your parents thought Danny was beneath your station in life. Did they actually object to a marriage because his parents are farmers?"

"Yes, vehemently. But not because of that. Danny's father runs a metal and auto graveyard. In other words, a junk yard. That's mostly what my dad objected to."

"Oh, I see. Police will probably ask you about that, you know."

Holly turned her face away. "I know. That's why I need you."

"What do you think I can do?"

Astrid dreaded to hear the answer. It could only lead to an involvement that she'd rather not have.

CHAPTER 5

She was right. Driving home after leaving Holly, Astrid envisioned a black hole of poison snakes just waiting for her to fall in. "Damn, damn, damn." This was trouble no matter how she tried to think otherwise. Holly wanted her to find out if Danny killed her parents.

"Don't let the police know you're investigating," Holly had said. "Don't tell anyone."

As she thought about it, Astrid went on arguing with conscience.

"How can I do all that, I'd like to know," Astrid said, outstretching her hand as if talking with someone sitting on the hood of the Jeep. "You tell me, how can I do that?"

Then why did you say you would? Her conscience replied.

"Because I couldn't say no to her. She needs my help, that's why."

Conscience kicked in again: She may need help, but sometimes it's better to be honest up front than take a plunge you know will end in disaster. If the sheriff learns you're asking questions of a most probable suspect, he'll have you shot at dawn. If Abram finds out, he'll blow his top. If anyone at the newspaper gets wind of it, they'll be all over you for not telling them.

"Dammit all to hell."

Just when she thought her life was calming down, that she was once again peaceful, not having nightmares about being shot, suddenly here she was up to her ears in another shooting. Worse yet, she agreed to investigate for Holly. It was impossible. Not doable. Way out of her realm.

But she had promised.

"If you aren't the idiot of the day--no, the year--I'd like to know who is."

She stopped at the supermarket, walked up and down the aisles in a daze.

"Hey, Astrid. Where are you?"

"Huh? Oh, Beth. I didn't notice you. I guess I *am* in a daze, all right."

"Something wrong?"

Astrid had heard that Beth had her own perilous experience before marrying Larry Knight. Of all people, she'd probably be the one who could relate to this problem. But it was tricky. If she confided in anyone, she had to know just how well they could keep it secret.

"It appears that I'm in a bit of hot water, Beth."

"I won't pry, but if you want to tell me, I'm a good listener."

In one of those moments of desperation when any twig on the ocean looks like a lifeboat, Astrid decided to take a chance.

"You don't have Howie with you?"

"No. He's with every mother's dream baby sitter, his aunt. She loves caring for him, and he adores her. I get away without being noticed."

"And is this close to your supper time?"

"Not tonight. Because of the double murder today, Larry's working late. We probably won't eat until eight or so tonight. I never can wait that long, so I grab a half sandwich when I'm hungry."

Perfect.

"How about having a sandwich with me at my house. It's not far, and I do need someone to talk to. Would you mind?"

"Of course not, Astrid. One good thing about this time of year, I don't have to worry about frozen foods thawing in the car."

"Not in this weather, especially. I wonder if it will ever warm up."

They agreed Beth would follow her. They arrived at a well cooled down house, so Astrid set the den thermostat higher and went to the kitchen to make sandwiches and coffee. Beth joined her.

"Anything I can do to help?" she said.

"No, thanks. I'll just make ham and cheese sandwiches and you can help me take it to the den. For now, sit and talk to me. I wonder if Larry has discussed the murders with you at all?"

"So far he hasn't."

"Well, as you likely know the judge and his wife were the parents of Holly Rutherford, the real estate agent."

"Yes, I know her. A real fine person."

"Ya. We're in the process of buying this house through her. The owners are in Florida, just back from China."

"Really? I thought you probably had inherited the property. It's absolutely lovely. Beautiful house, sweeping view. Boy, you lucked out getting this."

"We did. I love it here, though I own property in town. You know, my house was blown up a few months ago by an intruder."

"I remember. What a terrible thing. Why did he do that."

"He was creepy crazy. It's a long story."

"Never mind then. So you own the property. What will you do with it?"

"Coffee's ready."

Astrid turned off the coffee pot, set the sandwiches on a small tray for Beth to take, and carried another tray with cups and coffee pot into the den.

"I was going to have a new house built," she said, "but in the meantime, we rented this even though we knew it was on the market. We needed someplace to live, and Holly showed us this. We liked it. As we talked about it, we finally decided we wanted to stay here. Haven't really decided about the land. I have a couple of acres, right in town near the hospital."

"I'm sure you'd have no difficulty selling the land." Beth bit into her sandwich. "Mmm. This ham is very good. Not too salty. Where do you get it?"

"At Angelo's Deli on Cross Street."

"I'll have to go there. Anyway," Beth said, "what's on your mind?"

Astrid liked the ease with which Beth approached life. She never appeared to be hurried, especially not when she talked. She spoke softly. Even now with her mouth full of sandwich, she made no pretense of chewing delicately in a sophisticated manner, just let her cheek puff out and talked around the food as she chewed. She looked as if she'd be at home in a woodcutter's camp, heating up coffee in a tin pot over a woodstove. In some ways, she reminded Astrid of Dee, only a much taller version, with less sadness beneath the surface.

"I made a promise today that bothers me, in a way," Astrid said. "I promised Holly Rutherford that I would investigate her boyfriend to see if I could determine whether he had something to do with her parents' deaths."

"Seems like a good enough thing to do," Beth said.

"But it isn't, you see. And the reason is your husband."

"My husband! Larry? Why?"

"Because just today he advised me to butt out, in so many words. He doesn't want me to investigate. I offered to go to the beauty parlor and inquire about Mrs. Rutherford…you know, like the barber, the beautician hears a lot from her regular clients. I thought I could do that and give Larry whatever I might hear. But he said that he wasn't going to deputize me. I was a bit set back. So that's my problem. If I do some snooping and find out something, I might be crossing paths with Larry and then he'd lower the boom on me."

Beth looked dumbfounded, and suddenly burst into laughter.

"Did I say something funny?" Astrid asked. Her ears began to feel hot.

"I'm not laughing at you, just at the notion that my husband would lower the boom on you. I see him in a completely different way than you do, I guess. I assure you, he's not going to get too tough with you. He has been out of sorts since Chief Nolan died. They were like brothers, knew each other for many years. It was a hard blow to lose him."

"Ah. I see. So you think it's safe for me to find what I can."

"Oh sure. Go for it."

"Does he ever talk with you about his investigations?"

"Not unless I ask. In fact, if I find out anything, I'll let you know. And we won't have to say anything about it to him or anyone else. Okay?"

Astrid felt sheepish having put forth something that Beth saw as an asinine concern, but on the other hand she was relieved that Larry would likely not handcuff her and put her in a cell should she get involved.

"Okay. Thanks, Beth. I knew it was a good idea to talk with you."

"Any time. I like to be with someone for an adult talk. My days are mostly filled with baby gibberish these days. It's fun, but not too stimulating."

Later, after seeing Beth off, Astrid returned to the den, cleaned up the lunch remains, and waited for Abram to come home. If he weren't working as well as going to classes, she would get him to help with her sleuthing, but as it was, she would be on her own, and it seemed best not to tell him about it. No need to cause him worry at this time.

. . . .

WEDNESDAY 5 P.M.

Chris finished packing his few clothes, locked the case, and looked around the house to be sure he hadn't forgotten anything. He would be glad to settle into a different environment after learning as much as he had about this militia mentality. What scared him was that they intended to pull everything down around American citizens by revolution if necessary. They seemed not to have the slightest concern that men, women, and children would die if they carried out the plan. He understood prisoners who had a one-time anger so strong that they killed. But indifference to causing untold suffering was beyond comprehension. He would not live among these crazies. He'd been around enough of them in prison.

He was fortunate enough to get both a job and an apartment in Fairchance in this one day. It was almost unbelievable.

Chris had simply walked in and asked Chip, owner of the business, if he could use him. They talked a while, Chip called the Greenboro office for a recommendation, and the next thing Chris knew, he was in.

"We need someone like you with advanced computer skills," Chip said. "I sent one of our workers off to school this past fall, but he's slow, and he won't be ready for months."

"Does it mean that I would be replaced when he comes back?" Chris asked.

"No, no. The more expertise, the better. This is a growing field. What's out there today is just the tip of the iceberg."

"I couldn't agree more," Chris said.

From then on it was all a cake walk, and he left the store feeling like a kid on his first job. They already knew about his ability. Good fortune shone on him back when he first applied for the advertised opening in Greenboro. The store manager asked only about his training, how much he knew about the growing field of computer technology, nothing more. Chris outlined what he could do, and since it was more than any of the local help knew, he got the job. Had his prison record been revealed, Chris didn't know if he would have been hired. Now to be taken on so easily in Fairchance was a real bonus.

He was equally fortunate at the home of Mrs. Oswald. He rang the front doorbell, told her he needed a small apartment since he was moving to Fairchance to work for Chip's Computers.

"Come in," Mrs. Oswald said. She had a ready smile, white hair loosely curled. She moved with some difficulty, shifting her weight from side to side.

"My son went to school with Chip. I know him well. So you're his new man, are you? Did he send you here?"

Chris was not a liar, but he needed a place to stay, and he knew that he would have Chip's blessing if he asked. He was tempted.

"I'd like to say he did, Mrs. Oswald, but honestly I saw your ad in the newspaper."

Apparently his honesty impressed her, and she asked no more questions, but told him it was two rooms and small bath. She expected the rent the first day of the month, she allowed no smoking or drinking in the house, and expected her tenants to turn TV and music low after 10 so that no one would be disturbed.

"Sounds like a good deal to me," Chris said. "I have no problem with rules."

The rules were better than any he'd had in prison, he could add.

"What about parking?" he asked as they walked up the one flight to the second floor.

"Oh, yes. I have a large garage in the back. I'll show you. There's plenty of room for one more car, if it ain't too big. You don't have a Cadillac, do you?"

"Hardly."

They shared a laugh, as she unlocked the two-room suite. Not only was it suitable, it was impressive, with a small iron woodstove, bay window on front, leather sofa and matching recliner, TV, a student desk. The dark hardwood floor glistened.

"This is lovely. No bed?" he asked.

Again, Mrs. Oswald laughed in her high-pitched way, and pointed to a plain wall with a slender bookcase.

"Just watch," she said, sliding two casual chairs aside. She reached inside the bookcase and pulled a lever. A double bed, all made up, lowered slowly.

"A Murphy bed," Chris said. "I've never seen one before, but I've heard about them. That's cool."

"I thought you'd like it. So now come see the kitchen."

Appliances weren't modern, but they were clean, counters held necessities including toaster. At the single window was a yellow and white check curtain. Chris went to it in order to see what he would look at during meals, and was not disappointed when he saw a large snow-covered back yard, a clothesline on one side of the yard. He was looking over a roof, and presumed that was the garage.

"And in here is the bathroom. It's small, but has all you need."

He moved to the doorway and peeked in. Like the kitchen, it showed age, but everything was clean and white.

"Very nice, Mrs. Oswald. I'm satisfied, if you are with me."

"Oh," she said. "It will be a pleasure to have a responsible young man here again."

He didn't ask what that meant, but was happy she didn't inquire into his "responsible" background. He never would have seen that Murphy bed come out of the wall had she asked for references.

Now he decided there was nothing of his left in the duplex rooms he was about to vacate. He was ready to go to the parking lot for his car. At the knock on his door, he set his case down and answered it.

"Drew. Come in. I was just about to leave."

His friend wore an uncharacteristically broad grin, showing two gold-capped front teeth.

"You look happy," Chris said. "What's up?"

"I'm leaving today, too."

"Good for you. Where are you going?"

"To Fairchance. Despite what Les said, I'm taking that job in the attorneys' office. I didn't say anything before because I didn't want a fight with my brother, but you know I can't be choosy about where I work. I don't have a good resume, as you know, and the fact that they would even consider me is a miracle. I told Mr. Bertram about my record and how I studied law for 19 years in prison. He just nodded, asked me what I'd do about things like wills and deeds, and the next thing I knew he offered me the job. That's what I'll be handling mostly--deeds and wills."

"Terrific. Have you found a place to live?"

"I found a one-room efficiency on the south side of town. I think the landlord houses mostly students, but I don't much care, as long as I can sleep at night. How about you? Got a place yet? He may have another efficiency."

"I got a small apartment in the heart of town. Nice older lady. Looks pretty good. The rooms, I mean."

"I guess we're all set, then," Drew said with a chuckle. "Though it might have been even nicer if the landlady looked pretty good. I'm packed and ready to go."

"What about your brother?"

"He's on the practice range. Now's a good time for me to take off. I left him a note."

Chris wondered how Les would take that, but didn't comment. It was Drew's business, and more power to him if he took the job he wanted.

They shook hands, and both left. For Chris, despite his daughter's sadness today, just being nearby would mean that he was bound to see her from time to time. It was a good feeling.

CHAPTER 6

After Beth left, Astrid checked her watch and decided there was time to make a list of people to see, anyone who would have known the murdered couple. With any luck at all she would come across something that law officers missed. No doubt, they'd ask Danny questions, and if it had been someone other than Holly who asked for her help, she wouldn't have agreed to find out what she could about him. She shouldn't even be thinking about it. But she had promised. So, getting to it, she headed the list with Danny's name, and stopped with pen poised. She didn't know his last name. She picked up the phone and called Holly.

"It's Astrid," she said to Holly's hello.

"Thank you for calling, Astrid. I have something to tell you."

"All right, but before that please tell me Danny's last name."

"It's Gerber."

"Gerber. Isn't that ..."

"A Jewish name, yes."

"I was going to say a baby products name."

"Oh, yes, that too."

"Where does he attend church?"

"There's a synagogue in Portland. He doesn't attend regularly."

"Does that mean you will convert if you marry?"

"Probably. I thought I would, once. But that isn't why he…I mean, it's no reason for…I guess that's why I want to be sure. You know?"

"I do now. Ya."

"It's so horrible," Holly said. "What I wanted to tell you is that I got a call from Police Chief Raleigh late this afternoon. He wants me to have a body guard, 24 hours a day. I told him that was silly. I don't need anyone to guard me."

"Don't be too hasty. They don't know who the murderer is, or whether he intends to wipe out the entire family."

Oh, damn. Why did I say that? Poor girl will be scared to death now.

"I just don't believe that, Astrid. I think it was someone who knew Dad and for some reason hated him. I don't see myself in the picture. I mean he could have come to the agency and shot me if he wanted to."

And that would have been about the time Abram and I were there.

"Were there many who hated your dad?"

"I don't know. I heard him on the phone not too long ago, and he sounded very angry. I remember he said, 'You can't blame me for that.' That's all I heard, because when he saw that I had come into the room, he hung up. He never said a word about it to me."

"I'd still pay attention to the police," Astrid said.

"But that would mean that someone would be there at the agency with me. It would be embarrassing to have a policeman with me when I'm showing property. Worst of all, he'd be in this house all night. I just don't like that."

"Talk it over with the Sillers. See if they would be too disturbed by it. And you can just ignore the guard at work. But it's your decision. I just think that until the killer is found, you should be very careful."

"I will. And I'll ask Ginny and her parents if a guard here in the house would bother them."

"Good. I'll talk with you tomorrow."

Later in the evening, Astrid waited in the den for Abram to get home from the sheriff's office. She envisioned a scenario in which Danny went to see the judge to tell him he wanted to marry Holly. The judge got angry, maybe said he wouldn't let his daughter marry a Jew and Danny lost his temper, went home, got a gun, and came back and shot the man. Mrs. Rutherford walked in on the scene, and he shot her, too.

Don't be stupid. Unless Danny has a horrible temper, he wouldn't do that. He loved Holly. Killing her parents would alienate her. Besides, she would know about a temper that bad if he had one."

However, she would investigate Danny, and set Holly's mind at ease. That didn't mean that the sheriff and police chief would feel the same. The broader picture was that someone had a huge grudge, against the judge.

All the killers she herself had encountered came with inflated egos. They believed they could do no evil, and they shouldn't be punished no matter how many they murdered. Jason Trump had no conscience, the police said, when it came to killing. His own greed and craziness got him killed when he blew up the house. She recalled with a shudder how she thought Abram was the one killed in the blast.

Jimmy Farr had his little circle of followers who were like puppets in his hands.

General Metcalf had the biggest ego of all but, in the end, died when he thought he could kill Maine's governor, as well as others, and become a martyr, pointing the way for other terrorists to rise up and take over the country in the name of patriotism.

Like the police, Astrid worried about Holly's safety. There was no way to know if the killer intended to murder the whole family or just the judge and his wife.

Suddenly she remembered that she needed to contact her brother. Gunnar had called when she was out of the office, she was told, and she had meant to call earlier. She hoped he wasn't in trouble.

When he answered the phone, Astrid could hear stress, close to tears, in his voice.

"Thanks for calling, Sis."

Now she knew something was wrong. He called her Sis only when he was in trouble.

"What is it, Gunnar? What's wrong?"

"It's Charlotte." His hesitation was maddening, but Astrid waited until he was ready. She could almost guess.

"She lost the baby," Gunnar finally whispered.

"Oh no. I'm so sorry. How did it happen?"

"I don't really understand it, to tell the truth. She started to bleed ..."

Astrid heard him sob then. She couldn't remember hearing him cry, not since he was a very young boy. What could she say?

Finally, "I took her right to the hospital, but you know it's 10 miles away and there was nothing they could do for her when we got there. The doctor said that it wouldn't have helped if he had been next door. The baby was already dead when she started to bleed."

His voice broke again.

"Oh God. It was so awful, Astrid. It had to do with hormone production, he said. Apparently it's not awfully unusual. If the pregnancy is within 10 weeks, this quite often happens. He said after 10 weeks, the placenta takes over in hormone production. Oh God, I feel sick. She's so weak."

"I know. I know. Do you need me to come to you? Can I help?"

"No. Her mother is here. It happened three days ago, but I just couldn't talk. I thought I was all over this emotion."

"Don't worry about that. If Abram weren't going to school and working, too, we'd come. But it's just a bad time. We've had a double murder in Fairchance today, and I'm working on that, of course."

"Hey, I know. I don't expect you to come. I just wanted you to know."

"I hesitate to ask, Gunnar, but do you think you'll try again?"

"Right now, I don't know. Charlotte is still in a sort of shock. She sits and stares. She blames herself, but I try to make her understand that she didn't do anything to cause it. The doctor says she'll come out of it. It's just a brief period of depression."

"Understandable."

She heard the back door slam.

"Abram just came in, Gunnar. Look, thanks for calling. I'll call you this weekend sometime. And try to stay calm. I know it's a great shock, but after a while you'll feel better."

"I know. Thanks, Astrid. Talk with you later, then."

She hated to hang up, but now she needed to get back to her own life. It would be hard to shake off Gunnar's news. She had looked forward to becoming an aunt. Poor Charlotte. Could there be worse news for a woman, looking forward to having her first baby, and losing it, when her own body failed to cooperate. No wonder she blamed herself.

Damn. Life can be so cruel. I just don't know if I'll have children.

CHAPTER 7

WEDNESDAY 9:15 P.M.

Astrid heard Abram stomping his feet and making his usual racket when he came in. She smiled, feeling a certain comfort by that manly noise. They'd been married over a month now and she still found little things, like the sound of a man in the house, comforting. Right now, that was just what she needed.

"I'm home," Abram called, as if she might not realize that.

"In here, Abram. Get yourself a snack and come in by the fire."

"Be right there."

He came in with two Drake's Cakes in one hand and a glass of milk in the other hand.

"I see you went for the health food," Astrid said.

"Nothing but. Want one?" He held one out to her.

"Ya. Thanks."

"My healthy woman," he said, as he leaned over for a kiss before sitting beside her on the sofa.

"It's snowing?" she said.

"Coming down fast. Have you been outside?"

"No, I smelled it in your hair."

"You smelled it? What does snow smell like?"

"Oh, white, I guess."

"White!"

"It has an odor all its own, like rain does. Clean."

"You should apply for a weather forecasting job. You wouldn't need any expensive tracking systems. Just stick your nose out the door and smell."

She snorted. "Very funny."

"She smells snow and rain. Never heard of such a thing."

Enough of that, she thought. "You came home early tonight."

"Sorry to say, they're cutting my hours. I'll work from 4 to 9 now. So we'll see more of each other."

"Good. Anything new on the murders?"

"No. Larry was like a bull, roaring around the office. I think he feels frustrated since there weren't any clues to go on at the house, and no neighbors saw anything."

"I ran into the bull, myself."

"No one knows anything. But there are plenty of folks who were not exactly buddies with the judge. Professor Vinton talked at length about him and what a strict professor he was. He said Rutherford didn't allow conversation in class…not even discussions about a point of law. Whereas we talk and discuss in Vinton's class. He encourages it. Says if we question and discuss, we'll learn better. I have to agree with that. But Rutherford, he'd as soon as not kick a guy out of class for the semester if he thought he was smarting off when he asked a question. Odd. I wouldn't have expected Vinton to talk about a fellow professor like that, especially one that died the way he did."

"Sounds like he might be holding a grudge."

"I didn't want to say it, but I think the same thing."

Astrid reached for Abram's glass.

"You mind if I take a sip of milk?"

"No. Go ahead. Just leave me some."

"Mr. Generosity."

They fell silent until Abram asked, "How's Holly?"

"She's getting better. What are the police doing?"

"I don't know a whole lot. No one does."

"But I suppose the sheriff will find something to incriminate someone."

"You sound cynical." Abram turned to look Astrid square on. "Tell me."

"It's just that Larry practically threw me out of his office today and told me not to get involved in his investigation. He's being a horse's ass."

"Don't hold back, dear. If something's bothering you, just let it out."

"It's not funny. I offered to talk with someone in the beauty parlor for him, and he told me not to. His whole attitude was that I shouldn't help. It never bothered him before."

"Ah, I see. Maybe, just maybe mind you, that's the problem."

"That I helped before?" She was ready to jump off the sofa to vent her disgust at the thought. "I was always a big help, and you know it."

"Maybe he figures you've survived each time and doesn't want to take a chance on one more killer getting hold of you. He's smart enough to know about the law of averages."

"That's just silly."

"I'd say cautious. I feel the same way. I'd like to have you stay out of the middle of things. I've gotten rather used to having you around, you know."

Astrid opened her mouth, but quickly closed it. He did have a good argument, and she couldn't deny that getting into it was just what she planned to do. The close calls she'd had in the past were all too alive in her memory.

At last she said, "Would you like coffee now?"

"No. I think I've had enough coffee today. We had a new man come in to train as a dispatcher. That's one reason they're cutting my hours."

"Ya? You two drink a lot of coffee, did you?"

"Good one. No. But he's eager and smart. Name's Hunter Thompson. He's older but not old enough to retire as a mailman."

"Did he lose his job?"

"He broke his leg and it didn't heal just right. He couldn't walk the rounds any more, and he couldn't stand at the window, so this job is something he can do."

"That's good. Family man?"

"Yup. Four children. All grown. And he has two grandchildren already. He said his only son is an engineer."

"Must be a smart one."

Abram looked at his watch. "Time for news. I'll turn it on."

"Before you turn on the TV, Abram, I have some bad news. Charlotte lost the baby. I just talked with Gunnar before you came in. He was all upset over it, of course."

"Of course. That's a real shame."

"I told him we would come down if we could, but there's just no way right now."

"We'll have to make a point of it on a weekend soon."

Astrid nodded and thought how glad she was that Abram had a sentimental, soft side.

"TV now?"

"Okay."

The major Maine channel carried its version of the double murder in Fairchance, with commentary thrown in.

"Fairchance may soon be known as the murder capital of Maine," the anchor woman said during the chat time before signing off.

The reporters at the desk all laughed.

"Anyone kept count of the recent murders?" the sports reporter asked.

"It hasn't reached an even dozen yet, I'm quite sure."

More laughter. Astrid jumped up and turned the TV off.

"That's damned insensitive," she said.

"Insensitive, but true, I'm afraid. It's hard to defend the area when the killings just keep piling up."

Astrid knew he was right, but she remembered when she came here, last year. The city appeared to be peaceful, and on the whole it was. The murders weren't hit or miss, but planned by unscrupulous types, some of whom just happened to come here.

"There are always mitigating circumstances," she said.

"Yeah there are, but I have to think Fairchance is a magnet to killers. I'm glad you're not getting into this one."

Astrid stared into the fire.

"Ya. Me too.

CHAPTER 8

Thursday

Drew spent his first night at the student rooming house listening to the sounds of young men talking, showering, playing loud music until midnight, before the landlord went from room to room telling everyone to quiet down. They did for the few minutes that he was on the floor, then it began all over again.

Unable to sleep, he thought, *I've got a new job to go to tomorrow. I'll be no good if I don't get sleep. This is too much. I can't stay here. I'm not a kid any more. I'll start looking for another place tomorrow. Maybe that place Chris found will have another room available.*

The alarm rang at six o'clock in the morning. Drew turned it off and listened. Just as he thought, there was no sound in the house. He felt like turning his radio on loud to give them a taste of disturbed sleep, but his vindictive days were long past. Now he wanted merely to get along in the world, to find peace and quiet, not to fight. He never was much of a fighter, which made the past 20 years he spent in prison even more cruel, he thought. He tried to leave the barroom when the brawl started, but someone--he thought a woman--shoved him backward and the next thing he saw was a fist coming at him. He ducked and kicked the man's leg, thrusting him forward too quickly to break his fall, especially in his drunken state. The man's head hit the corner of a table. Bleeding, he lunged at Drew and grabbed him, ready to fight. He recognized real trouble coming at him, and tried to back out of the barroom, but the jerk wouldn't let go. In the street, Drew found himself facing a gun. The struggle that followed resulted in the man's death by his own .38, and Drew had no idea how it happened.

"Damned judge," Drew muttered as he stepped into the shower.

At that time, Drew was not working, but he was soon to have a job on the docks where he had worked for four years previously. He had to accept a court-appointed lawyer, who turned out to be a weak, disinterested defense attorney. Judge Rutherford took into account that it was a barroom brawl and sentenced Drew to a minimum of 20 years. If anyone had reason to kill the bastard, Drew knew he would be one of the best candidates. But he got over it long ago and served his time.

Well, he wouldn't worry about the judge any more. In fact, Drew had not wasted his time in prison, but spent it in the library, not alone in his quest for more knowledge about the law. Several prisoners were doing the same thing, and he knew that some of them had retribution in mind, while others wanted to be cleared of their record. For Drew, the study led to his passing the bar exam, almost to his surprise. Now, he was being given a chance by these local attorneys, Levitch and Bertram, and he would always be grateful to them.

Walking the two miles from the rooming house, Drew found the Mid-Town Diner open and went in for a light breakfast.

"Mornin'. Welcome to Mid-Town Diner. What can I get you?"

The man at the counter must be the owner, judging from his long white apron and his hearty welcome. The skinny woman at the grill looked over and smiled. His wife, no doubt. One waitress worked her way down the row of booths taking orders. Taking care of all these customers had to be difficult.

"Good morning," Drew slid onto a stool and pushed aside the menu. "Just coffee and toast, with strawberry jam, please."

The man took back the menu and in doing so, looked Drew up and down.

"Toast comes with juice."

"Oh? Well, orange juice then."

Do I look so poor? Drew wondered. It was obvious that the man thought so when he saw the dated narrow lapels and thin necktie of the sixties. If it hadn't been for his brother, he wouldn't have even this skimpy suit and overcoat, but Les had picked up his clothes and stored them in a trunk.

When the coffee had been poured and the toast placed in front of him, Drew looked up.

"Thanks," he said. There were three slices of toast on the plate.

"You're new here."

"That's right. I'm starting a new job this morning. I guess I'm a bit out of style."

"Hey, you're okay. Where are you working?"

"I'm starting with Levitch and Bertram."

"Oh? Well, good for you. And good luck."

It sounded like he might have added 'You'll need it.' That wasn't a good sign, but Drew knew how the wind blew, even here in central Maine. Prejudice was not unique to southerners.

He didn't have much to leave for a tip, but put down a dime and a nickel, nodded at the diner owner, and headed up the street to the less-than-elegant offices of the partners. No matter what, he was determined to make a success of himself in this town, and that would begin right here, right now.

• • • •

Farther up Main Street, a left-hand turn onto School Street took Chris to Chip's Computers where he found the owner, Chip Rourke, just making coffee in the back of the shop.

"You're bright and early," Chip said. "We'll probably not have much to do today. People tend to hibernate when we have new snow. Can't blame them. I didn't much want to get out this morning, either. There's a closet in my office. Put your coat there and come have some breakfast with me. My wife makes a great pecan roll. I've got half a dozen here."

"Sounds good."

The office was a small room with desk, three chairs, a file cabinet and bookcase. Chris found the closet full of office supplies, and barely room for another coat. When he returned, the coffee was perking.

"I love the smell of coffee," he said.

Chip's grin gave him the appearance of a scoundrel right out of an old movie, not unattractive, just a twist of the mouth that created an expression of deviltry.

"Grab a paper plate and a pecan roll. Every day I'm afraid my wife might leave me."

Chris felt uneasy hearing that admission.

"Sorry to hear that," he said.

"Yeah. If she should, where would I get rolls like this? Or, for that matter, all the other great stuff she bakes?"

Now Chris laughed.

"I see. You had me going there for a minute."

"Don't mind me. You take me too serious and you won't know which way to turn. I'm what you might call a joker. At least that's what my kids call me."

"It's good to be able to laugh about things."

Chris meant that. He'd seen so much bitterness and anger in prison that being where someone could have a good time would be a treat.

"You found a good place to live, did you?"

"Yeah. And the landlady says she knows you."

"Who's that?"

Chris had already eaten one roll and reached for a second.

"Mrs. Oswald."

"Well, what ya know about that. She's my best friend's mother. Tommy and I must have added ten years to her life with all the antics we pulled. Now, my mother would have my dad's old belt at the ready for me if she knew some of the things we did. Don't get me wrong. She never used it. Just held it up for me to see. That was enough. I didn't tell her too much. But Mimi Oswald would scold and tell us not to do that again, then she'd give us cookies. I love that gal. Well, that's great. I'll have to go see her. Haven't heard from Tommy for ... let's see ... about a year, I think. After he went to college, we didn't have much to do with each other. You know how it is."

"Oh yeah."

Chris had no idea how it was. He had no friends that went off to college, any more than he did. They were all poor, living mostly on the street. Most of his friends ended up in jail.

The conversation and breakfast ended when the phone rang. Chip answered, talked for a few minutes, came back and said, "You've got your first job of the day. Over at the rectory. They bought a computer and have no idea what to do with it."

"The rectory," Chris said.

"Okay. It's the brick house next to the Catholic Church. You know where that is?"

"Just down the street."

He couldn't miss that ornate building. Its belfry towered over everything in Fairchance.

"They want you to come over at nine."

"In the meantime, I can straighten out the display case, unless you have other projects."

"No. That's fine. Go at it."

Chris worked until it was time to go. He gathered up a kit of tools and walked. At least the sidewalks were clear. Plows had been going most of the night. He looked up at the sky. It was so blue he could cry for the sheer pleasure of having fresh air, sunshine, and sky all around. If only his little girl could be happy and enjoy the freedom that he felt right now.

Each time he woke up in the night, Chris had thought about the murders. He tried not to think that Drew or his brother Les might have carried out that terrible deed, but he couldn't dismiss the grudge they both had expressed when they were talking one evening at the militia camp.

Walking slower now, he again felt the horror of seeing Holly fall apart while he worked on her computer at the agency office. The poor girl must have loved the judge and his wife, and because of that he felt only sorrow over the shootings, no sense of satisfaction that the hanging judge had finally got his due. If he were to assess his own feelings more thoroughly, he'd probably admit that there was a certain irony in the shooting death of a judge who sent so many men to prison. He didn't know how harsh he was with women, but he guessed it would have been no different. Still, the Rutherfords had provided a good home for Holly. She grew up without fear and most likely had a great deal of family love, so Chris had to be grateful to them.

Here he was at the brick house with white trim, a white double door in front, and a clear and dry walkway around to a side door where a discreet sign announced Office. He pushed the doorbell before he noticed the other sign, Walk In.

"Hello," the smiling woman at the desk said. "Are you the computer man?"

"I'm the computer man, at your service. Where is it?"

The fact that he didn't see it in his quick survey of the spacious office made him wonder where they expected to use it.

"It's in the next room."

She rose from her chair, started to walk toward the doorway at the other end of the office, and Chris blinked. He'd seen perfectly formed women in the past, but this one struck him as exceptionally fine, despite pure white streaks in her reddish brown hair. Then he noticed her built-up shoe. He also noticed how easily she walked with it. She must have had it all her life because she barely limped. He raised his eyes and hoped she hadn't noticed his momentary stare.

"We don't have a clue how to take it out of the box or where to put it," she said on opening the door.

This room could be made into a computer room, but it was dark, with no windows. The computer parts had not been taken from the big box. The top was open as if she had looked in and dared not touch the contents.

"Did you plan to use it in here?" he asked.

"I don't think so. Are you suggesting I should?"

"No. Not at all. What I should have said is where do you plan to use it?"

"I thought I'd like it on my desk, but it's so big I don't know where it could go."

Chris drew in a quick breath. She stood so close to him as they peered into the box that he could smell a lily-of-the-valley fragrance. Her soft, mellow voice stirred an emotion he hadn't felt in a very long time. There were plenty of women around, but none that had created this sudden turmoil in him. In fact, he hadn't felt this excited since his wife died. He had thought he'd never again experience it, but here he was, practically speechless. This one had an open personality that reminded him of a young child just finding out how something works, intent on the object at hand. He should run, leave before making a fool of himself, but his feet felt heavy as lead. He would be content to spend the day talking with her.

"Let's take a look," he said.

He walked ahead of her to the front office where he studied the desk top, all neatly arranged, with a document beside her typewriter where she had been working.

Clearing his throat, he said, "It doesn't look like you can have it on the desk. My suggestion is that you get a computer table to place on one side or the other so you can turn your chair and work at it."

She walked around the desk and studied that side.

"That's a good idea. Where can I get a computer table?"

For a moment he lost his train of thought.

"Where?" What was the question? "Oh. Well, we have a catalog I can drop off to you. I'd be happy to point out what I think would work well here."

Oh man. This was getting difficult. He needed air.

"That's fine. When can you bring it? Or would you like to have me stop at the store?"

"No. I'll bring it to you. That way we can take measurements and be sure everything will fit well."

His choice of words left him feeling embarrassed. Why was he the only one feeling as if he'd made a pass at the woman?

"You know, you want something that will leave walking room around it, but still be wide enough to place papers beside the computer if you need to copy something."

"Yes, I see. Well, then, tomorrow morning?"

"Right. Tomorrow morning."

He headed for the door, keeping his eyes focused on the door handle. Then he thought to ask, "I'm sorry. I didn't get your name."

She was sitting at the desk again.

"It's Sandra Brewster. Just call me Sandy. And I don't know your name, either."

"C-C-Christopher Benning. Call me Chris. Very nice meeting you, Sandy."

"Yes. Nice to meet you, too, Chris."

Outside, Chris let out a long, shaky breath.

Stuttering like a damned fool. What's the matter with you? You've seen pretty women before.

But he couldn't remember when he'd seen a woman like this one that he wanted to hold in his arms for a very long time. Not in 20 years anyway.

Stupid, stupid, stupid. You think a woman like her would be interested in you? Look at you. Just a worn out ex-prisoner who can't say his own name without stuttering.

CHAPTER 9

Astrid answered three telephone calls before Charlie and Will came in still talking about the murders. She would love to join in and tell them what she was up to for Holly, but she held her silence and listened to Will.

"Someone should be able to recognize that old car. How many rusted out old cars are there around here?"

"Not many. Which may mean that he came in from the country," Charlie said.

"I still can't believe no one saw his face, or even noticed him going into that house with a gun."

They headed for the lounge as if their sole purpose today was to drink coffee and discuss the murder. Astrid wrinkled her nose. Did they think they'd get the answers before the police did? Men could be so pompous at times.

When her phone rang, she answered, feeling left out and imposed upon.

Beth said, "Is this a bad time, Astrid?"

Now she was glad the others weren't in the room.

"Well, I just wanted you to know that last night I asked Larry if he had any leads in the double murder. He said they have very little to go on. The car has him baffled because the man who discovered the bodies can't remember the make of car or just how badly it's rusted."

"You'd think someone in the neighborhood would have seen the killer. Usually there's some gossip who doesn't miss a thing the neighbors are doing."

"I know. Larry said the woman next door, who usually sees people coming and going, was in Bangor for a doctor's appointment. So she couldn't help. They're going around to all the car dealers to see if they had an old car parked out back somewhere that might have been stolen. You know how they take clunkers in on trade. But no one had anything. So it's day one all over again. They start out today to see if they can pick up some new leads. I guess they're checking out of town and out of state to try to make connections with other similar crimes."

"Let's hope it's an outsider," Astrid said. "You hate to think that you're rubbing elbows with a murderer in a supermarket. Okay, well thanks for calling. I'll see what I can do today. By-the-way, have you two been invited to the party Dee's putting on tomorrow night for Mr. Cornell's birthday?"

"Yes, we have. We'll be there. I meant to mention it. What are you wearing?"

"Oh, you know me. Probably a pants suit that doesn't have holes."

Beth laughed and they said good-bye. Astrid hung up just as the two men came back to the editorial room.

"Anything new, Astrid?" Charlie asked.

"Just routine stuff. You solved the murders yet?"

Charlie looked at her over his glasses.

"Do I detect a touch of sarcasm? How about you? You have an insider. Has Abram learned anything?"

"No. I'll go to the college, though. Seems to be a lot of animosity toward the judge out there. Maybe one or two people would be willing to at least give us some quotable comments. Then maybe the church pastor would, too. I expect I'll hear two different versions of the man from those sources."

"You can be sure of it," Will said.

Astrid had suspected that Will had no church affiliation from one or two derogatory remarks he'd made previously about people of faith.

"Anyway," Astrid said, "unless you have something you want me to cover, I'll leave after I finish this routine stuff."

Charlie flipped a few pages of notes.

"Nothing pressing. Go ahead. This is a good time. TV news had an interview with that neighbor who found the bodies. Why don't you talk with a few nearby neighbors, too. I only got to one woman who's a widow. She would have talked all day if I hadn't said I needed to get back to the office. And how is the daughter? She ready to talk with you?"

"No. Holly is far too upset right now."

Charlie looked as if he wanted to say more, but lowered his eyes when Astrid focused hard on her work. What worried Astrid was that Sheriff Knight would go after Danny before she could find out anything about him. Then poor Holly would likely see the very thing she wanted to avoid, a lot of questions directed at her about the relationship between her dad and Danny

"Okay," Astrid said. "I'm out of here. I may return later today, but I have a lot to do. Are you two going to the party at Dee's tomorrow night?"

"I'm taking Jenny," Charlie said.

"And we've hired a baby sitter, so we'll be there, too," Will said.

"What about you, Astrid?" Charlie said. "Does Abram have to work?

"I'm going, and Abram will come along when he can get away."

"You think the party will really be a surprise?"

Astrid was at the door now.

"Ya, it will," she said. "Dee told me she hasn't said a thing about his birthday, and is pretty sure he doesn't think she knows his birth date."

She didn't dwell on Dee and Marvin long as she drove to the college. More important to her right now was the murder of a respectable judge and his wife, upstanding citizens in Fairchance, father and mother of Holly Rutherford. With absolutely nothing to begin with for clues, she could see only a blank wall. That's the way law enforcement officers must feel. How and where to begin investigating would be set out in an unwritten guide, she presumed, one that they followed routinely. Or maybe it was written. Anyway, one day Abram would likely be doing that very thing-- investigating cases beginning with nothing but slowly opening to a compilation of facts leading to an offender. Fascinating. Now she wished she had studied the process in school. Even studying psychology would have helped. As it was, she had to fly by the seat of her pants. Somehow she needed to collect bits and pieces that could either exonerate Danny or convict him.

"Damn. I need to get with it. Am I out to find the murderer, or am I just reporting for the newspaper? My job is to report. At least dig up some things to report on. Of course, if something leads to a suspect, then who am I to repress the information? We'll see."

As she approached the guest parking in front of the college administration building, Astrid realized she'd been talking to herself.

"I'm ready for the old folks' home," she muttered.

She started to open her door, when a thought stopped her. What was she doing here? Before Astrid could interview Danny's professors, she should know more than she did now.

Where does he live? What are his hobbies? Is he a hunter? I should have asked Holly for more information about him.

Holly may have gone back to work. She was strong and she would become bored and distraught just sitting and thinking about her loss. It was terribly soon for her to return, but worth checking out. If she had pending real estate deals, she would want to take care of them. And if she wasn't at the agency, she'd be at her friend's.

Astrid backed out, and hoped no one saw her as she headed back to town or they'd think she'd lost it for sure. Truth be known she felt at sixes and sevens. Where to go, what to do first? She hadn't felt this muddled for a very long time.

Make a decision. As Grampa used to say, do something, even if it's wrong.

Arriving at the real estate office, she saw that she had guessed right. Holly's car was parked outside, and Astrid left her Jeep next to it, pulled her collar up against the strong, cold wind and ran to the door. The sharp wind hit her face like flying icicles. Inside, she found Holly and Chris head-to-head at the new equipment. Holly looked over at the door.

"Astrid. Come in. I was hoping I'd see you today. Chris came back to give me more instruction on this program. I don't know if I'll ever conquer it. They speak of computer programs not being compatible. Well, I'm not compatible with the computer."

"You and me, too. Do you want me to come back at a better time?"

"No. I just want to be sure I have this right first. Then we can talk."

She asked Chris a question and they discussed where to find what she needed. Yesterday Astrid saw how distraught he became over Holly's reaction to the tragic news. Today he was patient, but all business.

Holly looked up at Chris and nodded

"I think I understand," she said. "I need to have a few words with Astrid. Can you wait, Chris?"

"Sure thing. Do what you need to do."

Astrid went to the round table at the opposite end of the room and waited. As Holly approached her, Astrid said, "I'm surprised to see you back at work so soon. Didn't you want to rest a while in a peaceful setting?"

"It was hardly a peaceful setting, Astrid. Everyone was just plain smothering. I had to get out, and this was the best place to go. Besides, I wanted to get that computer clear in my mind so I could start using it. Chris is a very good teacher, very patient."

Astrid wanted to question her about Chris but knew he'd hear her, even though the table was at a distance from the business area of the room. Times like this, she wished she had been born with a soft voice, like Holly's. As it was, Chris was the only other person in the office, and he would hear their conversation--at least, he'd hear Astrid's end of it--but it probably wouldn't matter.

"Have you learned anything yet?" Holly asked.

"Not yet, but I'm working on it. I need to know a couple of things before I can move on."

"Sure. What do you need to know?"

"Where does he live?"

"Just beyond the city limits on the south side of town. It used to be a farm. His father's business would never be allowed in town."

"I think I saw the junk...er...the scrap dealership when I drove that way to Augusta one day."

She remembered seeing whole cars in the yard.

"Do any of the old cars still work?"

"Probably, but I'm not certain of that. Many people get auto parts or bicycle parts from him."

Astrid felt a tingle of inspiration. Someone could easily have bought or taken one of those old cars. Suppose that was what the neighbor saw, an old junk car.

"Danny is still in school, you said? And he doesn't have anything to do with his father's business?"

"That's right." Holly scowled. "He works part-time for the vet. This is all helpful to you?"

"Ya. I just wouldn't know who to see or what to ask if I didn't have a place to start. And right now you're the only one I know who can give me answers. Then, when I know where to begin, I'll ask some discreet questions."

"I see. Well, his father has been in that business a long time. I haven't really met him, but I know from Danny that he's an honest man and everyone says so."

"So Danny's parents hadn't met yours?"

"No. Dad never would allow Ma to invite them to dinner. I shed some tears over that, but it did no good. My father was a strict man."

"Do Danny and his dad hunt?"

"Hunt? I don't think so. He's never said they do. Danny loves animals so much that I doubt he'd be able to shoot a wild one any more than he could a domestic one."

Astrid glanced toward Chris and found that his gaze was fixed on Holly. He quickly turned to the computer. Very odd, she thought. He didn't appear to be a danger to Holly, but he did seem to have an unusual interest in her.

"I've kept you talking too long, I think," Astrid said. "But I wonder what you and Danny do when you're together."

Holly had been close to tears as they talked, but now she stifled a laugh. At first Astrid didn't understand, but when she got it, she felt warmth rising around her neck.

"You know what I mean. I wasn't being personal, not like that. I meant do you go to movies, go dancing, or to bars?"

"Never. Neither of us drinks. We do dance once in a while. But most of the time we take in a movie, or go get an ice cream at the Social Center at Maple Ridge. You should go there sometime, Astrid. It's the one I mentioned when you took me to Ginny's house. We usually get her and her boyfriend and we all go have an ice cream soda or banana split. Just like the old days, you now."

Astrid doubted that Holly knew much about those old days, but nodded and said she would like to go there sometime. Then Holly got to her feet and Astrid followed.

"Thank you, Holly. Don't overwork yourself just yet. You really do need to rest as much as possible after the shock you had."

"I know. And I will go back to Ginny's early today. I'd like to go to my own home, but the sheriff said I should wait until...until things are cleaned up."

"Ya. That's best. I'll call you when I know anything about Danny."

Astrid looked directly at Chris and was startled to see his hazel eyes boring into hers. He rubbed his chin in a thoughtful manner as if he wanted to say something. He dropped his gaze and said nothing.

She left with a feeling that he knew something pertinent to the murders, but if anyone should ask her, she couldn't possibly say why, only that body language often said as much as words. Problem was, she wished he had actually spoken.

CHAPTER 10

D rew needed a place to stay. No way would he spend another sleepless night at that rooming house, listening to nocturnal noises of college kids. His brother's house at The Kingdom was out of the question, too. The parole board likely would object to that housing arrangement anyway, given the group's reputation. Besides, Les would probably shoot him if he showed up there. Drew wanted to wait a while before telling his brother that he took the job with Levitch and Bertram considering his reaction when he mentioned applying for the job in the first place. No need to rush the outrage. His brother's objection to the position was unreasonable, especially since it was Mr. Bertram, not Levitch, who hired him. In fact, he hadn't seen Levitch yet.

Why had Les turned into a bigot? They weren't brought up that way. But he had noticed that the militia group as a whole displayed racist bias. Les never explained how he became attached to that gang, but when their father died and left the bulk of his fortune to him, he lurched along paths that led finally to this camp of men and women with a superiority complex. Drew had thought Les would go to Florida and retire in luxury. Instead he ended up at The Kingdom, playing soldier with a bunch of malcontents.

The only person he could think of who might be able to help him until he had time to find his own place on the weekend was his old prison buddy, Chris Benning. If Mr. Bertram didn't object, he'd call Chris at his shop and ask that they have lunch together.

Mr. Bertram was a hard man to read. When most employers might have questioned, or objected to, that 20-year prison term Drew served, and what he did that put him there, Bertram looked over the application form and resume, breathed deeply, and said, "Looks like you accomplished what many under better circumstances have not been able to. You passed the bar exam. That's good enough for me. We needn't speak of the rest."

He had explained that duties at first would include greeting people who came in, deciding who should take care of each person's need, as well as routine deeds, wills, filing, and answering the phone.

Drew mumbled, "Secretarial work."

"Pretty much. When our secretary left, we thought rather than hire two people we could get someone who knows the law, but who could do the general work, as well. In fact, I do some of the same work."

"Do you ever go to court in criminal trials?"

"No. If a court case comes to this office, Abe--Mr. Levitch-- handles it. We don't get many court cases, to tell the truth. But we manage to survive with what we do. People know him and often come to us because of his social contacts."

Mentally reviewing all that previous conversation, Drew felt certain there would be no objection to his phoning Chris, but still he would ask. He went to Mr. Bertram's door and knocked lightly.

"Come."

Drew opened the door but didn't walk in.

"Sir, I wonder if I may use the phone to call a friend? I'm badly in need of a place to sleep tonight. My accommodations last night just won't do. Can't sleep because of all the noise the college kids make."

"Come in, Drew. You may use the phone whenever you want to, as long as you don't abuse the privilege. Now, this friend. Have you known him a long time?"

Drew understood what he was saying--did he know Chris in prison.

"Yes, sir. I've known him almost 20 years."

"I see. He's not apt to return to his former housing?"

"No. He has a daughter living here, and was anxious to see her. He has good reason to remain here." He quickly added, "But that's not a thing he wants people to know. She doesn't know that her biological father is alive, and he doesn't want to upset her, especially now."

"Why especially now?"

Mr. Bertram settled back in his soft tan leather chair, looking every bit like a country lawyer in old brown suit, loose tie, white fringe of hair, and sad eyes with sagging lids. Drew thought him far too quiet to defend a person in court. Of course, as he well knew, the quiet ones sometimes surprised.

"You probably heard about the murder of Judge Rutherford and his wife.?"

"Yes, I heard."

"Well, the Rutherfords had adopted the one they called their daughter. My friend is her birth father. The judge adopted her when he…"

Drew hesitated. How he hated to say it.

"Went to prison?"

"Yeah. When he went to prison."

Mr. Bertram made no expression of disapproval, once again surprising Drew. The first time was when he had applied for the job and said right up front that he'd been in prison, and that he had permission to come to Maine and find work. Nor did he now raise a questioning eyebrow when Drew spoke of the Rutherfords and their daughter.

"And both of you did the same thing," Bertram said. "You turned your lives around by studying. That's commendable. I want you to understand that what we say in this office will stay here. And that goes two ways. Understand?"

"Yes. I understand."

Mr. Bertram twirled his chair toward the windows. "Believe me. I know that you both will have a hard time to come back."

"Yes."

And just how would you know what we went through, how we spent hours in the library, when they'd leave us alone, and how we begged for more competent instruction? It took years, but we finally won and we both got the second chance we wanted.

Turning back, Mr. Bertram studied Drew for a full minute. Drew never lowered his eyes in embarrassment or shame. He'd learned to look into his jailers' eyes without emotion, being as determined as they were. He found that it sometimes angered them, but demanded respect in the long run. While he meant no disrespect to his employer, he would not show weakness here, either. He paid the penalty for an unwanted fight. He didn't believe that crime should forever require repentance.

"What's your friend's name?" Mr. Bertram asked.

"Chris Benning. He took a small apartment in a home owned by a Mrs. Oswald."

"Uh, huh. A good place. I know her. And you want to room with him there?"

"For a night or two. Just until I can get my own place."

Once again Mr. Bertram lapsed into silence. Was he always like this, always cautious in choosing his words? When he saw Mr.

Bertram quickly rearrange pencils on his desk, he knew the man was about to speak.

"This Chris. Tell me more about him."

"Chris? Oh, he was like me back then. Drinking, dabbling in drugs. He passed out one day on his bed, and he woke up to the sound of a gunshot. When he got to the kitchen, he found his wife dead on the floor. He did what anyone would do, went to see if she was still alive, got her blood on his clothes and hands. His little girl was in her bed, crying. He never knew who did it, but he was convicted of the murder because they could find no evidence that anyone else had been in the room. Judge Rutherford sent him up for 20 to life."

"Judge Rutherford. Same judge who sent you up?"

"Yeah. But, you see, I was guilty. The man who attacked me had the gun and in the fight that followed, the gun went off. The judge considered the circumstances and gave me 20 to 25. Both of us were convicted on the same day."

"Why did he attack you?"

"We had an argument in a barroom over some trivial thing, as far as I remember, but he wouldn't let it go. He came for me. I never was a fighter, so I left the bar, and he followed, and we ended up fighting in the street. When I saw that he had a gun, I tried to disarm him, but it discharged, and he was the one who was shot and died."

"Did you and Chris share a cell?"

"No. We met during exercise one day, and at first we were both pretty angry. We talked a lot, seemed to understand each other more than most prisoners do. After a while we realized we'd better do something with our time in there, or else we'd be there to the limits of our sentences."

"And what does Chris do?"

"He's a computer expert. Took to it like a fish to water. I don't think there's anything about computers he doesn't know. He works for that store here, Chip's Computers."

Mr. Bertram nodded. He fiddled with pencils some more. Finally he spoke.

"The living quarters at Mrs. Oswald's are cramped and suitable for one person. I have a large house on Cottage Lane. Never knew why they called it Cottage Lane. There are only a half dozen houses on it and no cottages at all. I live alone and have several unoccupied bedrooms. What would you say to renting one of the rooms? We can share the kitchen. I have it well stocked, overstocked for just one person. It might be nice to have someone else in the house. We don't need to get under each other's feet. Probably won't want a whole lot more to do with each other after working together all day, anyway. The room's on the first floor, and there's a back hallway, so we wouldn't have to be bumping into each other at all."

A room of his own and back hallway. Almost too much to hope for.

"What do you charge for rent?"

It seemed almost impertinent, considering the generous offer to begin with.

"I rented it once, and charged three hundred a month. Is that too much for you?"

"No. That's…that's fine." *Cheap, in fact.*

"Do you want to see it before you take it?"

"Yes. And thank you."

"Let's go now. I'll just lock the office for a half hour. It won't take long."

Drew soon found himself in a fine old Colonial with rich tapestries, and a sunny room on the first floor, east side of the house on Cottage Lane where traffic was light.

He could have hugged Mr. Bertram. Instead, he said, "This is a great place, Sir. I can't thank you enough for it. I'll work better and easier with a good night's rest."

"That's the idea."

"I'll get my things and bring them over after supper. I'll use the back door so I won't disturb you."

Mr. Bertram nodded.

Before he left, Drew just had to ask the question that had bugged him all day.

"You know, I've never seen your partner. Is it the *late* Mr. Levitch?"

The throaty little chuckle surprised him.

"Oh no. He's very much alive. He was on vacation, and now he's in Boston defending a man charged with murder one."

"He goes that far then?"

"He's a good attorney, has a high rate of acquittals in cases. And, yes, he goes that far."

It sounded as if he had more to add. Drew waited.

Then, when he half turned to leave, Mr. Bertram said, "Also in New York State."

The barely audible words suggested there was more Bertram could add. His detached gaze saw something amiss beyond the door. All at once Drew felt the prickle of uncertainty. The new position, the room, the absence of Mr. Levitch in the three times he had been in the office. In fact, now that he thought about it, there was nothing in the office to suggest that anyone else worked there. Mr. Bertram had a phone and the pencils, as well as a stack of documents, and a row of books, piles of notebooks and papers on his desk. Behind him was a large bookcase for an overflow of similar books. But Mr. Levitch's office in the back contained very little except for a telephone, as if everything had been cleaned out. Being too grateful for job and living quarters, he said no more about it. He would pay close attention to the activity and try to learn the reason for what appeared to him as the very odd absence of the partner in the firm.

Getting last-minute instructions about the bathroom and his landlord's expectations concerning noise and late hours--all landlords seemed to hold the same standard--Drew returned to the office.

Mr. Bertram brought out case files and piled them high on his desk.

"Study these, then file them," he said.

A little past five, he went back to the college housing and collected his few things, paid the requisite fee for early departure. This time, he piled into his Chevy, mentally thanked his old man for leaving him five thousand dollars and the car, and drove off. When he called earlier to tell Chris he had new living quarters, they agreed to meet at the Mid-Town Diner for supper instead of lunch. Chris was already there.

They gave their orders before Drew opened with his burning question, "So, how did you find Holly today?"

"I'll give her this, she's a spunky young lady. She acted as if nothing had happened. At least, she did until Astrid Lincoln came in. Do you know anything about her? The tall, blond, handsome Swede?"

Drew picked up his coffee cup.

"She writes for *The Bugle* doesn't she?" he asked.

Chris nodded. "She's friendly with Holly, and I think she's doing some investigating for her."

"Who's she investigating?"

"I'm not sure. You know, I couldn't very well ask questions. I'm just the computer man. But I did hear some discussion about Holly's fiancé."

"You have a more interesting job than I do, I think. It was quiet in the office. Mr. Bertram asked me a lot of questions about what got both of us in prison. I think at first he thought I shouldn't consort with you now. But when we finished talking, he seemed satisfied that all is well. My room is real nice, light, well furnished. It's great."

"I guess we both lucked out. Hey, I met a very nice lady today. She's secretary at the Catholic Church office. I'll be installing a computer for her. I'd like to ask her out, but I don't know if I should."

"She pretty?"

"When she talks and smiles, she's really lovely. I don't know that she's a beautiful woman, though. Just a very nice personality, considering."

"Considering?"

"She has a club foot with built-up shoe. She walks easily enough, though. And when you talk with her she's…well, she's just about perfect."

"Why *not* ask her out? It's time to start living, man."

"We'll see."

Drew had seen that reluctant streak in Chris before and decided he needed a prod.

"You may think you're young again, my friend, but believe me, you're not. Now's the time to snare a woman, especially if you've found a good one."

"Wonder why I didn't think of that."

"Okay, okay. I wash my hands of it. Just don't let me hear you pissing and moaning some day that you just found out she's getting married to some other man."

Chris sat back while their meals were served, then took a forkful of spaghetti. "This is good," he said, as if he hadn't heard Drew's reproach.

. . . .

79

Sitting on the edge of the bed before turning in, Drew looked around at the valuable antique pieces. For a rental room, Bertram might have gone to the Salvation Army store and bought some cheap stuff. However, he was one who appreciated the finer things of life, obviously. The furnishings were fine, indeed, all in pristine condition. If he wanted to study a bit, he found the bookcase filled with law books. Strange that Mr. Bertram should have the *Penal Law of The State Of New York.* The more he looked, the more law books he found for New York.

"That's odd. Why New York?"

He could think of no good answer to his question, except that his boss may have practiced law in New York before coming here, and he stored the books in this room rather than his office.

"That must be it."

He also wondered why a single man had such a big house filled with fine antiques.

"Must have been the family home."

He dismissed the question as being Mr. Bertram's business, not his.

Then he thought about Chris and Holly and the woman Chris met, the one with the pretty smile. He understood why he was reticent about asking her out. Sometime it would have to come out that he was an ex-con, and who wants to admit to that? Was she understanding enough to overlook it?

Having investigated his quarters and come up with more questions than answers, he crawled into bed. Just before sleep overtook him completely, he raised his head from the pillow to listen. He could hear voices coming from the kitchen, and he'd swear one of them was a woman's voice. To say the least, the voice had a high pitch that sounded excited. Well, none of his business. Mr. Bertram wasn't dead, after all.

CHAPTER 11

Friday

This would be a busy day, topped off with Dee's surprise birthday party for Marvin. While she ate oatmeal and coffee at breakfast, Astrid thought about Dee. No one deserved a good man in her life more than Dee. She had lost her husband in a hunting camp fire, and then for several more years supervised the alcohol rehabilitation camp they had established on the outskirts of Twin Ports.

Few saw her hard edge, most likely developed working with often abusive alcoholics, but Astrid did one day when the two of them were alone in the office. A man burst through the door and demanded to know who wrote the story about his son's arrest for drunk and disorderly conduct. He failed to mention the rest of the charge against the son--endangerment when he pointed a gun at a crowd of shoppers on Main Street. He swore at Dee repeatedly and threatened to kill her if she ever wrote anything about his family again, shook his fist in her face, and called her a bitch. Dee stood up with such ferocity that the man took a step backward.

With martial command, her voice took on uncharacteristic depth.

"Perhaps police should have locked you up instead of your son. You reek of booze, you come in here and threaten my life for reporting public information taken from the police blotter. With any luck at all, you'll get out that door before the police arrive and take you off to jail where you belong. I have a witness to your threat on my life. That should fetch you a fine, at least, if not some jail time to think about how you can help yourself as well as your son get onto a civilized track."

Despite his angry growl, she straightened her arm and pointed to the door.

"Get out. NOW."

She picked up the phone and began to dial. The man may have feared the police more than Dee, but it looked like a toss-up.

After that incident, Astrid respected Dee all the more. When she came to *The Bugle*, Astrid had little going for her by way of social skills. She wasn't unaware of her shortcomings, especially her over-use of profanity. She had never shaken off callous talk she learned from rough farm hands and then the all-male staff that referred to themselves as the Vermont Rough and Ready Reporters. She didn't even know what was appropriate to wear as a member of a more sophisticated newspaper staff. But by observing Dee and talking with her, Astrid soon began to shape up. She felt better about herself, though she never was shy about speaking up, even in public gatherings.

From the start, her relationship with Dee blossomed into mutual trust and confidentiality. Astrid would always be grateful for Dee's ready advice when she needed it. Although they were from opposite social poles, they shared the special independence surrounding wealth-- Dee's being from social pillars of the community, and Astrid's from immigrant farmers with a strong work ethic. Astrid had learned that Sheriff Larry Knight also inherited a fortune.

Invited guests to the party were told not to bring gifts. Astrid decided she wouldn't take a gift but would send flowers, just a bit of color to brighten things, she thought. As she cleared the table, she heard Abram coming downstairs.

"Good morning," he said, coughing. He wore only pajamas.

"Good morning, dear. Aren't you cold? Shall I get your robe?"

He stretched and yawned. "No. I'm going back for an hour. Just wanted to see you off."

"How sweet of you." She kissed him and tousled his hair more.

"Mmm. Sweet or not, I remembered I forgot to tell you that we had a visitor yesterday after you went to work. I got so busy myself that it just slipped my mind."

"God. He's got dementia already," Astrid said as an aside, parodying his remark last night about her smelling snow.

"And I married a wit. I should have remembered since the caller was a complete surprise to me."

"Oh?"

"Someone by the name of Geraldine Thorpe. Sound familiar?"

"Omigod. Geraldine. Ya. Of course, she's my niece."

Abram cocked an eyebrow.

"Niece? Pardon my ignorance, but don't you have to have someone older than 27 to be the father of a girl of 18 or 19? Or is this one for Ripley? It really shouldn't surprise me if it is."

Astrid plunked herself into a chair and leaned across the table. With her fingers, she rubbed away the milk carton mark on the wood table top. The answer was no problem, just difficult to sum up in a few minutes.

"You see, Gunnar and I have an older brother."

"You never told me."

"No. I just never gave it thought, to tell the truth. Hell, it's such a long story."

"I'm in no hurry. I'm sure it will be interesting enough to keep me awake."

"Ya. Well." Astrid looked into Abram's cynical eyes, and tried to think of how to shorten the explanation. "Years ago my father and mother had a son. His name is Nels. That was ten years before I was born. Gampa called him a hot head, said he had been that way from his early years. He fought with our father and insulted our mother. When he became a teenager, he couldn't stay out of trouble. Once he was held overnight in jail for drunkenness. But it didn't cool him down any."

Astrid got up and poured coffee for the two of them.

"When he was 18 he said he was going to marry a girl who was 20. My father gave his consent, though he didn't approve, of course, and the two of them lived with her parents until their baby was born. Then he came back to the farm. Grampa tried to get him to work with him, but Nels never would. He just hung around the house until Father kicked him out, baby, wife, and all."

Astrid studied Abram's reaction, but saw only interest, no sign of disapproval--yet.

"Somehow he got together money enough, and I suspect Grampa gave it to him, to get them to California. And that seemed to be that, for many years. Then when I came back to the farm a year ago, I found his daughter, Geraldine, living there under Gunnar's roof, in order to attend the University of Maine. He said she arrived without first contacting him and he couldn't refuse her housing. But I found that she was as bad as her father. And the day I went back to the farm after my interview for the job at *The Bugle*, I found her in my bed with one of the farm hands. I fired the worker, and told her to pack her things. I didn't care where she went. She was not welcome there."

"What did Gunnar say to that? Wasn't he the one who should fire the farm hand?"

"He was happy I did it. He just didn't have the heart to do the firing. And he couldn't bring himself to make her leave either. After it was all over, he told me that she'd been stealing from him."

She took a sip of coffee and thought that she probably should have told Abram about that part of her family.

"I would have told you, Abram. It's just that the family sort of disowned Nels, never talked about him or his family. I didn't think about Geraldine ever showing up here after she left the farm because I made it quite clear that we didn't want to see her again."

Now she saw a glimmer of disapproval in Abram's eyes and wished she had told him long ago.

"So," Abram said, "it seems that she wants to have words with you now."

"Well, I'll tell you one thing. She will not camp here. And if she comes to the door again, you damned well better tell her she isn't welcome here."

"Yes sir."

"Don't be smart. I'm serious. She's trouble."

"I get it."

Hollow joking, if ever she'd heard it. She needed to get out of here before she completely lost her temper. To think that he wouldn't understand why she hadn't told him about the side of the family that she and Gunnar wanted to forget was too much.

Astrid jumped up. "Good lord, look at the time. I've got to go. See you later."

She gave him a quick kiss and ran out the door, leaving Abram with a blank look on his face.

． ． ． ．

Pretty well drained of arguments, sometimes shouted as she drove to work, Astrid was ready for her third cup of coffee when she arrived at the office. Abram was sweet most of the time. Then there were times when he was so aggravating. Just because she didn't tell him something. Oh, he was angry all right. She knew that. Well, he must be perfect. The hell he was. He must not have any skeletons in his closet. Ya. Of course. He probably could tell her enough about his family to turn her face red, too. Well, hell's bells. Everyone has some relative they don't talk about. Don't they?

She could smell it from the back door. Charlie had made coffee already. Just as she reached the office door, the business office door swung opened and Kit Carson nearly ran into her.

"Sorry Astrid. Gotta go for a big ad. Can you believe it? Old man Gushee is having a jewelry sale. He hasn't done that in ten years. I'll get a good ad out of this one, finally."

She grinned at his enthusiasm, and entered the office, only to be met by Charlie, shaking a newspaper under her nose.

"Now what?" she said.

"Did you know about this?"

"Since I don't know what you're talking about, I guess I didn't."

"Here." He shoved the Bangor morning paper in her hand. "Read about it. Sheriff's Detective Green made an arrest in the Rutherford murders. They've caught the killer."

"Oh my God." Astrid started reading the story. "That's what it says. I wonder why we weren't told."

"Yeah. So do I. Maybe you ought to find out, Astrid."

"Wha…? You blame me? Why? What did I do?"

"You're the only one who's had a falling out with the sheriff."

"Well, ya, but I don't think he'd leave us out of the picture for that if they have the murderer."

"Just find out, will you?"

"Sure."

She went to her desk and pulled the phone toward her. As she pressed the numbers, she thought that she should have stayed in bed this morning and pulled the covers over her head.

She was put through to Sheriff Knight. She took two deep breaths before speaking.

"Good morning, Larry. It's Astrid. Just reading about the arrest in the Bangor newspaper this morning."

"I just got off the phone to the editor up there. I don't know what kind of idiots they're hiring these days, but that one's a real screw-up."

"Are you saying you don't have the murderer?"

Astrid looked straight at Charlie and tipped back her head to look at him over her nose.

"No, we don't have the murderer. He's a would-be thief. A neighbor saw him sneak under the crime scene tape at the Rutherford house, and she called us. By the time we got there he was in the house, and we booked him on breaking and entering with intent to steal. Look, you know we'd tell you if we arrested the killer. You'd be the first to know."

Astrid felt a load lift from her shoulders.

"Thanks Larry. I appreciate it. Can I see you this morning to get the rest of the story?"

"Come over at about 11. We have another arrest we're processing. I'll tell you about it all then."

She pushed the phone back and stood up to get herself that third cup of coffee.

"So? What was it?" Charlie asked.

"Someone broke into the Rutherford house and a neighbor saw him and called the sheriff. He's not the killer, just someone trying to steal a few things. I'll go over to get the rest of the story, and possibly another one on an arrest that they're processing."

She stood at the lounge door and looked over at Charlie, hoping she looked as self-satisfied as she felt.

"Other media don't always get the story right, I guess," she said.

"Ayuh. I guess."

As she poured her coffee, she giggled. *Score one for me this morning, if nothing else.*

CHAPTER 12

The sheriff could wait an hour. For now, Astrid drove to the animal shelter a mile from the center of the city. Snow banks had melted so that visibility was improved and roads were mostly clear, with only a slick icy patch now and then. The sky seemed bluer than ever, without a cloud this morning. Astrid loved winter in Maine, when evergreens stood out in *bas relief* against white birch trees and crisp, cold air felt clean in her lungs. A flock of pure white snowbirds sailed across the road in front of her Jeep, settled down on a white field, then soared again. As one, they swirled like a white sheet flapping in the wind. Unlike most area roads, this one lay flat, appearing to meld with distant purple mountains. A few stiff spikes of hay stood in the ice fields as reminders that it was still February, far from spring.

It'll probably snow tomorrow and we'll be shoveling again.

All of a sudden the road curved sharply, and Astrid saw the shelter on the right. Not expecting it, she overshot the driveway, and had to back up to make the turn in. It was a long, white set of buildings, with a pristine appearance, not at all what she expected for an animal shelter. She parked beneath a sign declaring it the visitor's parking space, and walked to the steps, opened the front door. Her heart felt unburdened of self-doubt for the moment.

Larry Knight had given her renewed hope that she wasn't on his black list. Just as Beth had said, he didn't harbor grudges.

She heard barking dogs and hoped she would see them. Every once in a while she desired to have a pet. She liked both dogs and cats. Most men seemed to prefer dogs, as she recalled. Well, she could just forget it. The worst shock she'd give Abram would be her short hair, and she planned to see to that this afternoon.

"May I help you, ma'am?"

The young man with rusty hair and red freckles, wore a white coverall that needed laundering. Astrid sensed that he was Danny.

"Are you Danny Gerber?" she asked.

"Yeah. Can I help you."

"I'm Astrid Lincoln, a friend of Holly Rutherford."

He looked up at her as if he doubted her statement.

"I'm a reporter. Holly told me she's engaged to marry you, and it occurred to me that you might be willing to talk with me about her parents. I'm writing a follow-up story for *The Bugle*, and am interviewing everyone I can find who knew them. Obviously, you did."

He swept his hand toward a straight back chair for her to sit, and he took a similar one facing it. He brushed the mass of wavy hair out of his eyes.

"Well, I don't know a whole lot about them," he said. "I met them a couple of times. They seemed nice enough."

"You found them amiable?"

"Yes." The hesitant answer sounded more like a question than a statement.

"It must have been a shock when you heard about their murders."

"Sure was. Here we're just planning a wedding ceremony, me and Holly, and they get shot. Gosh. Can't imagine who'd do such a thing."

He threw a jeans clad leg over his knee and started kneading it, like a kitten with its mother. Astrid wondered if he had injured the leg.

"Were you here or in class when you got the news?"

"Oh, I was here. Working."

"I see. So you and Holly have set a date for the wedding?"

"No, not yet. I don't know when it will be. Of course, I have this job, but I also go to a class at Fairchance College. It doesn't leave me a lot of time to do much courting."

His grin pulled at the left side of his mouth.

"I expect not," Astrid said. "But now that the parents can't object, do you think you'll want to make the wedding sooner?"

His back straightened.

"Object? They didn't object to the marriage. Did she say they did?"

The question was obviously meant to find out what Holly had told her.

"I just thought maybe they were the hold-up."

"Oh. No. Well, they didn't exactly want to have us jump in too soon. Mr. Rutherford thought I should be settled in a steady job first. And he wanted Holly to get a new business established. He was going to advance her a large sum of money to do that, you know." His eyes readjusted to the window. "Imagine having a parent who hands you that kind of money without question."

A wistful thought? Had he felt that he couldn't support her, or support her business, like the parents could?

"But don't print that," he added quickly. "I wouldn't want her to think I noticed how he controlled her."

"I won't write it, but you think he controlled her?"

"Oh yeah. Be in by eleven. Don't go to an R-rated movie. Don't wear short dresses. Yeah, he controlled her. I'll bet she's relieved that he's gone, if you want my opinion. I know I am. But don't print that either."

"Definitely not." She was glad he was opening up this way. "You don't know how she feels now? You haven't talked with her?"

His face flushed and he studied his busy hands for a couple of seconds.

"Well, I thought I'd give her space. Well, you know. Just lost her parents. She don't want to shoot the breeze with me right now. I can't do much, anyway. I'm too busy here. I guess…that is, well, I've been thinking what I could say. I'm not good at that sort of thing, you know. I thought I'd wait and let her call me when she's ready."

Very supportive guy, Astrid thought.

"Actually," he added, "I don't know where she is. I shouldn't think she'd go back home where her folks were shot. Of course she might. There's no blood anywhere but in the living room."

Astrid refrained from asking him how he knew that. No mention of where police found blood was made in anything she'd seen or heard, and she had checked all stories.

"Do you know where she is?" he asked.

"I'm not sure. I do know she returned to work already."

"Oh. I suppose I could call her there."

Don't put yourself out.

Astrid started putting pen and pad into her bag.

"You know, Danny, I love animals. Are you too busy to show me what you have in the pound?"

He jumped up, all eagerness.

"Come this way. They're out back, of course. We have half a dozen puppies, four full-grown dogs, and eight kittens and six cats. Quite an assortment. You interested in taking one home?"

"I am. But I'm not sure my husband would look kindly on my bringing an animal home. I'd better leave that for another visit."

"Sure."

As they walked slowly past the animal shelter's upper and lower kennels, Astrid thought how much more enthusiastic Danny was for the animals than he appeared to be for Holly.

The dogs were mostly mongrel, some in worse condition than others. She hated to see the remnants of a dog that had been abused, all the liveliness beaten out of him. Then they arrived at the section for cats. A few had weepy, dead eyes, but some were downright adorable. Astrid stopped in front of a cage where three kittens played together, ignoring Danny and Astrid, as if there were no life beyond the cage.

"They're a happy bunch," she said.

"I think they're the cutest of all we've got here."

She studied each one. An all gray puff ball, one with the yellow, brown and white markings of a money cat, and a short-hair black and white.

"I'd really love to have that black and white tuxedo kitten. He looks so alert. Look at the black patch over one eye."

She laughed when the kitten stood on hind legs, widened his front ones, and pounced on the gray kitty.

"I call her Patch as a matter-of-fact."

From behind them came another voice, with the wheeze of a man suffering from either a bad cold or emphysema.

"You gonna take our Patch away, Miss?"

Looking at the thin man, Astrid decided he was very sick.

"Oh, I doubt it," Astrid said. "I'm Mrs. Astrid Lincoln."

"And I'm Dewey Ryman. Saw you just recently on TV."

"Ya. When the governor was here."

"You almost got shot yourself," he said.

Danny looked at his watch.

"Hey. I gotta go. Class starts in fifteen minutes."

"You bettah hustle, Danny."

As she watched him run to his car, Astrid said, "He'll never make it on time."

"Yup. He will. Drives like the devil's afta him."

Astrid turned back to the kittens rolling about the cage, just about able to keep from grinning at the man's very strong downeast accent. He outdid Charlie in that department.

"Does he have classes every day at this time?" she asked.

"No. He works full days some. Heah on weekends to give me a couple o' days off. Then I give him a full day off on Wednesdays since he don't have classes then and it gives him a break."

"I see. Well, he seems like a nice young man."

"Ayuh. Nice enough. He has his moments. I've seen him get kinda nasty with some o' the animals. Had to kick his ass outa here once. Told him if he wants to work for me, he can't be abusing the animals."

"So he has a temper."

"We all have a tempah, but you go out and kick a block o' wood if you need to get it out of your system. He strikes out at anyone or anything neah him."

"And yet you keep him on."

"For now. I've got my eye on someone else who wants to work heah. A girl. I dunno. Nevah had a female workah, but she'd be moah gentle with animals, I'm thinkin'."

Astrid walked to the other end of the room when Dewey began to cough long and hard. When he finished his hacking spell, he took a flattened pack of cigarettes from his shirt pocket and lit one up.

Well, why not? Wouldn't do much good to stop now, I'd say.

"I thank you for the tour," Astrid said after returning to his side. "I have to go now."

"Come back, Missus. That kitten won't stay small many weeks, ya know."

"I know. If I decide to take it, I'll be back. It's a girl?"

"Yup."

"They're the best."

"If you say so."

Out on the road again, Astrid regretted that she'd learned Danny was a liar with a bad temper. If she told Holly this, it might be the end of a perfectly good relationship should it not actually mean he was the killer. But even if he weren't a murderer, no woman should have to live with someone with a violent temper. For that matter, no one would want to be married to a liar. At that thought, she screwed up her face, wondering if Abram thought she was a liar by omission.

Well, he can just get over it.

In the meantime, she had another stop to make before going to the sheriff's office. She let her mind picture a grim scenario. Danny could have gone to the Rutherford house. He had access to junk cars so he might have driven a rusted car there and returned it to the junk yard. And that's what she was going to find out right now.

CHAPTER 13

She saw him coming toward her, but kept walking along frozen ruts between the two long rows of junked cars poking through blackened snow banks. This place gave new meaning to dreary. Intertwined huge old oak trees blocked the bright sky so thoroughly that it could be dusk. Black snow covered questionable humps. No doubt Mr. Gerber could locate whatever he wanted beneath these mounds. Astrid put a gloved hand over her nose against the biting air.

Taking long strides, she just might make it to the end before he caught up with her. She wasted no time looking at cars with broken axles, no tires, and missing doors. This car would be operable, without so much wrong with it as to attract a cop along the way to Fairchance. She was coming to the end of the frozen dirt driveway before she saw it, clear of snow unlike all the others, no tires missing, everything apparently intact, except that it was rusted below the doors and around the edges of both fenders--a rusted, faded, brown vintage Dodge.

"You want something, miss?"

He'd caught up with her, and he wasn't smiling.

"I'm not sure. I have a young brother who thinks he wants an old car to work on to see if he can get it running. He's a teenager, and you know how they are. He says he'd like to become a mechanic. Well, I must say he is very good at taking things apart and putting them back together again without anything left over. And generally they work, too. So I'm wondering if this car would be something that he can work on. What do you think?"

Now he stopped scowling and started scratching his head. Astrid thought his hair must be full of grease, since everything else about him was. Danny, with his red hair, did not resemble his father. In fact, Danny looked more Irish.

"If he wants something that isn't working, this isn't it."

"Oh? I noticed that it has a lot of rust. But you say it works?"

"That's right. If he wants a working car that he can do body work on, this will fit the bill."

"Oh no. That's not the direction he wants to go in. He's mechanical. Anything else that might do?"

"Not really. Anything that can't move, is all apart. I sell parts, you know."

"Well, I'll tell him he probably should find something else to put together. Frankly, I don't think he'll ever be a mechanic. Dad wants him to go to college. He'll end up there, I'm sure. Thank you, anyway."

"Uh, huh. You're welcome," He stopped scratching, pointed at her and said, "Say, aren't you…?"

She ran back to her Jeep before he could finish asking his question. He was going to ask about her TV appearance, she was quite sure. That was the trouble with notoriety.

Can't get away with anything.

But maybe she had. Maybe he wouldn't mention this meeting with his family tonight. Wouldn't matter anyway. The important thing was that she found out about the car. It had to be the one that the neighbor saw in front of the Rutherford house that day.

And, putting two and two together, it must be that Danny was the killer.

Wait a minute. You don't know that. It's circumstantial. You need more than the fact that he's a liar, has a temper, and his father has a working rusted car in his junk yard.

Unless Danny had been seen in the car, unless he could be identified as the one who held the gun that shot the couple or that he even had a gun, she had no more than a hunch that he was guilty of murder.

"Dammit."

She should have looked around inside that car. If Danny had used a gun, he'd have had to hide it somewhere. Maybe he hid it in the car. Only problem there was that she would have been rather obvious, looking under seats and in the glove compartment.

"I wonder how well he guards the place after dark."

She didn't see any dogs or signs of electronic alarms. If it weren't for the fact that they had to attend the party, she'd go out there tonight and take a closer look.

Probably ought to tell Larry about what I found.

She pondered on that for a while, weighing the chances that he'd go look anyway. For all she knew he might already have the car that was used. Or he could have the gun. So no need to check in with him just now.

After all, I was checking out Danny for Holly. I'll just leave it at that.

The little voice told her not to do any more probing, not to poke her nose into an ongoing investigation by authorities. But her own big voice said, "It won't hurt to look around a bit more."

Back in town, she drove directly to the sheriff's office. It was always busy, but today it was busier and noisier than ever. A woman sat on the floor, her back to the wall next to the desk, her knees pulled up to her chin. She was crying, not even trying to cover her face.

Astrid looked around at the chaos and went to the front desk. "What's going on, Archie?" she said.

"A madman barged in just two minutes ago. You just missed him, Astrid. He was waving a shotgun and shouting, 'Someone's going to die here today. I'll find him.' I hid under the desk. Damn. I thought he'd shoot through it, but he just went on by and headed down the hall. I couldn't see, but I heard the gunshot ..."

Gunshot! She ran down the hallway toward Abram's office. Was he hurt? She pushed aside two people who appeared to be in a trance. At Larry's open door, she skidded to a stop.

"Oh my God. Is he dead?" She needn't have asked.

Still clutching a .12 gauge shotgun in his right hand, the body that sprawled just inside the doorway wore a dirty sheepskin jacket. Blood outlined a hole over the heart area. The thin face had frozen into a look of complete surprise.

Larry's expression was no less dramatic, still flushed and wild, as alert as if a lion had charged him.

"He's dead." Larry said. "Well, I knew you were an aggressive Lois Lane, but what were you doing? Dogging my attacker?"

Astrid swallowed a few times to hold down the bile. She didn't want to become ill and draw the attention of all these officers and clerks.

"No, of course not. I came to see you. What's this all about, Larry?"

"Who knows? Deputy Smith here says the police have been called to his shack at the edge of town several times. He's Guy Platt. They tell me he was a heavy drinker. I don't know why he came in here looking for me. I heard him yelling that he was going to kill someone, so I had my weapon ready when he pulled the door open and as soon as I saw the shotgun aimed at me, I instinctively pulled up and shot him. I hope someone can shed light on his reason for coming here."

"I've seen this man. He came into our office and gave Dee a hard time several weeks ago."

Behind her, she heard, "Astrid? You all right?"

Abram's voice relieved her tension. Now she could almost cry to see him all in one piece, concerned over her welfare.

"I guess we're all a bit shaken up, Abram, but the only one feeling no pain is the gunman."

Abram glanced down at the face, did a double take, and said, "I know this man."

"You, too?" Larry said. "How well do you know him, Abram?"

"When I was a kid of about eleven, he lived next door to us. One day a couple of friends and I were down by the stream not far from our homes. We were throwing rocks into the water. Guy was fishing just around the bend in the stream, We didn't see him until he came charging at us like a bull, yelling that we were disturbing the fish. We told him we'd stop, but that wasn't enough. He picked up a long piece of wood and ran after us. I tripped and fell and he walloped me a couple of times across the back. I wasn't very big then. When I got home, I took my shirt off to wash up at the sink and my brother saw the welts. Well, I had to tell him what happened, and he got real mad, went over to the Platt house and pulled Guy out. I didn't see the fight, but Guy never troubled me again."

"Still doesn't account for his coming after me."

"Maybe he wasn't after you, Larry. Maybe he was after me."

Astrid reached for Abram and fell into his arms.

• • • •

Chris left the real estate agency with a heavy heart. How he would like to tell Holly about their relationship but he mustn't do that. She wouldn't be happy to know that her father was a graduate of a New York State prison, convicted of killing her own mother, and that he had come here solely to see her. She might even think that he had been instrumental in having her adoptive parents murdered. That was a disturbing thought, and this wasn't the first time he'd had it. Authorities knew about him of course. Would they arrest him? He'd likely be under suspicion. Every day he expected a police officer would come to take him for questioning. Drew was in the same boat. Maybe they'd both be suspected of conspiring to kill the couple.

Chris felt that he could be facing a bad time of it. He probably shouldn't have come to Maine. There were plenty of places he could have gone. After all, his computer skill was exceptional and he knew it. A good many places would have taken him on. He had excellent references from prison authorities.

A wild thought hit him. It might be best to go to the police station and give them a statement about where he was at the time of the murder. Then again, he might appear to be too eager to clear himself. Sometimes that was worse than just waiting for them to make a move. He needed to talk with Drew. They left prison at the same time and came to this area together. It was unlikely that they wouldn't be viewed as dangerous.

The irony for him was that he had the perfect alibi. He was with Holly Rutherford, the daughter of the murdered couple. How much better could it get? Of course, it gave him no pleasure to say Holly was someone else's daughter, but legally she was.

Feeling lighter now that he thought of the obvious, he went to the office before going to the church office where he'd get to talk with the lovely Sandy Brewster. As he put together the pamphlets and catalog he would need, Chris looked down at his old clothes, having removed the uniform. Well-pressed and clean, they were new when he wore them in court. Personally, he liked the neat black suit with trousers that looked like trousers and not the current look of flared pajama bottoms. No platform shoes for him, either, or long vests. What were they calling the modern style? He just saw it mentioned in a magazine. Oh yes. The disco look. Well they could keep the disco look. He noticed that Sandy didn't wear mini skirt or platform shoes.

Oh dear. Well, of course she is wearing one raised shoe. I wonder if the club foot bothers her.

It didn't bother Chris. If she had a prosthetic leg, he wouldn't care. She had a fine face and figure, and appeared to be a gentle soul. He liked all that.

"You headed out again, Chris?"

His boss didn't have a tight rein on him, but probably wondered what was taking him so long to gather up a few brochures.

"Going over to the church office. The secretary needs a computer desk, and I told her I'd take her a catalog of what we can get for her. I'll give her some of these brochures about computers, too. I'll need to do some measurements."

"Okay. Tell her for me that I'll be in church Sunday."

"I doubt she gives a damn, to tell the truth."

"No, but my wife does."

They laughed and Chris left, glad to have a respite from thoughts of Holly, her dead parents, and possible harassment by police. Later he would call Drew to meet him at the diner for supper, and they could talk over the less pleasant aspect of being here in Fairchance at the wrong time, two parolees trying to put their lives together. For now, he left his car parked out back and strode toward the imposing Catholic Church, his heart racing as he got closer.

I feel like a teenager picking up a girl for the first time. Gotta stop this nonsense.

CHAPTER 14

By mid-afternoon Astrid had talked with Danny and the director of the animal shelter, she'd seen the old car in the junk yard, and she had walked in on a shooting at the sheriff's office. That was about enough to fill anyone's day, she thought as she pored over her notes and listened to conversations on the tape recorder.

"Okay you two," Charlie said, in a weary voice. "I'm going home and take a couple of winks before that birthday party. Jenny's shopping today. I dread to see the credit card bill. She said she didn't have a thing to wear, but I could swear her clothes take up three-quarters of the closet."

Will guffawed. "Know what you mean. I think my wife is with yours, Charlie."

"What about you, Astrid?" Charlie said.

"I don't have a wife."

With a groan, "Aren't you going to get in on the shopping frenzy today?"

"Maybe. Haven't given it much thought."

Out of the corner of her eye she saw the look that passed between the two men. She thought, *Okay, wise guys. You just may get a surprise when I walk in tonight.* But she told them nothing. Better they think she would show up in jeans or pants suit.

After both men left, Astrid finished writing up notes for the shooting story, cleared her desk top, and headed out to the parking lot. She stopped first at the real estate office, where she hoped she wouldn't find Holly. But she did.

"What are you still doing here, Holly? You were going to go home and rest."

"Well, I got busy, and I just wanted to finish a few things first."

Puffy eyes, limp hair, deep frown, all reflected the ordeal Holly was trying to handle. It seemed a pity to have to tell her about Danny, but it had to be done. Astrid had a strong feeling that he was not a good choice for a husband, but Holly should decide for herself.

"If you aren't too busy," she said, "I can tell you about the conversation I had with Danny today."

Holly reacted in such a deadpan, unconcerned manner that Astrid wondered if she wanted to hear the worst possible news. Could it be that she really believed he killed her parents?

Turning away from the new computer, Holly motioned for Astrid to sit next to her.

"Tell me," she said.

"Understand, I was careful not to allude to the murder in a way that he'd think I was fishing."

Holly nodded. "Good."

"After he left to go to school, I talked with his boss. Holly, I have to say that Danny lied to me. He told me he got along well with your parents and that they didn't object to your plans for marriage."

"Oh lord. Well, they did. What else did he say?"

"He told me he worked Wednesday, but his boss said he didn't. It's his day off each week."

Holly pulled in her lips, as if she were trying to keep from crying. Her voice was hoarse when she spoke again.

"I had doubts that he really loved me, but I didn't think he'd lie like that. I still don't think he could have killed my parents."

Astrid decided to leave it like that. No need to tell her about Danny's temper. She was sad enough.

"Holly, may I make an observation about him?"

"Sure."

"I don't think he's as ready for marriage as you are. You know what I mean?"

"I think you're right. Thank you, Astrid. I appreciate your help. You know, my mother was making a formal gown for me to wear at the real estate convention in Augusta next month. The material is the most beautiful royal blue velvet. My dad was helping me study contract law. And we had planned … Oh, God. I just want that insane killer, whoever it is, to pay for what he did."

She began to sob. Astrid waited. She studied the cross-stitched wall sign, *Welcome,* set amid red and pink roses. Probably another gift of love made by her mother.

What kind of person would shoot a man and a woman in cold blood? And why did that Guy Platt go berserk today and get himself shot for no reason at all? Why all this madness? She understood General Lee Metcalf's motivation. He sought power and recognition. Worse than that, he was plain crazy. Well, there it is, Astrid thought. Madness for one reason or another. She tried to concentrate on Holly, to put away the awful dread that hit her when Abram suggested he may have been the one Guy Platt was looking for. What if that were the case, and Platt had found Abram? He'd have been defenseless with no gun like the sheriff had.

When Holly seemed calmer, Astrid offered her a ride home, but Holly said she would be okay to drive.

"I need to make a phone call before I go back to Ginny's for the night," Holly said. "You know, Danny hasn't talked with me yet. I did think he might call and tell me how sorry he was that I lost my parents. Seems like that's the least he could have done. I realize now just how much, or how little, he cares. My dad said I shouldn't trust him. I guess he was right."

Astrid nodded. "I have to agree. Again, Holly, if you need anything, just let me know."

In her Jeep, Astrid hoped that Holly would be tactful. Danny had a quick temper, and apparently a destructive one. Whether he was a killer or not, he could conceivably harm Holly.

I can't trust a man who professes to love animals and yet hurts them. I just have to believe he's not beyond murder.

But, for now, she had her own agenda. She pulled away from the agency and thought, *Okay. It's now or never.*

She chose now and headed for the finest dress shop in Fairchance. She figured she should be able to get something nice within the hour that remained before her next appointment.

• • • •

Drew tried not to be obvious about watching Mr. Bertram through the open door, but each time he looked up, he saw the repetitive motions--moving pencils, picking a file from the stack on his desk and studying it only to put it back, turning his chair toward the window and craning his neck as if watching for someone. Finally, Mr. Bertram stood, paced, came to the door, turned and paced again. When he came to the door again, he walked over to Drew's desk.

"He's coming back today, you know."

"Pardon?"

"Mr. Levitch. He should arrive any minute now."

"Oh. No, I didn't know. Is there anything I should do?"

"Do? No. Just wait for him to come over to you. He'll introduce himself, I'm sure."

Drew felt uncomfortable just watching Mr. Bertram's obvious discomfort. Why? The two had worked together for a long time. Why should he be nervous now that the man was coming home? It suddenly occurred to him that maybe Mr. Bertram had not told Mr. Levitch he had hired a junior attorney.

He was about to ask, when the door opened and a short man in fine black coat with mink collar walked in, a real-life male fashion plate, all in black. He looked down to see if this man was wearing spats. He wasn't, but guessing by the visible part of black leather boots, zipped on the sides, he wore expensive Italian leather.

The partners shook hands, ignoring Drew. Without preamble, Mr. Levitch said, "You have a report for me?"

"I do. We can discuss it whenever you want to. How did the case go?"

"It was a tough one, but I won. The prosecutor was a lightweight."

Mr. Bertram congratulated him, and nodded toward Drew, directing Mr. Levitch's attention in that direction.

"Who's this?" Levitch asked. He still wore his fully buttoned coat.

"This is Drew Godfrey. I've brought him in on a temporary basis for a month. Drew, this is Mr. Levitch."

Mr. Levitch nodded, and Drew took off his glasses before standing up.

"Nice to meet you, sir," he said.

"Yes." To Bertram he said, "Come into my office, H.J.,"

Still standing, Drew watched as the two entered the tidy tomb. The door closed. He sat down again and thought that he was likely the topic of discussion. Maybe he should start putting things away, judging by the look he got from the senior partner. What surprised

107

him was that Levitch looked about 10 or 15 years younger than Mr. Bertram. They were very different--Bertram, the country lawyer; and Levitch, the suave city attorney with a stern face.

It was the first time that Drew had heard the word temporary, and for a month, at that. He had thought his job was secure, unless he screwed up. Maybe that was Bertram's way of breaking the news. Maybe he did this all on his own without Mr. Levitch's approval.

Now came the question, what would he do if Mr. Levitch said he was out?

Oh boy. Well, I won't go back to The Kingdom with Les. Maybe I can go to Augusta and try for a governor's staff job that requires paralegal knowledge.

Then, again, they might not welcome an ex-convict. That damned stigma. He was excited when he came to work here because Mr. Bertram accepted him for his qualifications, and allowed that he had paid his debt to society, or rather that he'd taken his punishment.

Drew learned in those hallowed halls of hell that few would help you and that you couldn't trust even the man who had your back. By all rights he should have come out more cynical than he did. Now here he was, once again getting used to the fact that on the outside you could trust a man's word, only to hear that the position might not last more than a month. Some men would just exit right now and…before he could complete that line of thinking, he listened. The voices behind the closed door rose and fell like tidal waves, making it impossible to hear full sentences.

"I told you …" That was Mr. Bertram's voice, louder than Drew had ever heard him talk. "You think that I won't …" His voice faded again. Later, he thought he heard the word murder, but it was muffled, could have been something else, maybe mother.

The other voice was firmer, but also rose and fell, and Drew could picture Mr. Levitch pounding the desk. At any rate, something sounded like pounding.

"No damned way that I'd let …"

What? Drew wondered. After a few seconds, he heard Bertram's voice again.

"This is your mess, not mine. And I'll tell you this …"

Drew's eyes were glued to the door, as if that would help him hear better. He'd never heard Bertram shout, never would have guessed that he could be anything but softspoken and even-tempered.

Are they arguing over me? I could rap on the door and tell them I'm leaving. But I won't. I want to see how this plays out.

The door swung open and Drew bent his head over his work. Without a word, Mr. Bertram crossed the room to his own office and slammed the door. Instinctively, Drew looked to see where Levitch was, but his limited view of the office didn't reveal the man. Returning to his work, it was only a few seconds before Drew jumped when Levitch slammed his door, too.

The two hours remaining in the day dragged, with no sign of either partner. At five o'clock, making as much noise as he could, Drew straightened up his desk, put on his outer clothing, and reached for the door handle, all the while expecting Mr. Bertram to come out and say goodnight or goodbye. But he didn't.

Maybe I'll see him tonight.

As prearranged, he met Chris at the diner, at a booth in the back. After the diner was destroyed by fire, the new owners built it to the original state, plus an added section that wrapped around the kitchen and rest room areas. The two booths in that section provided more privacy than any other place in the diner, and today that's what they wanted.

"How's it going with you?" he asked.

Chris hesitated, read the menu quickly, then laid it aside and leaned over the table.

"I got a bit worried today, Drew. Thinking about the murders. You know, we're both felons, new in town. We could be high on the list of suspects."

Drew thought about that before answering. The prospect had crossed his mind, but somehow he felt secure. But, maybe he hadn't thought it out as thoroughly as he should.

"You have the better alibi of the two of us. You were with the daughter. But I suppose I could be right up there on the list. I didn't go to work for Mr. Bertram until yesterday. I was with my brother at The Kingdom, of course, but I don't know how much credibility he would have should they ask him. He's part of that outlaw militia, took training from the man they called General Metcalf."

"Before he attempted to assassinate the governor."

"Yeah. So what do I say if I'm taken in for questioning? I don't care to make a connection to Les, and otherwise I don't have an alibi."

"Damn. When I thought about it at first, I thought I might be in trouble. But now, I don't know what to say. Probably, good or bad, you'd better tell them you were with your brother. At least he can place you over there and nowhere near here."

"If they believe me."

They ate in silence, and when they finished and were outside the diner, Drew stopped Chris.

"One more thing," he said. "I may not be working here much longer."

"What're you talking about?"

"Mr. Levitch came in today. First time I met him, and he wasn't very friendly. When Mr. Bertram introduced me, he said he hired me as a temporary attorney. He mentioned a month. I don't know what's going on. I'll try to see Mr. Bertram tonight and get the truth from him. If I'm out of there in a month, I'd better start searching right now for a new job to go to. I can't be without work for long."

Chris looked shocked.

"That sounds underhanded enough. You just can't trust attorneys."

Drew landed a light punch to his friend's shoulder.

"Seriously," Chris said. "If I find out about anything open in your field, I'll be sure to let you know."

"Appreciate it, friend."

Drew felt as if someone had hit him in the belly. After the high of finding a law office that would take him and getting a great place to live to boot, now to know that he was lied to by the one man he trusted made him sick. The let-down took him back to when he was sentenced by Judge Rutherford who never let the defense attorney explain the circumstances of the fight. He should feel sorry that Rutherford was murdered, but in his heart he believed the man deserved exactly what he got. Not his wife, though. That was too tragic.

Drew told himself not to spoil these few minutes he had with his friend any longer. He had a life, too.

"So, tell me, Chris. How did it go with your church secretary?"

Chris grinned.

"I wish she was *my* church secretary, but I don't see that happening. She's a sweet thing, though. I have a hard time explaining the advantages of a particular computer stand when we both lean over the catalog, almost head-to-head, believe me."

"Yeah? Get a little warm around the edges, huh?"

"*Edges* be-damn. Whew. I feel like I need to go outside and jump head-first into a snowbank."

Drew roared.

"You'd better ask her for a date soon. You can't take that kind of excitement too much longer, I'd say."

Chris looked away, as if studying the traffic. Drew did feel sorry for him. It was tough, no matter what you tried to do, this being an ex-con.

"To tell the truth," Chris said, "I asked her to go to dinner with me tonight. Nothing fancy, I told her. Just a plain dinner at that restaurant, Lakepoint, that everyone talks about."

"I haven't been there, of course, but someone told me the food is good, and the view is great. I'd say it's a good choice. Since you're with me, I guess she said no."

"But she said she'd like to go another time. She has a special choir rehearsal tonight."

"Choir? So she sings, too."

"I may just go over and sit in the back of the church to listen."

Drew nodded. "Good idea. Could be time enough to take her for coffee afterward."

"Yeah. I thought of that, too."

Drew pulled his collar up.

"Is it ever going to warm up?" he said. "I read in the newspaper that the library is open until seven on Fridays. Think I'll go over and search ads for a position where I might fit in."

"You don't know yet if you'll be let go," Chris said.

"No, but I believe in being prepared."

"I always knew you were a good scout."

"Sure." Drew looked up at the darkening sky. "Enjoy the music. I'll see you Monday."

Chapter 15

What was Abram going to say? Would he be angry, or would he say it looked great, or even good? It didn't much matter now. It was done, and that was that. Astrid drove toward her house, debating whether to break the news of her change or to wait and let him see it when he arrived at the party. Deep down she knew it did not pay to spring big surprises on him.

As she approached home, she found a suburban in her driveway, unfamiliar to her. She slowed the Jeep. Not Gunnar, unless he traded for some reason. It was a new vehicle, so possibly he traded to please Charlotte and help her get over the loss of the baby.

"Might as well go find out," she said, parking the car in the garage. She grabbed up her packages and shopping bags, and went to the kitchen door. Inside, she could hear low voices coming from the living room. She dropped the packages on the table, looked toward the telephone desk drawer where there was a handgun, but thought better of it. Whoever was here would leave. She'd see to that.

At the living room double door, she struggled to find her voice. "Geraldine. What are you doing here?"

"Aunt Astrid. What have you done to your hair?"

"Never mind that. What are you doing here? First, tell me how you got in."

"If you must know, when I came out here yesterday, you weren't here. So I chatted with Abram for a while, and at the door, I pressed the lock button so the door wouldn't lock when he closed it. I guess he didn't notice."

Astrid fought for composure despite her fury.

"Don't ever try that again or I'll have you arrested, maybe not for breaking in, but for entering without permission."

"That's no way to talk to me, especially since I came to invite you to my wedding, which is more than you did for me. This is Preston Norman. We're going to be married next week, and I'd like to have you there. You and Abram, of course."

Getting married would undoubtedly be the best solution to settling this wild one. That is, best if the man was not wild, too.

"Where and what time?" she asked.

"A bit abrupt, aren't you?" Geraldine looked up at Preston and giggled. "She's always abrupt. Sometimes she's downright mean."

"Well?"

Astrid would not engage in conversation or react to digs, not with her niece.

"Why don't you sit down and be sociable for a change?" Geraldine said.

"I'll stand. You're not staying that long. So?"

Preston remained silent and unsmiling. He obviously was making a detailed study of Astrid. With coal black hair and dark eyes, he was good-looking enough, and a contrast to blue eyed Geraldine, who favored the Swedish side of the family. If she were to be honest, Astrid would have to say that they made an attractive couple. However, she wasn't in the mood to be congratulatory.

"We're getting married at The Kingdom. I guess you know where that is," Geraldine said.

"I saw you there when you came over to dig up dirt on the militia," Preston said. His tone was chilling.

As surly as he was, Astrid almost felt sorry for Geraldine--almost. She couldn't possibly know what she was getting into with these militia people.

"And when?"

"Next Saturday at 10 a.m.," Geraldine said. "Not too early for you, is it Auntie?"

"I'll see what Abram has planned. We'll make it if we can."

She'd been looking at each decoration in the room.

"Well, if you're not sure, you might want to give me a gift now. Maybe a pair of silver candlesticks?"

"Tell you what, Geraldine. I'll mail them to you. What I'd like to know is how did you get involved with someone from The Kingdom?"

"Your newspaper stories about the group, what else? I thought it all sounded quite exciting and something I'd like to join. You know, revolution. I'm revolutionary, always have been. Just like my father. I simply drove out there and talked with a few of the people, and Preston offered to show me around. When I said I had no place to sleep, he got me into one of the empty duplexes. Too bad so many of those good people moved away after you got General Metcalf shot."

"I ..." Oh, how Astrid wanted to take her on, but she didn't have time. "Ya. Too bad. So ..." She swept her hand toward the front hallway. "I guess we're done here. If I don't get to the wedding, I wish you a happy marriage, Geraldine. Preston."

"I think she's kicking us out," Geraldine said.

They exchanged disgusted looks but got to their feet and headed for the door, where Preston turned around and faced Astrid. His half asleep eyes never changed expression. His demeanor gave the impression that he didn't allow whatever compassion he might have to rise to the surface.

"Too bad you're a reporter, Astrid. I think I could like you. But as it is, best if we don't cross paths too often. You don't seem to understand the significance of the movement General Metcalf started. He didn't live to fulfill his ambition to cleanse the world of political and religious evils. But his ideals are not dead. We are re-forming, and we will overcome the hypocrisy that you and all the media and politicians and preachers wallow in. We'll see to it that your lies are silenced. The media will soon feel our power. Mark my word."

Geraldine waggled her head, taunting, as if she had a great sage at her side, about to become her husband.

"How soon?" Astrid said.

"Everything in order. One thing now, the next later. I'm not like Metcalf. He had no patience left. This time we're moving like the country's original Patriots, quietly and out-of-sight, striking where and when the enemy is least prepared. We'll make our stands one by one, and authorities won't know what's happened."

"Such mystery," she said. "As I recall, the general was stopped by a woman with nothing more than a gun look-alike. You may not see the banana peel, but one wrong step and you just may slip as stupidly as your wonderful leader did. Playing God is damned risky business."

"You already have an unsolved tragedy here in Fairchance. It's only the beginning."

"Are you saying you're responsible for the death of Judge Rutherford and his wife?"

She hadn't meant to show her surprise.

"Did I say that?"

He took Geraldine's arm, opened the door, and steered her outside. Before he closed the door, he said, "Just be careful what you print. It would be too bad to have to face court action for slander."

Astrid pressed her fingers against her temples, trying not to think that the community was being attacked again. As for Geraldine, she now wished she could have a long talk with her, but it was too late. Obviously she had bought the militia's propaganda. Considering her background and her attitude, as rebellious as her father's, it should be no surprise. Such a pity. With all the places she might have gone, she chose the most dangerous.

Returning to the kitchen, she put away groceries and sat down to a light snack. The one thing she needed to do in order not to give Abram a surprise that could turn embarrassing was to call him. It took her another 10 minutes to get up enough courage for the conversation, but finally she dialed the number. He seemed happy to hear her voice.

"What's up, dear? Let me guess. You don't want me to forget the party tonight. Oops. Hold on a minute."

He was gone only seconds. When he returned, Astrid said, "Ya, that's partly it. I need to tell you something, but first, is everything okay there now? Heard anything new on why that man wanted to shoot the sheriff or you?"

"Things seem to have calmed down. Guy was obviously very drunk, and I think that bothers Larry. He might not have been so quick to shoot if he'd known how drunk he was. But on the other hand, if he'd waited, Guy could have shot him in a split second, too. Larry has gone home already. I don't know if he'll be on temporary suspension, but I expect so. I believe it's customary under these circumstances to have a board of inquiry go over the incident. He doesn't have anything to worry about, though. There were enough witnesses to the whole thing."

"I wonder if Larry and Beth will go to the party tonight."

"We'll just have to wait and see."

"Ya."

After a long silence, Abram said, "Well? You said you have something to tell me. Please don't say you tried to make another custard pie."

They both laughed over his reference to her baking disaster a few days ago.

"No, not that."

"What then? Better hurry up before it gets busy here."

"Ahh, well, you see I went to the beauty parlor this afternoon. I had my hair cut."

Dead silence.

"Abram? You're mad at me."

His deep chuckle told her differently.

"Of course not. I told you once before that if you wanted to cut it, I didn't care. How does it look? You like it?"

"I don't know. I think I do. It just feels strange to have so little hair now. My head feels light."

"I'll see you at the party at about eight."

"Did I tell you it's at the Edge of Town Motel?"

"Only half a dozen times. I'll find it."

"Amazing. Please remember that I love you," she said, and realized that the reason she said it was to buffer his possible outrage later.

"Oh hell. How can I forget that? I love you, too. Even if you are bald."

"Abram! I am not bald."

CHAPTER 16

At the library, Drew looked first on the computer to see if he could find job openings. Not being schooled in the use of one, he gave it up as a useless search, and went to the newspapers and magazines. He wrote down addresses and phone numbers of what few openings he found calling for his expertise. He would take anything in a law firm.

Driving home, he felt less apprehensive now. If the partners didn't want him to stay on, there were options. He wanted to believe that. At least two ads looked promising, one in Maine and one in New Jersey. His problem was how to get around his record. Here, he just filled out a resume truthfully, and when he was called in for the job interview, he found that Mr. Bertram almost dismissed prison time as a minor incident. Why did he change his mind so quickly when Levitch came back?

One way to find out. Ask him.

At home, Drew found a dark house. Either drapes were all pulled or Bertram was not here. Out back, the empty garage confirmed his absence.

Okay. I'll just wait. He'll come home sometime tonight.

It was Friday night. Maybe this was Bertram's night to kick up his heels. Drew almost laughed at the picture of his boss doing that. Then again, he had heard a female voice once. Maybe he took her to dinner Friday nights. Whatever, he'd come home sometime, and Drew would confront him when he did. No sense waiting until later.

. . . .

The Edge of Town Motel looked like a mansion with its white fringe of Christmas lights still hanging over the front entryway and bright red sign aglow on the roof. To Astrid it felt almost like home, and she cherished the evenings she and Abram spent over that stupid puzzle during the weeks after her house was blown up and each had a room here before they found a place to rent. She enjoyed coming back where they were greeted like old friends.

She found the party under way when she got to the front conference room. The banquet would be in the room beyond, where round tables with eight chairs were set up. For a few minutes she stood just inside the doorway to catch the soft strains of Glenn Miller's rendition of *Under A Blanket Of Blue,* perfect background for this romantic evening. She slipped off her long coat and hung it on a rack with all the others. Stomping her feet to warm them in the beige dressy flats, she wished she had worn her usual boots, but they wouldn't exactly go with the new dress. It appeared that there were maybe 30 people here. She had met several of the community leaders, but not all.

She heard someone say, "Hey. Look at Astrid."

The room went quiet. Seemed like everyone turned to stare at her. Not for the first time in her life, she felt embarrassed. She thought she was over that shy phase of her life, but now she wondered if she'd gone too bold with short hair and flared knee-length gold dress, cut low enough to show a bit of cleavage. She hadn't thought twice about the left-over Christmas dress once she saw that it fit her and was marked down half price.

She automatically touched her hair, a short version of Princess Diana's flipped style. Those who knew her were used to seeing her in jeans or pants suit and hair braided and coiled around her head. Could it be that she looked like a giant lemon squeezed thin? She would like to escape and return home, but it was too late. Well, she refused to slouch in defeat. Let them stare.

"I'll be damned," she said, her voice loud and clear. "I thought I was coming to a party, not a wake."

Laughter filled the room. Charlie clapped.

"You look great, Astrid," he said. The entire newspaper personnel, wives included, came to greet her.

"We're so glad to see you." Dee, the perfect hostess, took her hand. "I love the hairdo, and the color of your dress suits you."

At her side, Marvin Cornell beamed his approval, whether it was with Dee, or her, Astrid couldn't be sure. Most likely, both.

"Tell me, Mr. Cornell, did Dee surprise you with the party?"

"Surprise me! She certainly did. But, then, Dee always surprises me."

He squeezed Dee close to his side.

"Happy birthday," Astrid said.

"It's a very happy birthday," he replied.

Dee steered her to the largest group huddled by the punch bowl.

"Everyone. For those of you who don't know her, this is Astrid Lincoln. I believe Mr. Lincoln will be along soon, and when he comes we can go in to dinner. For now, let me introduce you."

Astrid wished Abram would get off work early. She should have asked him to try. No way could she remember all the names as they were thrown at her, but she recognized a few, including bankers and attorneys. They were all people with whom Marvin associated. It was obvious that Dee had no difficulty blending in with his business associates, and no surprise. She had all the same type associations herself years ago in Twin Ports. She had that wonderful knack of smiling and looking interested, even with her worst enemy.

Once the introductions were finished, Dee went to the dining room beyond the double doors to supervise, and Marvin joined three of his friends. Astrid stood with a glass of punch, and sipped to be sure it wasn't spiked. It wasn't.

"Mrs. Lincoln," she barely heard the voice behind her, "I'd like to ask you a question."

Facing the man, Astrid recognized the lawyer, Abe Levitch. She remembered the name because of Abram. There were no similarities in more than name, however, especially in stature.

"What's that, Mr. Levitch?"

"Do you know anything new about that militia group you were writing about?"

"Not very much. But I understand some of the members have returned to their homes there in Greenboro. They created a town that they call The Kingdom in the middle of nowhere."

"You've been out there, have you?"

"Ya. I interviewed some of them before I wrote that first story."

"I meant recently."

"Oh, no."

He was probably the best dressed man she'd seen in a very long while. In college, she had a professor who always dressed to the nines like that. Students called him Sweetie behind his back. She treated him with respect, however. He was a good teacher.

"If Judge Rutherford were alive, he and his wife would be here at this party," he mused. "I just wonder if there's a connection between their deaths and someone from that militia. Have you heard anything more about the murders?"

She wouldn't think the question strange except that he appeared quite anxious, as if it were urgent that he know all there was to know.

"No, I haven't. But I see Sheriff Knight talking with Chief Raleigh. Let's go over and ask them. I would like to know the latest myself."

He looked in the direction she indicated, and his voice became almost a whisper.

"I'd rather not right now. I just thought if you knew something you might share it with me, considering my friendship with the Rutherfords."

"I see. Well, if I find out anything new I'll be sure to share it with you. Of course, I get only what they want to tell me for a newspaper story, so I don't always hear the whole story, you understand."

"I understand very well."

"You live here, so I expect you didn't know the judge when he was on the bench."

His smile looked almost sinister.

"But I did. I was in New York and defended someone I knew. That's when I became acquainted with the judge. He presided over that case."

"What a coincidence that you both moved to Fairchance and picked up your friendship here."

"He's the one who moved here. I'm a native of Fairchance." He looked around the room, obviously seeking out a particular face.

"I haven't spoken to my partner yet this evening. Will you excuse me?"

"Certainly. Nice meeting you, Mr. Levitch."

"Mmm."

I wonder what his problem is. Surely seemed nervous.

Astrid thought his real interest in the shootings wasn't as he presented to her. Obviously, he wasn't being open about his friend, the judge, if he was a close friend. And why did he want to know about the militia? What did he know that she didn't know and how could she find out?

She walked toward the two lawmen, and saw Beth first. As always, she was a vision of perfection, wearing black cocktail dress and silver necklace. Black was a perfect complement to her dark beauty. Tall like herself, Beth couldn't look more glamorous.

"Hi Astrid. What a surprise. I like your hair short. Gives you a less severe look."

"Thanks. I feel half naked. I came over to see if there's anything new on the murders."

"Not that I've heard. But Larry is being unusually quiet, I must say. He comes home and says nothing about work. Something's bothering him, and I don't know what to make of it. I thought at first that he was still mourning the chief's death, but it seems to be something more than that. And then today, that terrible incident at his office. I wanted to cry when he told me about it. He didn't say much, though. What do you know about that?"

"No more than you do, I'm sure. I was there to ask about the Rutherford murders, but the shooting incident sort of overshadowed everything else for the moment. Should I even ask him, do you think?"

"Why not. The worst he can do is tell you to go to hell."

"Beth! I can't believe you said that."

"I thought I might as well say it before you did."

They laughed.

"What's the joke?" Larry's voice startled them.

"Your wife is becoming vulgar, Larry."

Larry eyed Beth with a question mark.

"Now Astrid," Beth said. "You're getting me in trouble. Don't pay any attention to her, Larry. She's a trouble-maker."

"That I believe," he said.

"You're ganging up on me," Astrid said. "Okay, what I really want to know, Larry, is where you're at in the Rutherford case. Is there anything I can report from you next week?"

He sipped his punch, and sighed.

"I wish there were something, Astrid. It's a tough one. Of course it's early yet, but...and don't quote me on this...the case ran cold almost immediately. We're following every lead we can think of, and can't come up with anything that ties in. The neighbors seem not to have noticed anything out of the way, except for the one across the street and he didn't see much. We can't find the car. Anyone who might be a logical suspect has an alibi. So at the moment, we seem to be planted on square one."

"Mr. Levitch just asked me if I'd talked with anyone from The Kingdom. I thought that militia had disbanded, but I did hear that they are returning. Do you know anything about them?"

Astrid noticed Larry's twitch when she mentioned Levitch.

"Detective Green has been keeping an eye on the place about once a week. They have been dribbling back from wherever they went, though the camp is far from full again. I doubt that anyone out there murdered the Rutherfords. They're busy reassembling."

And I'm afraid my niece is one of them.

"I won't be working and I don't know how long I'll be off the job. It all depends on what the board of inquiry says. So talk with Detective Green. Are you working this weekend?"

"Ya. I'll be following up on both cases tomorrow. I expect tonight's news will carry your shooting."

"TV crews came in quickly after you left, but I left it to Detective Green to handle the interviews."

The door opened and Abram came in, looking fresh and dressed in his new beige jacket and brown slacks. He must have gone home to change.

Astrid excused herself and quickly went to his side by the entry, apart from the other guests.

"I'm so glad you're here, Abram. You look handsome. You must have gotten off early, after all."

"And you are …? Well, I'll be. Don't tell me you're my wife."

"Stop teasing, Abram."

He held her by both arms.

"You're gorgeous, sweetheart." He backed up and looked her up and down, still holding her hands. "Wow. I can see that I'm the luckiest man here tonight."

"Oh, Abram, stop it."

But she smiled, so very glad he liked her makeover.

"Here you are, Abram," Dee said. "Good. My, what a handsome couple you are."

She turned around and faced the other guests.

"Everyone. Now that Abram Lincoln is here, we can eat. You'll find place cards for your seating."

CHAPTER 17

The dining room was festive, with lit candles at each table, light blue napkins, white and blue streamers and balloons hanging from chandeliers. The buffet table displayed a lavish variety of foods. Astrid found her table first and laid her consignment shop gold evening purse next to her place card.

It was obvious that Dee had been careful to seat the newspaper couples at different tables, no doubt so that they could talk with people they didn't see often. Abram and Astrid returned from the buffet with their dinner plates, and waited for the table to fill up before starting to eat.

"You shouldn't have waited. Go right ahead and eat. It's allowed at a buffet dinner."

The woman speaking identified herself as Daniella Caton, president of the Fairchance Women's Club. She sat at Astrid's right.

"I am so glad to meet you," Mrs. Caton said to Astrid. "You write so well. I was an English teacher, and I watch the grammar of newspaper writers. Most writers are careless. Sometimes, I think, they're just plain ignorant. I don't know what they teach children in school these days. I said as much to Mrs. Levitch one day and…"

"The attorney's wife?"

"Right. I saw you talking with Mr. Levitch. Yes, they are my neighbors and I talk with her often. She's a dear woman. Always doing for others. Generous to a fault, you know. Only now she seems to be ill. She has been for a few days. He came back from defending a case in Boston. I think that's right. Yes. I'm sure that's what she told me. He was defending someone in Boston. I expect he won. He always does. If you ever need a good attorney, go to him. He's the best. Well, just ask Mr. Bertram. He's sitting next to your husband."

What surprised Astrid was that Mr. Levitch was married. She never would have guessed.

Just shows that you can't judge a person by appearance.

When Mrs. Caton said the partner was next to Abram, Astrid leaned forward and said, "Hello, Mr. Bertram. I met your partner earlier. So nice to meet you."

"Good to meet you, Mrs. Lincoln. Your husband was just telling me that he is a dispatcher for the sheriff and a student, too. Commendable."

Astrid looked at Abram and smiled.

"I believe you're right."

Daniella Caton was not finished. Her piercing voice went on and on until all other conversation stopped among the seven others at the table.

"...the neighborhood. She should see a doctor. I just hope it's nothing too serious. I told her to see a doctor, but she said she would get over it by herself. I never let my health go like that. Do you, Astrid? Of course not. You just can't be too careful. My mother was like that. She had a cold that got worse and worse, and by the time she saw a doctor, it was too late. She had pneumonia and died two hours after she went into the hospital."

For a couple of minutes, Daniella took the time to eat a few mouthfuls before starting up again.

"She finally took to her bed today. Lou Levitch, that is. To tell the truth I'm surprised to see Abe here. But then, he's seldom home. Always off for a court case somewhere. I wouldn't put up with it myself. Would you? Of course not. Couples need a family life together. I think this is her second marriage. Well…"

While she hesitated in order to take another bite of food, Astrid jumped in with a question directed at a man across the table, the owner of Light's Chevrolet agency. She had met him once when she had a flat tire and he tried to sell her a new car.

"How's the auto business, Mr. Light? Does the cold weather slow business down?"

Looking relieved to have a chance to say something, he wagged his big, white head in a so-so attitude.

"The weather doesn't have as much influence on sales," he said, "as the economy. Some of my old customers are saying they don't want to trade for a new car because they're worried about interest rates. They're hanging onto their old vehicles and waiting to see what happens next. This up-and-down economy scares people. You should do a story on it, Astrid."

At that, Abram laughed.

"Yeah," he said. "Why don't you do that, honey?"

She wanted to kick him under the table, but thought quickly.

"I would. But we're a county newspaper. We don't get into political issues, generally speaking. The editor may back candidates for local positions, but state and national politics are left to the dailies."

The woman sitting next to Victor Light joined in.

"Do you think the new president will keep his word? You know, 'no new taxes.'"

Light said, "This is my wife, Sheila. She's a frustrated political analyst."

129

"Well, Sheila," Abram said. "if we pay attention to history, I'd say it's doubtful."

"That's just what I think," she said. "It was a campaign lie. Ann Richards, in my view, got it right when she said, 'Bush was born with a silver foot in his mouth.' People like that don't understand the common person."

Everyone nodded, and Astrid looked from one to another to see how many of them understood the common person. Attorney Bertram? Mrs. Caton? The couple that hadn't said a word and whom she didn't recognize? But most likely the car dealer and his wife had worked hard to get where they were. Then again, she decided, she should be careful about judging. She knew nothing about any of these men and women.

"I find it interesting that the ones who take the most interest in politics are those in that army group over in Greenboro."

That was from the quiet man. Who did Dee say he was? Astrid couldn't remember and didn't want to ask and possibly sound rude. Abram took care of that for her.

"I came in late," he said. "so I didn't get your name."

"I'm Jerome Cobb and this is my wife Patsy. We operate Cobb Insurance next to the theater."

Astrid asked, "Does the militia worry you, Jerome?"

"It sure as hell does. You wrote about it. It should worry you, too. They don't talk about taxes or Medicare or anything else except to do away with it all and create their own type of government. Patriots, they call themselves."

He didn't have to stand up to be heard. He had an orator's voice and a fighter's anger. So much for the quiet couple.

"I served in the Korean War. When I hear bastards like those guys talking like little Hitlers, threatening to take over the government, bet your life I get worried. You said in one of your stories, Astrid, that the man calling himself a general, the one that got himself killed, told you they were preparing to eradicate freedoms and our republic. Right?"

"That's right. He was delusional, thought he would rise up and lead a huge movement against Washington."

"There you are. Men like that have to be stopped. There may be war with weapons, but some of them won't need to raise a rifle. They'll worm their way into the government through elections, calling themselves Patriots. They'll campaign against big government spending and waste. They'll become so powerful that they'll shut down government as we know it. And the United States will begin to weaken, until finally that very thing you wrote about will happen. What was the name of the book you quoted?"

"The Turner Diaries."

"Yeah. That one that described destruction of all but white supremacists. Who knows? Maybe the prediction of destroying other nations will also come about."

Now Jerome's wife Patsy gently touched his arm.

"I think you've made your point, my dear," she said quietly.

He patted her hand. Apparently this wasn't the first time she'd spoken to him about pontificating.

"I know. I got carried away again. But I'll tell you this, and then I'll shut up. Those people out there are planning something, you can be sure of it. I would not be surprised if we learn that they killed Judge Rutherford and his wife. The police should haul them in for questioning."

When he finished, everyone at the table became quiet. Astrid looked over at Abram, who raised his eyebrows but said nothing. Mr. Bertram stayed focused on the beef tips he swirled about in gravy, not eating, just swirling.

Daniella, however, wasn't finished.

"I don't know personally, but Mrs. Levitch told me she knows a member of that compound, and that they aren't the monsters they're painted to be. Sorry, Astrid. I'm just repeating what she said. The one she knows does chores for her--you know, plows the driveway, mows the lawn--and he has been gentlemanly and kind to her, Mr. Levitch being away so much and all. She thinks they had one or two bad apples, as it were, but that they aren't planning any revolution or bombings in high places. They're just trying to live together quietly and create a safe place for their children to grow up. That's what she says. I myself like to give people the benefit of the doubt. Don't you, Astrid? Of course you do. People can't be painted with one broad stroke, now, can they? Of course not."

Obviously no one wished to dash this woman's fantasy about the militia members. Astrid could rebut her words, but also decided to leave it there. However, she determined to see Mrs. Levitch and learn why she felt so kindly toward a group whose avowed goal was to destroy the status quo.

What Jerome said rang too true in her opinion. She saw the group as they practiced their assault techniques, and she heard their bold boasts that they would take over the country one day. Could it come true? Was Jerome right? Was it possible that a Patriot group could gain control of Washington and shut down the United States through the democratic voting process?

It couldn't be. It's just too ridiculous.

CHAPTER 18

Ready to ask hard questions about his employment, Drew waited for Mr. Bertram to return. For the second time he went to the garage to check whether the car had come in. He had dozed, but didn't know how long he'd slept. This time he wandered about the four-car garage to see if his host was a hobbyist. It looked like an ordinary garage with wood benches all around. Tools were neatly lined up on the bench or hung up on peg boards, and a red chest with glass front drawers filled with screws and nails sat on the longest bench. When he reached the far end, he stopped in front of a covered auto. He'd seen it before and wondered if it was a vintage car of considerable value. Just as he was about to lift the cover to look, he heard Bertram's car coming down the driveway. He smoothed the cover back where it was and ran down the hallway to his own quarters.

He listened at the door, heard the footsteps go by and down to the kitchen. He waited another few minutes before leaving the room. He rapped lightly on the kitchen door, and pushed the it open. Mr. Bertram held a bottle in one hand and a glass in the other.

"Good evening, Drew. Just pouring myself a nightcap. Join me for a brandy?"

"Don't mind if I do, thanks."

"I just got back from a birthday party. Most dull affair. But in our business it's best to meet people whenever possible."

"I expect so."

Drew would be willing to do that, but without being known in the community it might be hard for him to break in. As if guessing his thoughts, Mr. Bertram said, "I should have asked you to accompany me."

"Oh. Well. That's nice of you."

He pulled out a chair and sat at the table. Everything in this house was big, including this room--big and dark. The yellow and white check oilcloth looked so much like linen that he ran his hand along it to be sure.

Settling himself opposite Drew, his host said, "No lace tablecloth for me. I decided I wouldn't get too fancy in my own kitchen,"

After an air toast without words, Drew gulped his drink and choked. He hadn't had anything harder than beer for a long time, and the brandy burned in a rather soothing way.

"You okay?"

"Yes, sir. Fogot how warm brandy is."

"Well, I guess I know why you're here, Drew. Have you given this careful thought?"

"Sir?"

"About leaving the firm?"

"Oh. I've thought about it some."

"I was hoping this wouldn't happen," Bertram said while studying his drink.

"So was I, frankly."

"But you've decided."

"I guess so. I just wonder why you didn't tell me the job was temporary."

Now Mr. Bertram looked baffled.

"Because it wasn't."

"Then why did you tell Mr. Levitch I was only temporary?"

"Merely so that he'd get used to having you there. I never meant it to be temporary."

Drew couldn't quite comprehend.

"I see." He mulled over what had just transpired between them. "Then why did you think I was leaving?"

"Your brother called me. He told me you weren't planning to stay with us."

"My brother! Dammit. What's he doing? I didn't know he called you, Mr. Bertram. I thought you were about to let me go, and I came in tonight to find out for sure before trying to locate another position. Since you told Mr. Levitch that I was hired as a temporary employee, I thought I should start sending out inquiries if I was going to be out of a job."

Bertram nodded.

"I see. Well, I said that because he was in a low mood, and I thought it best if he thought he would have some say in the hiring. He'll come around to the efficacy of keeping you permanently. Like I said, I hired you as a permanent attorney in the firm. What you need to understand is that Mr. Levitch has some personal issues to sort out right now. He's disturbed by that."

Neither spoke for a full minute, then Mr. Bertram said, "So your brother told me wrong. Why?"

Drew didn't want to say anything that might give the wrong idea, but he should be honest.

"You know about the militia at The Kingdom?"

"I do."

"Well, you see, my brother is one of its members, sorry to say. I don't share their views and I have no intention of ever doing so. I hate to tell you, but Les tried to stop me from taking this position, based solely on his own anti-Semitic stance. He's a white supremacist and believes that Patriot militia groups will overturn our government, and a whites only class will rule."

He looked into the eyes of his boss and drew in his breath. What should he read from the blank stare? Was he angry?

"I see," Bertram said. "I heard a good deal about all of that this evening. It sounds like a very dangerous group."

"I believe it is."

"Abe--Mr. Levitch--is a bit difficult to get close to, but he's a good man just the same. I wouldn't want him to hear of this conversation. It would disturb him greatly. Understand?"

"Yes, I understand."

"As far as I am concerned, we'll forget it. But what I want to know is just how much of a problem Les could be to you, and to the office. Is he likely to set off a bomb there or to barge in some day and cause a ruckus? Call out Mr. Levitch? Demand that you leave with him? What do you think?"

Drew lifted his glass to the light and studied the amber color of his drink.

"Would you mind if I had an ice cube in this? I'm not used to the strong drink now."

Bertram nodded toward the refrigerator.

"It's in the door."

Ice in the door was new to Drew and at first he wasn't sure what to do. When he figured out what needed to be pressed, the gush of ice filled his glass.

"Damn," he said, and looked around for help.

"Here," Bertram said. He got to his feet, went to a drawer and took out a cereal spoon. "Take out what you don't want and put it in the sink."

Once Drew was settled again, he moved the glass in his hands and thought how to answer Mr. Bertram.

"I want to reassure you that none of that will happen," he said. "I'll go to The Kingdom tomorrow. It's time I told my brother to get out of my life. I've been reluctant to do that because he's my only living relative, but he has taken too many liberties."

Drew lifted his glass and downed the rest of his drink.

"He won't be disturbing your law office or troubling any of us again, rest assured."

· · · ·

Saturday

Saturday morning, under a dazzling sun and blue sky, Drew headed for The Kingdom. Uppermost in his mind were the words he'd rehearsed half the night. It wouldn't be easy. Les had never been an easy one to reason with, and this whole new obsession with making radical changes in the country brought about a change in his whole personality. Drew had noticed it the day he arrived from prison. Instead of a happy reunion, it turned into a boot camp orientation of what he could and couldn't do. Les wanted his brother to become one of the militia. But Drew felt only repulsion at the idea. More importantly, the connection would be against conditions of his parole. Above all, he intended to stay outside prison bars.

He left his car in the wide parking lot and walked onto the town plaza. Three doors down he rapped on his brother's duplex quarters, not surprised when a woman answered.

"I'm Drew Godfrey. My brother home?"

"Come in. He's in the bathroom. He'll be right out. I'm Robin."

She was a wiry woman of medium height, with a mannish haircut. Drew felt the strength in her hands when they shook. He was surprised that Les, a decidedly handsome man, had chosen such a homely woman. Then he realized she might not be his woman, merely one of the several women in the militia.

"Sit." She was also a woman of few words.

"Thanks. Have you been here at The Kingdom long? I don't recall seeing you before."

"Not here long. I came over from the Kent Militia."

Since he didn't know where that was, he said no more. It was only seconds before Les came out, rubbing his hands together.

"Drew. Good to see you, brother."

"Yeah? Well maybe not."

Les looked at Robin.

"Hey, we're through for today. Why don't you go back to the range. I'll see you there later."

After she left, he and Drew sat at the dining room table.

"Well? You have something to say to me?"

"Yeah. I had a talk with my boss last evening, and he told me about your phone call to him."

"So?"

"I'm not about to leave the firm of Levitch and Bertram. It's a good place for me. You don't seem to realize that I'm not long out of prison. I have to be working. Mr. Bertram overlooked my background. There's no place for me to go, even if I wanted to leave."

"You can always come here. We don't care where you're from, prison or pigsty. We have some millionaires here, but also some very poor. Robin, for instance, is from a wealthy family, but you'd never know it. She's a good woman. On the other half of this duplex are two people who were living in an old barn that leaked. The house had burned and the owners walked away, let the fields grow up to trees."

"The point is," Drew said, "I don't want you interfering with my life again. I like my position. Even if I didn't, I'll decide whether to stay or not."

"So you won't come here and live a free life?"

"No thanks. I don't like your politics."

"Why not? You don't know anything about our politics."

"And that's the way I want to leave it. Look Les, I'm the older brother here, not some kid that you can push around. You've been acting like I don't know what I'm doing. This stops now."

"Why shouldn't I be interested in helping you out? That's what brothers do, you know. They help each other out. I wouldn't have called your boss if I didn't think it was right that you leave that place."

Les had mastered the art of deceit and persuasion long ago by using loyalty, family, duty, anything at all to twist logic and lure Drew into his web of control. Not today. This was independence day. Time to break away.

"I don't want us to part enemies, but if that's what it takes to get you to stop meddling in my life, then that's how it will be. This militia outfit of yours borders on the illegal. I can't live with law breakers. The rest of my life will not be lived behind bars. I've had my fill of outlaws, thieves, and killers. I'm working within the law and I'm staying within the law."

He stood up to leave, but Les wasn't finished.

"Have it your way, Drew. But just how much do you know about your two employers?"

"What do you mean by that?"

"I mean, it'd be a good idea for you to do some quiet investigating. You might be surprised at what you'd find."

"What? What would I find?"

"No, no. I won't say any more. You've taken your stand. You go ahead and bow to that Jew and that hypocrite. When the day comes that you have an epiphany, let me know. I'll still be here, and despite your attitude now, I won't turn my back on you. Just remember that."

Confused, Drew hesitated at the door. He'd like to know what Les meant, but he also knew how his brother could dissemble facts to suit his own agenda. Best to leave now before he was trapped into begging once again.

"Thanks for the advice, Les."

He left, not quite sure if he really should attempt to investigate his employers. He recalled the scene between the two when Mr. Levitch returned, and how they secluded themselves behind closed doors afterward. Perhaps Les really did know something. He seemed to know everything going on around these parts. For now Drew needed to get back to Fairchance and have lunch with Chris. It would probably be best to ignore Les's negativism. After all, that's what the militia was all about--being negative, distrustful, hateful. They could keep it.

. . . .

Chris waited for Drew outside the diner for a while, until he decided he was cold enough. No need to freeze out here. He went inside and took the usual, more private booth that they liked at the back. So far, so good. As yet, he hadn't been questioned by police. With any luck it would remain so. He had called his parole officer and explained the situation, and she told him she'd inform local law enforcement. When they concluded their conversation she said not to worry.

He recalled how Astrid Lincoln had watched him at the agency when she talked with Holly, and wondered if she knew he had served time as a felon. After all, she was a reporter. The thing that bothered him most was his own conscience about the prison time.

He felt like his forehead was stamped with the word FELON for everyone to see.

As much as he was attracted to Sandy, that guilt feeling surfaced each time he talked with her. He could easily fall in love with her, but could she overlook his record? It would be easier not to learn the answer to that question. He could take rejection, but for now it would be better to enjoy seeing her once in a while rather than being cut off entirely from that pleasure.

"That's a mighty big daydream you're having."

He turned from staring out at traffic to see Drew slide into the opposite booth.

"You're late," he said.

"Yeah, well, I had business at The Kingdom to settle."

"With Les?"

"With Les. I told him he'd have to stop trying to run my life."

"How'd he take it?"

"Not well. He wants me to go live there again and join their crazy cult. I couldn't do that even if I had the inclination to."

The waitress with the husky voice arrived and stood with pad and pen in hand.

"How're you guys today? Decided what you'll have?" she asked.

"I'll have a ham salad sandwich," Chris said.

"Make that two. And coffee now, please."

"Be right up."

She left the half-sheet menus for them to slip back into the slot next to the juke box song selector.

"How about you?" Drew said. "You see Sandy's rehearsal last night?"

Chris felt like a fool to admit what happened.

"I went to the church."

"And?"

"She didn't tell me she sang for a different church."

Drew laughed.

"A different church! So you didn't hear her sing?"

"I hunted all over the Catholic Church and finally found a maintenance man who knew her. He said she's Baptist, not Catholic, and to try there. So I got to the Baptist Church just in time to hear the last song."

"Well? Could you tell if she has a good voice?"

Chris sighed with a whine like an infatuated teenager.

"She had a solo part to sing, and yes, she has a very good voice, just like I expected."

"And did you take her out for coffee? Or whatever?"

"No whatever, that's for sure. They served refreshments there, so I got a glass of punch and a cookie and sat at a table with five others, all older women. She was sweet, though. Introduced me all around and told them that I'm an expert computer man."

Now Drew bellowed.

"An expert computer man, huh?"

"She was nice about it."

"What's not to be nice about? Not many can make that boast."

"Can it. Here comes the food."

They settled down to their sandwiches, but Drew kept chuckling.

"You know, I just hope you find a nice woman you want to date one of these days," Chris said. "I'll remember this harassment."

"Who's harassing? I'm just enjoying the picture of you sitting at a table surrounded by older women, dying to cozy up to Sandy, and being introduced as an expert computer man. Not a dear friend, not my date, not..."

"Okay. Okay. You made your point."

Chris tried not to laugh, but he had to admit it was a lot different from what he hoped the evening would be. And the title of expert computer man didn't have the same sophisticated ring that attorney did.

"We can't all be white collar hot shots," he said in his own defense. Nevertheless, the chuckle won out. "At least I walked her home. Not that she lives far from the church, just a couple blocks."

"And a goodnight kiss?"

"No. I thanked her for a pleasant time, and left."

"Not even a kiss at the door? See you tomorrow? I'd like to take you to dinner?"

"Well, no. I guess I lost my nerve."

"She'll think you don't like her."

"I don't know what to say when it comes to personal stuff. 'I got to be a computer expert by studying in prison for 20 years?' That'd go over big, like a lead balloon."

"You should stick to questions about her, and let the conversation go where it will. If she wants to know about you, she'll ask. But my advice is not to avoid the truth. The longer it takes to tell her, the worse it will be. If she asks about your training, for instance, just tell her that you were in prison for a crime that you didn't commit and you made good use of your time by studying."

"Sounds good. I'll keep it mind."

I could do that. Or I could also just go and jump off the nearest high bridge.

He needed to have some physical activity. The thought just struck, and out of the blue he said, "I'm going to the Fairchance College fitness center this afternoon. I hear that the public is welcome on Saturday afternoons. You have plans?"

"Yeah," Drew said. "I'm going to the library. Want to do a bit of research."

They parted outside. Chris drove off to find the college, a place he had not visited yet. He'd be the oldest person in the gym, no doubt, but it didn't matter. No one knew him anyway.

CHAPTER 19

Chris had worked on the treadmill only a few minutes when he looked toward the stationary bikes where he saw Astrid Lincoln working out. She nodded. He should have a chat with her to learn more about Holly, if nothing else. He left the treadmill and went into the bike section, separated from the main fitness workout room by a half wall. The other two bikes were idle.

"Mrs. Lincoln," he said, "how are you this afternoon?"

She climbed off the bike and held out her hand.

"I'm doing well, thank you. Did you get Holly all set up?"

"Set up, but she's too distracted to concentrate on what I told her. I'll go back Monday. Have you seen her today?"

"No. I thought I'd give her some space. She's been under so much stress. Problem is, she won't stay put. I'll bet she's back at the office."

"I would expect that, too. She's nervous and grieving."

He noticed the intense study she made of him. Was she trying to determine if he was the person she'd seen in a police photo?

"Of course she is," Astrid said. "She likes you. Have you known her long?"

"Only since I was assigned to her for the computer installation." *And when she was a baby.* "You're doing some investigative work for her? I couldn't help overhearing part of your conversation about her fiancé. Didn't mean to, but there wasn't much choice."

"Ya, and you'd have to cover your ears not to hear me."

"Well, I didn't mean to …"

Astrid waved it off.

"Think nothing of it. I'm loud, and that's it. I've been on that bike a half hour and am ready to leave. Can I buy you a cup of coffee in the coffee shop?"

"They have one here? Yes, I'm a coffee addict."

"Grab your coat. It's in the Student Union."

Outside, they walked along a sidewalk that wound around the campus, past a long classroom building and into the Union, where several students were having lunch over open books.

"Students here work hard," Astrid said. "They cause very little trouble in town. Nice to see young people dedicated to their studies. It's not all about environmental protection, but much of it is."

"It's an interesting campus," Chris said. "I should think the wood buildings dangerous, though, wouldn't you? I mean, if a fire should get started, it might go through all of them in no time."

"You're probably right. They have plenty of water from the lake, but not in winter. So it could happen, I suppose."

At the buffet counter, they picked up coffee mugs and each took a brownie, went to the end of the counter, past the sandwiches, soups, and salads.

"Work hard to burn off the calories and then eat brownies," Astrid said with a laugh. "Makes sense, huh?"

"As much as anything else, I guess."

They paid a cashier after waiting in line for students to go through. Astrid nodded to one empty booth by a window and they hurried to get it before someone else did.

"You asked about my investigation," Astrid said. "I'm not sure I should tell you this, but you seem interested in Holly."

"I hope you don't get the wrong idea about my interest. I once had a daughter who'd be her age, and I guess I look on Holly as I would my own daughter. You understand?"

Astrid didn't respond at once. He could see that she was thinking it over. He would like to tell her the truth but it could be risky considering that she was a reporter. Well, what of it? Would she write a story implying that he had every good reason to kill Holly's adoptive parents? Best to leave it the way he put it.

"I understand. But still I don't think I should say too much about Holly's personal business. I hope *you* understand."

"I do. I guess I should confess that I heard you mention her fiancé, and that he lied to you. What concerns me is whether you think he killed her parents."

"I can answer that. No, I don't think he did it, even though he lied about being at work that day. His boss said it was his day off. Something about him strikes me as too indifferent to commit murder. I don't think he has the passion for that or for much of anything else. At any rate, I do think Holly would be wise not to marry him, considering his temper. I don't think he'd kill, but I do think he'd hurt. It sounds to me like he has a tantrum-like temper that passes quickly. The judge and his wife obviously died at the hands of someone who had thought about it a long time."

"Do you think Judge Rutherford opposed the marriage? May I ask that?"

"Ya. He did."

"I see."

Chris knew more about the judge than just about anyone else did. In prison, he and Drew shared reports coming through the grapevine concerning Rutherford's callous use of his authority. Almost daily someone vowed revenge for unjust punishment.

"The judge was a bigot, you know," he said.

What brought that to mind, he didn't know, only that it seemed to be the worst he could say at the moment about a man who sentenced people to die by the drop of his gavel.

Astrid's eyes opened wide.

"You know that, do you?" she said.

"For reasons I can't divulge right now, let me just say that I have friends who had dealings with the man. And, yes. They all ageed that when he was a judge in New York he was harder on certain ethnic groups than others. Although I must say, it was barely noticeable."

"How interesting," Astrid said. "Then it will be no surprise that he opposed Holly's marriage because her fiancé is Jewish."

But it did surprise Chris. He should have guessed. And maybe he shouldn't have revealed that he knew that much about the judge.

"That would definitely make him unacceptable to the judge. From what you just said about the boy's temper, though, I wonder if she'll break it off now. Didn't she know that about him already?"

"She didn't, but she was put off by his attitude, not just that he lied, but also because he didn't call her or see her after the murders."

"Not much of a man, then."

"No, not much from what I could tell."

Silence, then Astrid said, "Holly has a ready smile and the patience of a saint, judging from my dealings with her. I find it way beyond belief that anyone could just wipe out her family for no reason."

Chris hesitated for only a minute before he said, "You know she was adopted, don't you?"

"Ya. I know. Did she tell you?"

Now he had to think of an answer but not exactly the truth.

"I heard someone speak of it downtown."

"The gossips are having a field day, I expect."

"TV, too. Did you see the news last night?"

"No. I didn't watch, "Astrid said. "I had already seen how they were speculating and making assumptions that are way afield of truth. For instance one TV reporter actually quoted someone who said Judge Rutherford was disliked by everyone in Fairchance. I find that hard to believe. Everyone I've talked with liked him and said he didn't have an enemy in the world."

"Funny thing how people will exaggerate under the right circumstances."

Chris was thinking of his trial. People who didn't know him and his family testified that he was an evil man. He guessed they were neighbors along the street, people he'd never met. Most likely the prosecutor's staff convinced them it would be best to put him away. Yes, he knew how cruel and dishonest people could be.

"Are you from around here, Chris?"

"No. I'm from New York State."

"Where? I worked here and there in the state for eight years."

Chris smiled, feeling quite pinned down. He couldn't tell her where he'd been for the last 20 years. This conversation was becoming difficult at every turn.

"It was an out-of-the way place. You wouldn't know it. I'm going to have another coffee. Can I get you another cup, Mrs. Lincoln?" he asked.

"No. I'm all set. I must get moving. It was nice talking with you, Chris. And please, call me Astrid. I'm just barely used to my new last name."

"A newlywed?"

"The first of the year, ya."

"Congratulations. Many years of happiness."

Her blush seemed out-of-place. Chris concluded that he liked this Astrid. He understood why Holly trusted her. Maybe some day he'd tell her about his own daughter, as he remembered her and as he was getting to know her now.

. . . .

Leaving the warmth of the Student Union, Astrid stepped into a blast of cold air. Fidgety wind lifted tiny spitballs of icy snow and spun them across the open campus. They pricked her face. Young men and women with various degrees of skill skated around the ice that likely extended the depth of the lake. Could it possibly thaw by summer?

Will this winter never end?

She pulled her sheepskin collar tight around her neck, trying to protect her face. Her thoughts dwelt on Chris and why she sensed he was hiding something important. She saw sadness creep into his eyes when he spoke of his daughter. She'd like to have learned more. If it had been the right time she would have pressed him further for answers. He avoided her question about where he had lived. Why?

As she approached the classroom building she decided to walk through the hallway in warmth toward the parking lot and ran up the ramp to the back door. The college was way ahead of a lot of places in Fairchance with handicap access, she noted. Ought to write a story about it sometime. Half way down the long hallway, she saw an open door and read the name, Professor Vinton.

Abram's law professor. Why not?

She went to the doorway and saw him in a big swivel chair, his feet crossed atop the desk. He ate a sandwich in one hand and read a book in the other. He looked like a cartoon character with hair spiked after a lightning strike. Possibly 50, he appeared to be a hundred miles away, and didn't hear her clear her throat at the doorway. She walked in slowly, not wanting to surprise him all at once.

"Excuse me," she said. "Professor Vinton? I'm Astrid Lincoln."

His feet uncoiled in a flash, and he shot straight out of his chair, all five-eight of him. Built like a pretzel, the professor reached her in a dash and grabbed her hand.

"So this is the exquisite Astrid that I've heard so much about," he said, raising his eyes to meet hers.

"Astrid, ya."

He motioned toward the chair next to his at the desk and pulled her along to it. Abram had never mentioned an eccentric side to his professor, just that some of his teaching methods were unique.

"What else does a young man talk about but his lovely bride? Abram has a good head on his shoulders even if he is love-struck. He doesn't just have stars in his eyes. He's set to make something of himself. No doubt that's a good deal your doing. Now you take me at his age." He nudged her arm. "I wish someone had. Ha, ha. I fumbled my way along and finally got the knack of things, how to study and what to study. Of course, I also found a woman who could put up with me. Oh, she makes me toe the mark, don't think she doesn't. If I get too shaggy and baggy, she lets me know it's time to spiff up. Clean up my act, as she puts it. But I believe you came to see me for a reason. What can I do for you?"

Astrid blinked a few times when the professor hoisted himself into a sitting position atop his desk, pulled a knee up and locked onto it with both hands. She couldn't hold back a smile. He was a perfectly charming professor, unlike any she had in college. Not a surprise, then, that Abram talked about him so much.

"I don't know if there's anything you can do for me, Professor Vinton. You know I'm a reporter, so anything you say is not confidential."

"Ha. I should have known. I'll wager you want to talk about Judge Rutherford. Am I right?"

"Ya, you're right. You knew him …"

"You bet I knew him. And confidential or not, I didn't like the man. My wife would be happier if you didn't print that, but I don't give a damn. A rotter dies and all of a sudden everyone loved him. I am sorry that his dear wife had to die. She was a good woman. How someone like the judge can charm a woman as kind and charitable as Winona into marriage, I'll never know. I suppose he might have been less intolerable when he was young, but he garnered no respect from me. And I've been told that he had a less than sterling reputation on the bench. More than one man was sent to life or death in prison under questionable negotiations with rogue lawyers. I say good riddance to the likes of him. Like I said, it's a pity Winona was there. Maybe if she'd been out, she would have been spared."

"When he taught here," Astrid said, "did you ever hear him say he feared for his life because of a particular person or action?"

After careful thought, Professor Vinton said, "Not that I heard personally. But he told our college president that he had to stop teaching this year because he needed to keep an eye on his family. Not many here know that, but I have the ear of our leader by virtue of coincidental problems. We both have a teenage daughter. He let it slip one day that Rutherford needed to watch his family, and we thought it odd at this stage of Holly's life, since she's in her twenties now. Ha. Unless, of course, his wife was fooling around with a younger man. Ha, ha. I doubt that. She was nice, but she was the homemaker type, if you know what I mean. Nothing wrong with that, mind you. My wife is, too. But the homemaker type that I mean is always doing needle point or sewing clothes or knitting. Now my wife goes to the gym, shops incessantly, has women friends in for cards and gossip. Can't see Winona deviating a whole lot from the more staid life. As far as I know, her biggest joy in life was to take care of pre-school kids. I do know that Holly plans to marry a Jewish boy. That wouldn't bother me any, but Rutherford was almost violent talking about it one day right out in the hallway where everyone could hear."

"Ya, I know that he objected to the marriage."

"Objected! He wanted to kill the guy. You know, it could have been self-defense, for all I know. That's a good one to figure out, huh? A man comes to your house to try to make friends because of his upcoming marriage to your daughter and you fight a bit, maybe, and bam, the gun that is in your hand goes off, and there it is, one dead body. Only now the wife enters the scene, sees who the trespasser is, and he knows she'll get him arrested if he doesn't do her in. So he does. Now, how's that for solving our mysterious double murder?"

"Probably a little more bizarre than the reality, but not bad," Astrid said with a grin. "At first I thought the boyfriend might be the killer, but after meeting him, I now think he's innocent. Do you think anyone here at the college could have had a grudge bad enough to kill him?"

"God no. We may be an odd lot of professors, but we're all civilized. The worst we'd do is talk about him--behind his back, of course--but no one would kill him. If we were capable of doing that, we'd go after an in-town attorney. And I don't think anyone will do that."

"An attorney?"

"Not many know about this. When Rutherford was here, a local attorney filed a lawsuit against the college for hiring this man who was, in his words, teaching students his anti-Semitic opinions. It was all done very quietly, and before action was actually taken, the judge vowed he wouldn't profile Jewish people in class or advance his own religious views. I never heard any students say the judge injected his own prejudices into class work, but that lawyer claimed to have first-hand evidence. Interesting, huh?"

"Very," Astrid said. "May I ask who the attorney is?"

"You may ask, but I won't answer. I'm clean, and I'm keeping it that way."

He held his hands up, palms out, to indicate a wall of silence.

"Okay," she said. "I thank you for talking with me. It has been interesting."

"Indeed. Now I can put a face with the name when Abram mentions some unusual thing his wife has done. I must say, you give him a lot of material."

"Oh? I'll have to find out what he's been saying about me. Again, thanks professor. I'm very pleased to have met you. Abram took an extra shift at the sheriff's office today, and he'll want supper when he gets home. I need to get it ready."

Was that a snigger from the professor? Had Abram been talking about her cooking? The pretzel untangled himself and walked by her side down the hallway to the end door.

"Come back and talk with me any time, Astrid. You're a good listener."

She nodded but refrained from saying he was a pretty damned good talker.

CHAPTER 20

Astrid began re-heating the beans when she heard Abram's truck drive into the garage. She would say nothing about his being late, even though she was anxious to tell him about what she'd learned today. After all, he had a busy life, too.

"Hi, dear," he said as soon as he opened the door. "What a day. Sorry I'm late."

He threw his coat on a chair before grabbing her and landing a cold smootch on her cheek. She could see that he had news to tell, so she waited before launching into her day.

"We had a breakthrough today," he said, rubbing his hands together. "Seems…"

He looked over at the phone when it rang.

"I'll get it," Astrid said. "Better stir those beans, Abram."

Before she could say hello, the barely audible voice said, "I need help, Astrid."

"Holly? What's the trouble?"

"Please come to the office. It's Danny. He's acting crazy. I've locked myself in the back room, but he's pounding on the door."

"Did you …?" Not to alert Abram that something was wrong, Astrid did not go on to ask if she'd called the police.

"I'll be right there, Holly."

She went to the closet for her coat and on the way out the kitchen door said, "Gotta go give Holly a hand, honey. I'll be right back. Go ahead and eat while it's hot."

"Yeah. Thanks. Looks delicious."

Before he could ask what the problem was, she slammed the door behind her and ran to the Jeep. The hillside road had been icy, but road crews had come by earlier spreading sand and salt over it. As she gunned the Jeep down the hill and into the city proper, Astrid asked herself why Holly hadn't called the police. Obviously she was scared to death. It must mean that Danny lost his temper and she'd managed to get to the back room and lock the door. She hoped he hadn't hurt her. Would he attempt to break down the door? Astrid pressed the accelerator harder, stopping only for the one red light in the middle of Main Street. Two blocks beyond, she drove into the real estate office parking lot and saw Danny's car. She switched the engine off, jumped out, rushed to the office entrance, but stopped to look through the side window. Danny stood in the middle of the room yelling. She could see no gun. The back room door was still closed.

By quietly turning the door handle, then quickly crashing into the office, she surprised Danny. He whirled about, his mouth still open on his last words.

"What're you doing here?" he said.

"You're the one to answer that. What are *you* doing? Giving Holly a bad time, are you?"

"No. She's giving me a hard time. She won't talk with me."

"Seems to me you were yelling at her. What do you want?"

"I want her to marry me, and she says she won't. What business is it of yours anyway?"

Astrid had dealt with men who yelled at women. Moving quickly to him, she grabbed his coat lapel and pulled him up against her body. Since she was the taller, she leaned over him so that his head bent backward. His arms flapped as he attempted to get her off him, but she pressed harder.

"It's my business if I say it's my business, you loudmouth punk. Now you get out of here, leave the premises, and leave Holly alone. She has made up her mind. You understand?"

"You call me loudmouth? What are you, a cross-dressing man, or somethin'?"

That was just too much. Astrid hurled him toward the door. He stumbled, caught himself, and looked up with a tinge of fear in his eyes.

"I'm the one who says get out. That's all you need to know, Danny boy."

"Okay. Okay. I'm goin'. You tell Holly she hasn't heard the last of this."

"Just a minute. She'd better have heard the last of this. The next time you won't deal with me. It will be uniformed men with guns who come after you. Just remember that. You got your answer. Holly said no. Leave it there."

"Huh!" He left without further argument, and Astrid turned around just as Holly came out of the back room.

"You all right, Holly?"

"Yes, I'm all right. Thank you, Astrid. I knew you could get rid of him. I didn't really want to have him arrested, you know."

"Might have been better if you had. You heard me tell him that if he approaches you again, the police will come. So be sure that's the case. Call the police. They'll keep him away from you. And, by the way, where's the guard Chief Raleigh assigned to you?"

"I told him to leave me alone. He was a distraction. Always in the way."

"Well, now you see how much better it would have been if he'd been with you."

"I suppose."

Fighting the urge to shake Holly into realization that her life was in danger, Astrid put an arm around her instead and walked her to a chair. She pulled a chair to sit in front of her, in order to hold eye contact.

"Listen to me, Holly. You must stop this. Go home and be with your friends. You need to grieve, and all you're doing is trying to run away from the pain by working. It's unfortunate that the funeral couldn't be held soon, but when they're through with the autopsies and the investigation, it can all go forward, and your life will get easier. I've been through it more than once. When my mother died, I tried to run away from the reality. I left the family and hung out in Boston. I went to movie after movie just to keep from thinking about the tragedy and how miserable I felt. Finally, my dear grandfather came and got me, took me home, and he and I talked for hours. We both cried. I had to face the loss. I thought I'd die, but that didn't happen. You won't die either, unless you put yourself in harm's way. If the killer wants to take your life, too, he knows where to find you here at the office. So I'm pleading with you. Get out of here and stay out for as long as you can."

Tears spilled down Holly's cheeks. She tried to hide her face from Astrid by turning sideways in her chair. Astrid let her cry before saying more. When she turned back to Astrid, Holly took a handkerchief from her pocket and wiped her face.

"Sorry about that, Astrid. You're right. I work so I won't think about it all. You see what happens when I do think about it. I cry."

"That's okay. The horror and suddenness are still very raw. But, like I said, it will heal. You won't forget, but it won't hurt so much as time goes on. Now let's get you back to the Sillers. I'll follow you there and see that you're inside safely. Also, Holly, you get the chief to reassign that guard to you. Please don't fight it."

Holly looked worn out. Her shoulders slumped, and her eyes, red from crying, were barely visible. She studied the monogram on the handkerchief in her hands, as if she could see her mother sitting for hours to make every stitch even.

"I won't," she said with a sigh. "I'll do like you say."

. . . .

After Astrid watched Holly go into the Sillers' home, she drove back to town. At the stop light, she waited and thought how winter days turned dark much too early. In fact, it seemed extra dark today with no moon.

"I wonder …"

Was it dark enough to check out that car at the junk yard? Should she? Abram was waiting for her to return. Should she take the time now? If not now, when?

"Easier to ask forgiveness after the deed than seek permission beforehand," she recited.

It wouldn't take long to get there and back, and all she wanted to do was look inside and in the glove compartment to see if there was a gun. It would be a perfect place to hide one. Who'd think to look in a junk car right out in the open. Earlier she had decided that Danny wasn't the shooter. But now, she began to have doubts. Maybe his temper did molder inside, and maybe he finally decided to confront the judge. Perhaps she gave him too much credit for being a quick-tempered person who was soon over it. His aggression at the real estate office seemed to indicate a deeper brooding personality than she had thought. Suddenly he was at the top of her list of probable candidates based on motive.

Turning thoughts over and over, Astrid soon found herself within sight of the scrap yard. Rather than drive right up to the place, she looked for a spot off the road to park the Jeep. Finding a turn off partly hidden behind fir trees, where no one at the house would be able to see it, she parked, and took her flashlight from the glove compartment, locked the door, and started off along the road in the dark.

Pot holes made walking difficult, especially since she needed to keep an eye on the house to see if lights came on.

"Ow!" The outburst was loud. She had tripped when she stepped into one of the pot holes. She stood up and rubbed her knee reflecting on the wisdom of wanting a dark night to do this. Tonight on a road with no lights, it was like being in a cave.

"Damn." She hoped no one was outside the house where they could have heard her outcry. When she left to go to Holly, she was in such a hurry that she didn't take gloves with her. Now she wished she had. Not only did her hands hurt from the cold, but it felt like she had scraped them on the rough road.

Continuing on, she came to the entrance. Except for the dull yellow lights in two windows, the house was dark. She walked farther on in the road until she could make out the vague shadows of scrap cars lined up. The one she wanted was at the far end. Rather than take a chance on going down the plowed out driveway and being seen by someone, she continued on the road until she thought she was at the end of that row of cars. Just one problem now. Snow.

Where the hell is the end of the lot? They must have more than one entrance.

But apparently not. She didn't want to spend more time looking for it. All she found was a high wall of snow. In the dark, it was hard to tell how high it was. It appeared to be the dumping place for snow that was plowed after each storm. She felt along the wall and realized that it was, indeed, a wall. Couldn't be too far up to get over it.

Can't let a little thing like this stop me.

She felt like a mountain climber once she started up the snow bank, only she had no equipment. A harness or an ice axe would help, to say nothing of the right boots. There was nothing to grip. She dug her fingers into the icy snow as deep as she could and lifted one foot after another, until one sank into a soft spot.

"Whoa!" she cried. "This isn't good."

She looked upward and then back to the road. The top was closer as far as she could tell. She could make it if she could ever get her leg free of the hole. She pulled and wiggled it, winced when her hands slipped. Now she had to stop and breathe. Her lungs ached. With her whole body and face against the hard, cold mass, she envisioned a horrible scenario. What if she couldn't get free and had to yell for help? How could she explain this?

"Just let me get out of this mess," she said under her breath.

She tugged harder, nearly lost her grip, and with one great effort pulled the leg out.

"I can make it. I can."

The final struggle took her to the top, where she lay flat to catch her breath again. If only she had stopped to put on one of her warm jackets instead of this lightweight rain jacket. She raised her head to look at where she was, then ducked when lights came on, illuminating the whole junk yard. Would they come all the way down to this end and find her here? She couldn't very well turn and run. If Abram knew what she was doing, he'd kill her. He was so overly cautious about everything. What was it he said when he came home? There had been a development? No, he said there had been a breakthrough today.

Wonder what he meant by that.

She didn't dare move, just waited for what felt like 15 minutes. Finally, a voice called out, "No one's out here." And the lights all went out. Astrid let out a long breath, and raised herself up.

I'm not going back now, she thought, while crawling along the top of the blackened snow to where she thought she could make out the car.

They must have piled the snow up here after every storm. Had to have used a backhoe to get it this high.

She might break a leg if she jumped. Moving mostly on her stomach, she edged herself over to one side hoping to find a safer place to get down. Not any better, as far as she could see. Frantic to get off the snow hill, Astrid said, "Oh, hell," and, dragging her nails along the side of the rough, cold wall, slid and fell to the bottom, landing on something hard and sharp that tore her right pant leg.

Oh, for godsake.

Feeling around, she discovered that she had landed in an old bathtub filled with iron objects. At least she could get out of this. Unable to tell if her leg was bleeding, she crouched and moved forward, hoping to come to the rusty car. And here it was. She turned the handle. Locked!

"I don't believe it."

She reached in her pocket for the flashlight. It was gone. She had stuffed it into the coat pocket before she started the climb. Where could she have dropped it? Impossible to find it in the dark. Besides that, time was moving on. She needed to get back to the Jeep and go home before Abram called the police to find her. She looked at the high snow pile. No. No more mountain climbing. She was cold enough.

Only one way out. Run to the main gate.

She started off, not quite sure where she was. Usually a bit of light would be shed by snow even at night, but the snow here was soot black. She caught her toe again and fell. Her hand landed on something that felt like a frozen animal.

"Yuk. Who runs a junky junk yard like this?"

She would have laughed at her thought if she weren't so anxious to get out.

How can they live here?

She glanced at the outline of the house. In a dim light from a window she could see the outline of junk cars, refrigerators, sinks, toilets. Their view? Could they possibly live like this? Perhaps there was a field on the other side. That would relieve the morbid atmosphere.

Must be the most depressing place this side of a cemetery. At least cemeteries are clean and usually pretty.

Trying to hunch down low while running slowed her progress. When the lights blazed again, she didn't try to hide, but stood up and ran. She was almost at the entrance.

"Someone *is* out here, Papa. Bring the shotgun."

Oh, God. Move!

She just got through to the road when a shot rang out. Nothing like gun shots to give wings to feet, she thought, quite certain that she surpassed her college track record in getting back to the Jeep. She unlocked the door, turned on the engine, and backed out before she slammed the door shut.

"Okay," she said after a mile of top speed down the country road. "Okay, you can ease up on the gas now."

Her foot felt like lead on the pedal, difficult to pull up.

"Oh, man. Is Abram going to be furious. And all for what? Didn't get a damned thing for all that trouble."

She took her time parking in the garage, closing the door, finger combing her hair, and brushing off her clothes before entering the kitchen. Abram had gone to the den. She peeked around the corner in the doorway. He sat in his recliner, comfortable and cozy in front of the roaring fire. He looked up from his book.

"You're back? That didn't take long."

Never even missed me.

"Only an hour and a half," she said as she walked into the light of the room.

"Really? I didn't even...for godsake, Astrid. What happened to you? Did someone attack you? A dog? Are you all right?"

He was on his feet now. His look was one of sheer horror. Good lord, she thought, I must really look bad. She tossed her short hair back with a flick of her head.

"Look at you. You're bleeding. Your hands."

He turned them over and now Astrid saw the injuries, too. As she looked at her hands, all scratched as if someone had taken a grater and scraped back and forth, she began to shake.

"What happened?" He asked again. "You're cut, bleeding, your jeans are torn."

He knelt down and looked at the tear.

"Your leg is bleeding, too. What have you been up to?"

"I need to sit down," she said.

"Well, tell me. What happened? Surely Holly didn't attack you."

She laughed at the suggestion.

"No. I...ah...I sort of fell...a few times."

"Fell! Where were you? In a coal bin?"

"You could say that. I guess I'd better take a shower and change. I'm a mess."

"You can wait long enough to tell me the truth. What happened?"

Astrid felt like Lucille Ball, conjuring a lie that Ricky would believe. She blew on her hands trying to cool the sting. She'd better make it good. He was not in a happy mood.

"I had occasion to go to Danny's house. You know. Holly's boy friend. She told him she was breaking the engagement off, and he didn't want to take no for an answer, but he did, and he left, and after I saw Holly home, I went to his house. It's a dump. That is, his father runs a scrap yard, and while I was there I sort of looked around, and tripped a couple of times. That's how I got scratched up. It was dark outside, and then there was a shot..."

163

"A shot! Were you hit? Wait a minute. Why did you go to his house? And why were you looking around in the dark?"

"Oh. Well. They have a lot of old cars there, and…"

"Old cars! You went there to see if you could find the old car that was seen at the Rutherford house?"

"Ya. That's kind of what I did. But…"

"What am I going to do with you, Astrid? You know better than to put yourself in danger like that. No wonder Larry didn't want you to jump into this case. If you had come right back home like you said you would, I would have told you about the sheriff's breakthrough."

"What breakthrough? Did he get the killer?"

"No. Not that. But they found the old car."

CHAPTER 21

Holly knew that Astrid's advice should be heeded, but she hated being watched day and night. When the guard returned to the house, there was no escaping his watchful eyes though she and Ginny were trying to have a confidential conversation. She wanted to tell him to go somewhere else, even if he couldn't hear them where he was, just beyond the kitchen doorway. He looked about ready to fall asleep in that chair.

She leaned over to Ginny and whispered, "Let's see if we can sneak to your room."

Ginny nodded and they made a quick dash down the hallway to the end room. However, Police Officer Mailer wasn't asleep. He followed them to the bedroom door, where Holly stopped.

"You're not going to come in here, are you?"

"No. I'll just get a chair and sit outside the door."

"Good."

Inside, she went to the chaise by the window. Ginny flopped on her belly across the bed.

"So what will you do if Danny comes back?" Ginny said.

Holly looked out the window. At night the Sillers had a light on in the back yard to dissuade anyone who might want to prowl about. Most of the neighbors followed suit, so that it looked almost like daylight. In order to have oil delivered at the rear of the houses, an alley way had been provided, and co-op owners paid for snow removal in winter.

Holly watched two squirrels chasing each other around a maple tree just beyond the alley. She hardly knew herself what she would do if Danny came back. Astrid had insisted she have this guard. Would he always be with her when she needed him?

"I don't know. Astrid was very firm with Danny, but I still hate to be mean to him. I was so sure he was the man I wanted to marry. Now I would feel rotten if I called the cops on him. You know what I mean? I'd be betraying the man I thought was the love of my life."

Ginny looked like a princess with long, flowing red hair. Her room was still decorated for a young child with dolls and teddy bears, and ruffled pillows. Even though surrounded by the fantasies of childhood, Ginny had a solid outlook on life, wisdom beyond her years, and a heart of gold which endeared her to Holly.

"Maybe you need to think how he betrayed you," Ginny said. "He didn't show empathy for your heartbreak, did he?"

"No. He didn't even call me."

"Then I don't think I'd worry about hurting his feelings. He seemed to think he could waltz back into your life, ignore the fact that your parents had been killed, disrupt your mourning period, and demand that you marry him. I don't think I'd have needed help getting him out the door with that attitude."

Holly found that amusing. She remembered Ginny's reaction to a boy on the playground at school, when they were in fourth grade. He had come up behind her and pulled her red braid. She whirled about and hit him with a right hook that landed him on the ground and in need of the school nurse's attention. No, Holly doubted that her friend would have the same conscience about Danny that she had.

"You're probably right, Ginny. I feel so weak."

"You're suffering, my dear. Did you talk with your minister yet?"

"Not yet. I just couldn't talk about it to him. I knew I'd break down."

"Well, of course. That's what you're supposed to do."

Holly looked away again and watched the squirrels still cavorting in the back yard.

"You feed the squirrels, do you?" she asked.

"No way. We put food out in a feeder for the birds. But the darned squirrels get up there and clean it out every day. Dad's going to make a slippery aluminum cone under the feeder so they can't get up there."

"Clever idea."

In the lull between them, Ginny got off the bed and went to her dresser.

"Mom said she left my mail here, and I forgot to look."

She thumbed through a few envelopes and a magazine.

"Oh, Holly. Here's one for you."

"For me? Who's writing to me? And how did they know I was here, I wonder."

She joined Ginny, took the envelope, and looked at the hand printed address. A feeling of anxiety ran through her. No one should be writing to her here, and obviously whoever it was didn't want the handwriting to be recognized. She took the letter opener that Ginny held up for her and slit it open.

"Oh," was all she could say when she read the block printed words.

"What is it, Holly?"

"Look."

She handed it over, and Ginny read aloud, "SORRY. HE DESERVED TO DIE."

Holly's legs felt weak. She tried to speak, but couldn't breathe.

"Are you okay, Holly?"

"I…I'll be okay. Just a minute."

Wild thoughts raced through her mind. Did she know anyone who would feel that her dad deserved to die? What about her mother? Did she deserve to die, too. At first, Holly wanted to cry. Then as she considered the message, she became angry.

"Who is this monster?" she said. "Who is he to judge that my father deserved to die? What did either of my parents do to him that was so bad he killed them? Who made him God?"

"I know, Holly. It's terrible. Do you want to show it to the police?"

"I don't think so."

"There might be fingerprints on it."

"Yeah. Mine, no doubt." Holly turned to the window again. "I wonder if he will think I deserve to die, too."

"Oh, Holly. I don't think so. He did say sorry. He must be feeling guilt to have done that. Maybe his conscience is getting to him and he'll confess to the police."

Still watching the back yard, Holly realized that the squirrels were gone. Why did they leave so suddenly? Was someone out there?

"Your windows are locked, aren't they Ginny?"

"I think so. Let me check."

Ginny went from one to another.

"This one wasn't. There, I've locked it. I don't think you have to worry, Holly. No one will come in through the windows."

Comforting words, but not necessarily true. Holly had a foreboding that something was going to happen. Despite the 'sorry' in the note, she didn't believe a killer was ever really sorry. Maybe he was out of his mind. And maybe, even though she couldn't see anyone out there, he was lurking somewhere outside just waiting a chance to get in and kill her.

"Oh," Holly said. She put her hand over her mouth.

"What?"

"I'm thinking wild thoughts. I need to do something. Maybe I should go back to the office."

"No. You mustn't do that. You're safer here. If you want something to do, let's go down to the family room. Dad said he was starting a fire in the wood stove. We can shoot some pool."

Holly glanced out the window again. For a fleeting moment she saw a movement, not small like a squirrel, but the size of a human. She walked closer to the glass and peered out. If it was a man, he was gone now.

"You're so jumpy," Ginny said. "Come on. Let's go downstairs."

. . . .

Astrid slumped into a chair and drew a deep breath. Why had she been so foolish? What in the world did she expect to find? It made no sense to think a murderer would leave a gun in a car for police to find. Sometimes she couldn't explain her own actions even though they seemed reasonable at the time. Like when she went out to The Kingdom alone and faced all those armed men. What was she thinking?

"Where did they find the car?" she said.

"So you're interested now. You showed no interest when you ran out the door to go to Holly."

"She needed someone to get rid of that no-good Danny."

"And you sent him home and then went after him?"

"No. I got him out of Holly's office, and then I followed her home to be sure he didn't go there. After that, it just occurred to me that it was a good time to check out that car in the junk yard while it was dark and no one would see me. Only it wasn't easy. I lost my flashlight, the car doors were locked, and I had to give up."

"Well that explains everything. And so reasonable, too."

169

She hurt too much to take his smugness.

"Oh, go away."

No use trying to hide her disappointment that she hadn't found anything for all her struggle.

"I thought you'd be glad to hear about finding the real car," Abram said. "But if not, then I won't tell you the rest of it."

He knew how to press her buttons. Of course she wanted to hear the whole story. She just wanted him to notice the pain she was suffering.

"I guess I need to clean up and put something on these cuts," she said.

"Here. I'll help you. You sure you don't want to go to the ER?"

So he really did care. With his help, she got up and walked to the stairs where she hesitated.

"Where did they find the car?" she asked with enough humility that he put his arm around her waist to help her up the stairs. "And how do they know it's the right car?"

"It was abandoned just off the Greenboro Road, but in plain sight. It's true that they're going on the color and rust, but they're 99 percent sure it's the one."

"Anything found in it? Anything to give a clue to the murderer?"

"Not a thing. A couple of deputies went out to fingerprint everything before it could be moved, but they came back with nothing. I should say they had a lot of prints because the car is old, and has had a lot of people in it. They lifted a couple of prints that appeared to be recent, but had no matches. I expect it was driven around back roads so no one would notice that it had no license plates."

"Seems impossible. It could be a respectable citizen. Someone who never got into trouble with the law."

"Exactly."

"That makes the murders even more awful, then. To think someone hated them enough to kill them. Someone who apparently upheld the law enough to stay out of trouble until now."

"We don't know that, any more than we know where the driver of that car went and why he wasn't seen."

With him following, she went into the bathroom, where she ran warm water into the tub.

"I want to soak a while in a warm bath instead of a shower."

"Those cuts and scrapes will hurt when you get into the water," Abram said.

As if she didn't know that. She smiled at him.

"I'm tough. I don't think they're deep enough to worry about."

"How about your leg? Is that a scrape? It's not a gunshot wound, is it?"

"No, no. They were using a shotgun. Never touched me."

"God in heaven. A shotgun. If you don't get killed one of these days, you'll at least be the death of me."

"I was never in great danger."

Not too great, anyway. How can anyone shoot at a person, even if it is a prowler? Doesn't it prove that the person is capable of murder? Did Danny and his father go to Judge Rutherford's house in that car? Maybe each one had a gun and maybe both of them are the killers. Or maybe just Danny went to the house alone, like I thought before. Or maybe his father did it. He was the one that shot at me, I think. Unless he handed the gun to Danny, which I doubt.

Abram touched the leg wound and his expression softened.

"That seems pretty deep to me. You get into the tub and I'll clean it and take a closer look. Come to think of it, I may take a closer look at more than the leg."

He waggled his eyebrows like Groucho Marx, then ducked.

"Just stick to the wound, thank you."

But Astrid liked his attention to detail, especially when it was her body.

"Are they going to search the car more?" she asked. "Maybe there's a tiny detail they missed."

"You think like a detective. Sometimes you do, that is. But not when you barge out into the night and trespass and invite gun fire. Larry said they've called a forensics expert to see if he can find something they've overlooked. He's worried that the investigation is going so slowly. Each day lost gives the killer more time to get far away. I hate to say it, but I think he's worried that this is one case he may never solve. What a shame that would be."

"Larry's back to work already?"

"Not officially. He came in to pick up a few papers, and stopped by to ask me more about Guy Platt. I couldn't tell him much more than he already knows."

Astrid began to tremble again when she thought that Platt might have been after Abram.

"Why did you think he'd come after you, honey?"

She grabbed his extended arm to step into the tub of warm water.

"Ouch. Oh. Ouch." She said.

"Told ya it would hurt."

"Okay, you did. But tell me why?"

"Because the water is a little too warm and…"

"Hey. You know what I mean. Why did you think Platt might have been out to shoot you?"

The water he sponged on her back soothed her shakiness. After a few minutes of soaking and sponging, she relaxed.

"Probably because we met one day on the street and he stopped me to say that he never forgot his enemies. I suggested it was a long time ago, and he should forget it. I guess my exact words were, 'Get over it, man.' And that hit a nerve. He said, 'I'll get over it when I see you laid out in your coffin.'"

"Abram! You could have been killed. Why didn't you tell someone? Did you tell Larry?"

"No, of course not. The man was a falling down drunk. I didn't want to aggravate his hate for me by having a deputy out there telling him to cool it."

"I suppose not. But that was too close. I think you're right. He must have meant to kill you, not Larry. But see? Now there's a case of someone with a long-standing grudge, and if he'd killed you and no one saw him, we wouldn't know anything that would lead us to him. Just like the Rutherford murders."

Abram stopped sponging her back.

"Now that's something to think about. Guess I'd better check my list of boyhood fights and make sure someone else isn't out to get me."

"Ya. I think so." Astrid said with the same tone of sarcasm. "I didn't know I was marrying a man possibly wanted by the Mafia."

They could laugh about it, she thought, but had Guy Platt found and shot Abram, how could she go on?

"I couldn't."

She realized she'd said it aloud when he responded.

"Couldn't what?"

"I couldn't go on without you, Abram." In a whisper, she added, "A good man is hard to find."

"A good woman, as well."

He slipped his arm around her bare shoulders and kissed her with such tenderness that she could have cried if she weren't so emotionally drained. Then she thought.

"Abram, promise me something."

"Anything. Anything reasonable, that is."

"Promise me you won't tell Larry about this."

"My dear. I never tell Larry about holding you naked."

"You know what I mean. You are so aggravating at times."

CHAPTER 22

Sunday

Drew had been awake for several minutes, not anxious to get out of his warm, soft bed. *How many people really appreciate a good bed?* It would be a long while before he'd forget the backaches he endured for many years and the longing for relief he could have if he could sleep on a soft mattress. He was right. Once he sank into this pillow-soft bed at night, the arms of Morpheus cradled him until daylight.

If he should be forced to leave here, he would ask to buy the bed. He sat up, drew up his legs, and crossed his arms on his knees. Why did he think he would be forced to leave? Something happened, but what? Before going to sleep last night, what was it that he heard? It wasn't a dream. Noises. People talking loudly. If he hadn't been so weary, he would have gone to the hallway to listen. He told himself to remember. Think! Yes. He did remember. Mr. Bertram and Mr. Levitch were going at it again. This time he heard a single word. That was what he wanted to remember. Murder. And there was another voice. Lighter. Possibly a woman's. Hadn't he heard it before? Could it be Mr. Bertram's woman friend that he heard a couple nights ago?

Why did the two lawyers get angry and speak of murder? They did it at the office, too. He couldn't even speculate. They couldn't be involved in murder, but they might have a murder case to defend. Then why fight over it?

All at once he thought of his brother's words about the attorneys he had joined. "You might be surprised at what you'd find," he had said about investigating them.

Damn you, Les. Why did you say that? What's going on? And how can I find out without tipping my hand?

He needed to talk with someone he could trust. That would be his old friend Chris. They hadn't planned to meet today, but Chris shouldn't mind if he dropped in to see him.

. . . .

Drew found him home, and as he expected, Chris was glad to see him.

"It's awfully quiet," Chris said. "This is a good little apartment, but not much going on, and I don't feel like going downstairs and pestering Mrs. Oswald. She's always busy."

"Why not go find your girl friend?"

"I don't have a girl friend. Not yet, anyway."

"You could have if you'd be a little more aggressive."

"Yeah, well. I'm not aggressive with women. Even in better circumstances, before I had a record, I didn't force myself on them or even get overly friendly. My wife did the proposing. Otherwise, I probably would never have had the fam…"

He choked up, and Drew walked to the kitchen window to give him a minute to compose himself. How different the two places were. His had the rather heavy feeling of antiques, light enough but not bright like this one. He was glad for his friend to have found a comfortable place, just as he did. Drew liked old things. Maybe it suited his desire for the sedate life that made him happy to have furnishings of historical significance around him.

"It's still hard, you know," Chris said. "And I worry about Holly. She doesn't have anyone to watch out for her. Although I think that woman reporter, Astrid Lincoln, is sort of a protector. Seems like a very nice lady."

When Chris had poured coffee for both and brought out a package of molasses cookies, they sat at the kitchen table.

"I had a chat with her at the college. She was there to work out, too. Seemed very concerned about the murders, and I don't think she was gathering material for a newspaper story."

"Maybe she could help, then," Drew said.

"How's that? Something wrong?"

"I don't know, to tell the truth. I came here to see how crazy this all sounds when I speak of it out loud. You know that I live in Mr. Bertram's house. He's a kind man. Let's me pretty much have the run of the house, but of course I don't go beyond the kitchen. I finally asked about my position, whether I should be looking for another job in light of what he told Mr. Levitch about his hiring me for temporary work. And he said not to worry about that."

"That's good news. Glad to hear it. Finding another position as easy as you did here might be hard."

"It would be downright near impossible. So after you and I talked about that, I waited up for him to come home from a party. I got a bit impatient and went out to the garage and walked around a bit. He's got everything for tools. On the far side of the garage he has a car covered up, and I went over to look at it when I heard his car coming, so I went back to my room. But I can't help wonder if that might be the car they spoke of having been seen outside Rutherford's house after the murders."

Chris looked genuinely shocked.

"You think Mr. Bertram could have killed them?"

Drew shrugged.

"Damned if I know. I didn't see the whole car, only a bit of the rust around the lower part. It's not much to go on. Doesn't seem likely that he'd kill anyone. He's what I'd call a gentle man. But I do know that I've heard voices in the night a couple of times. They came from the kitchen, I thought. The first time, before Levitch came back, sounded like a man and a woman talking. I chalked it up to a rendezvous between Mr. Bertram and a woman friend. He's not too old, you know."

"Who is?"

"Huh! Yeah, I guess you're right. Then last night, again I was in bed just about to go to sleep when I heard voices again. I was just too tired to go listen in the hallway, but it sounded like the same woman and Mr. Bertram and Mr. Levitch. They got pretty animated, and a couple of times I distinctly heard the word murder. I couldn't hear complete sentences. I don't know what's going on, but it seems that the two attorneys are at disagreement about something."

"The more you say, Drew, the more it sounds possible that they, or at least one of them, had something to do with the murder of our beloved judge."

Drew grinned.

"Beloved. Yeah. Well, I don't know what to make of it, but here's a scary part about it. When I went out to The Kingdom to see Les and tell him to stop meddling in my life, he said I should investigate the lawyers I was going to work for. He made it clear that he knew something I didn't know about them and even said I might be surprised at what I'd find if I did investigate."

"Wonder what that's all about."

"So do I, and I can't very well go searching for information on my bosses. That would be a sure way of getting fired if they found out. But maybe there's someone who can dig into their background a bit."

"Don't look at me. I'm no investigator."

"Not you. But you mentioned the name just now. That Astrid woman. I know she's a reporter, but if you could swear her to secrecy in doing it, she might be able to find out if there's anything in their backgrounds that's serious enough for me to consider leaving them now. I can't afford to get into any kind of questionable dealings, any more than you can. I need to know what Les meant."

"Why not ask him?"

"If I did that, he'd try to convince me to join him, no matter how insignificant the history, and I just don't want to battle it out with him again. I left, and I'm not going back. He's a control freak. Better if I stay away."

"I had him pegged for that, myself," Chris said. "Well, I guess I can give it a try. Astrid may not like the idea of playing detective, but I'll see if she'll talk with me in private. I'll think of some reason to look into the firm for me."

"You can say you want to have a will made out but want to feel perfectly confident in the lawyers before going ahead with it. Huh?"

"I guess I can do that and sound sincere enough. I wish I knew what we're looking for."

"So do I. It may be no more than a bribe that Les found out about. Or it could be a lawsuit against the attorneys themselves. I just don't know. What I heard last night sounded to me like they were involved in a murder case. Could be they had a disagreement about taking the case."

Chris stared into his coffee cup, obviously disturbed about his role in deceiving Astrid.

"You don't have to do this if it bothers you, Chris."

"No. That's not it. She can't do any more than say no."

"So what is it?"

"It's just that I'm so close to that murder, and I guess that's all I can think of because of Holly. You don't believe your bosses could be involved in the judge's murder, do you?"

"I don't want to. But I don't want to work with them if there is a shadow of doubt about their integrity, murder or not. I'd like to know before next week when I have to report to my parole officer, because if there is doubt, I need to be able to tell her my reason for leaving the firm, if I do that."

"I'd be just as careful myself. Maybe one day we'll be excused from the oversight of the parole board."

Drew smoothed his mustache and considered that possibility.

"Mmm. But it will take some time and proof that we can be trusted to live peaceably and responsibly on the outside."

One thing Drew had learned in these few weeks of freedom… doing well and proving yourself after a crime was much more difficult than staying out of trouble in the first place.

CHAPTER 23

Monday

Headlines this week would tell of yet another murder in Fairchance, this one at the sheriff's office. Astrid re-read her story, and lingered over the quote from Sheriff Larry Knight:

"This tragedy saddens me as much as it saddens Mr. Platt's family. My deepest sympathy goes out to this family. It would be easy to dismiss the incident by pointing out that if Guy Platt had not entered the sheriff's office with a shotgun, and if he had not pointed that gun at the sheriff, he would still be alive. But the fact is that all of that did happen, he is not alive, and it is most regrettable."

And if he had gone a little farther down the hall, my husband would be dead.

She turned away and looked out the window. Main Street was busy this morning, not unusual for a Monday. How different all this would look to her if Abram had been the one to die that day.

Could I bear losing him? I'm not sure I could even remain in newspaper work. And he's studying to become an officer of the law. It's dangerous enough working as a dispatcher. How much more danger he'll face as a deputy. Will I worry every day he goes to work and wonder whether he'll come back to me alive? How does Beth do it?

In a sigh, the words "Oh God" slipped out.

"What?" Charlie said. "Something wrong, Astrid?"

"Just thinking aloud, I guess," she said. "Thinking about what a family goes through when someone is murdered senselessly. First the Rutherfords, and now Platt. The sheriff had no recourse but to kill Guy Platt. He was drunk and he was waving a shotgun at him. But Holly's parents--I don't know. That was a premeditated killing. Who has that much anger and hate? Even if they hate, how can they stand face-to-face with someone and shoot that person and watch him die?"

"You got a pretty good first-hand look at a man who hated everyone, Astrid. The general didn't kill you, but came awfully close to it. Cat Cotter died in your arms practically."

"Don't remind me. I had nightmares for weeks. Poor Cat. She just wanted to get guns out of the hands of people like that. She had a lot more guts than most people."

"Amen to that. You finished that story yet?"

"Ya. It's ready. I need to go out to see Mrs. Platt and get a picture of her husband, if I can get one. I'll call first. She may not want to let me have one. No knowing what her reaction will be. She's probably mad at all society, since her family was defined by an alcoholic husband. Don't you think so? If society had done more to protect her, if the police had put Guy away, or if he couldn't have had access to a liquor bottle, all the humiliation she has had to endure would never have happened. I guess I sound like the sheriff now. But I think I'd be upset with everyone if it had been my husband who drank and bullied."

Charlie nodded.

"You make a good point. You don't think she knew what she was getting into when she married him?"

"Maybe. Abram had a run-in with him as a child, and Guy never got over it. She must have had occasion to see his paranoid side before she married him. Well, I'll try to get the picture."

She felt Charlie's eyes studying her while she looked up the number in the telephone directory. When she looked up, he shook his head.

"Looks like you had a rough weekend," he said.

How typical of Charlie. Not an ounce of tact.

"Nothing like stating the obvious." She held up her bandaged left hand. "Ya. It was rough. I went skiing without skis."

Let him figure that one out. She wouldn't elaborate. He could give her that smug grin all he wanted to, he didn't intimidate her in the least.

"I don't doubt that," he said.

He could take as well as give, and he knew when to concede. She liked Charlie for that reason. At times, their rapport felt like sibling rivalry, a bit sharp but not mean-spirited. He would have been a rough and tumble brother, no doubt, a bit like her own as a youngster.

She dialed the number for Mrs. Platt and listened to four rings. About to hang up, she heard a click.

"'lo?" The woman's voice was weak.

"Mrs. Platt?"

"Yeah. Who're you?"

"I'm Astrid Lincoln at *The Bugle*. First, let me say how sorry I am for your loss. I…"

"You're sorry for my loss? Why?"

Oh dear. She's ready to fight.

"We don't know each other, Mrs. Platt. I have no axe to grind with you, and I sincerely hope you don't with me. I just need a photograph of your husband, if you have one and if you would lend it to me."

"Oh yeah? So you can plaster his face all over the front of yore newspaper? No. I won't *lend* you one. And I won't give you one, neither."

"It's okay. Is there anything I can do to help you through this? Do you need anything?"

"Need anythin'! Of course I need anythin'. I need my husband. Can you bring him back?"

"I wish I could. There isn't a whole lot I can do, I know, but I could pick up some groceries for you, or I could transport you if you don't have a car."

"I have a truck. I can drive my husband's truck. You one o' them sons-a-bitches do-gooders are ya? I don't need you or anyone else for help."

"Just one question Mrs. Platt. Do you have children?"

"Oh yeah. I got children all right. Five. I take care of 'em. Have for a long time, no thanks to Guy."

"You work, then?"

"You mean am I on Welfare. Yeah. I get Welfare. How're the kids gonna eat if I don't get it? No shame in that, is there? To feed kids?"

"No, of course not."

"Well, good. I'm so glad to hear it. Goodbye."

Astrid pulled the phone away when Mrs. Platt slammed hers down.

"Whew. Not much cooperation there," she said.

"I could hear her from here," Charlie said.

Astrid couldn't resist a little laugh.

"Ya. I think she was louder than me. You want me to go to the school and see if I can find his picture in a yearbook?"

"No. Let it go. He'd have looked a lot different then, anyway."

"Okay."

She started to write a caption for the page one photo she had taken of the sheriff's office where the shooting took place. Looking over at the empty chair where Will should be, she said, "Where's Will? Isn't he coming in today?"

"His daughter is quite sick, and he took her to the doctor. He'll be in about noontime."

"I could call the college and get a report on the women's basketball game Saturday. It would be that much ahead for Will anyway."

"Sure. Go ahead. He has a full load of games to write up. Where was it played?"

"At Farmington. Our team won. About time they broke their losing streak."

About to call, Astrid picked up an incoming call instead.

"Mrs. Lincoln?"

"Ya."

"Astrid, this is Chris Benning. You know, the computer man."

"Of course. We had a nice chat over coffee at the college. What can I do for you?"

"I wonder if you and I could have a private talk, sometime when you're not too busy."

"It's always busy here on Monday, but if you can come at about 12:30 when I take a lunch break, we can talk in our conference room upstairs."

"I'll be there."

I wonder what that's all about, Astrid thought.

She made the call to get stats on the college women's game. Coach Buddie Schram answered.

"Hi Buddie. It's Astrid."

She couldn't imagine naming a girl Buddie, but the coach had told her that her parents decided on a name they would use for either sex. Thus, she became Buddie.

"Calling about our game with Farmington I'll bet."

"You got it. Congratulations, by-the-way."

"We barely squeaked by, but it was a win, thank God. Before we get into that I want to invite you to play on a very special team."

"What special team?"

"Donkey basketball. Ever play it?"

"No. But I've seen it played. It looks like fun."

"It is. We're picking up adult players to go against our varsity team Friday evening. We wanted to just call on alumni, but there aren't enough in Fairchance, so we're including anyone who will play. Can you make it?"

"I can. I'll be there. So give me more about that, too. I'll write it up for the readers. You should get a good turnout for something like that."

Basketball on a donkey. Crazy, she thought.

They went through the stats and highlights of the women's game, as well as the upcoming donkey basketball, and Astrid soon had the stories written, ready for Will.

For the first day of the week, the newsroom was quiet. Usually there was a flood of notices and obits.

"What's going on?" Astrid said. "Never saw things so slow on a Monday."

"I was just thinking the same thing," Charlie said. "Will said doctors are very busy. A lot of this sickness going around."

He let the phone ring three times before answering.

"This is Charlie," he said.

As he listened, his scowl deepened.

"That sounds bad," he said. "Don't worry about the office. You tend to the family first. Anything we can do?"

A few more seconds, then, "All right. Try not to worry too much. And good luck."

Charlie's concern prompted Astrid to ask, "What?"

"It was Will. Julia seems to be worse."

"What's wrong with her?"

"She has a strep throat. They're worried it might develop into rheumatic fever. Will said his sister died as a result of childhood rheumatic fever."

"Oh God. Let's hope not."

"He said she's had a sore throat for several days. They'll know soon if it's worse than that."

"That poor little girl. Such a sweetheart."

Astrid recalled eight-year-old Julia with the huge personality and beautiful dark eyes.

"Yeah. She reminds me of my own daughter when she was that age."

"You never speak of her. She coping all right without you?"

"Sure. We talk with her each evening. I think she enjoys life without us."

"At her age, you may be right. But she'll always need you and Jenny." Astrid had yearned for her parents many times. "I know from experience. Even my granddad couldn't take the place of my mother."

"Looks like we're it for this week's news. You'll have to finish up the sports page. Will had a feature on the proposed start-up of a Youth Group. Look it over and see if there's the possibility of a sidebar to it. You know the routine. If you don't have enough copy for the page, dig out one of those cute photos of youngsters practicing at the hockey rink. Will wanted to use one last week, but there wasn't space enough."

"Okay."

Now it seemed that everyone remembered to bring in their club meetings, pictures, and even a lengthy speech given at a Woman's Club meeting by none other than the president Daniella Caton.

That must have been delightful–and long, Astrid thought.

• • • •

Just as she promised, Astrid set aside her work at 12:30 and headed up the stairs with lunch bag and paper coffee cups in one hand while carrying her usual work bag over her shoulder. She hadn't heard Chris come in, but that was not surprising with all the sudden traffic and phone calls. She opened the conference room door with trepidation. Would he be here?

"Ah, Astrid Lincoln," Chris said. "Thank you for seeing me."

"No problem."

She set all her goods on the conference table, motioned for him to sit and took the chair facing him. While she hauled out sandwiches and coffee thermos from the paper bag, she watched him.

"It's not very warm in here," she said as if he might not notice. "This room doesn't get used much, so the heat is kept at a minimum. I can't stay long, or I'd turn up the thermostat."

"I'm fine, if you are," he said. "I know you're busy."

"Help yourself to the sandwiches. They're all the same. Turkey."

She poured coffee for both. When he took his, his hand shook. Cold or nervous?

"Eating together is getting to be a habit. I didn't expect to be fed. Just wanted to ask a favor." He reached for a bagged sandwich. "But thanks. I am a bit hungry."

"Okay. Shoot. What do you need?"

"It's a favor, but not for me. I have a friend who needs information about a couple of lawyers in town, and we couldn't think of anyone with easy access to that kind of information, unless it was you."

"And what kind of information do you need?"

He swallowed, took a drink of coffee, and sighed.

187

"Oh, I don't really know, to tell the truth. Just find out if their pasts are clean of trouble, I guess."

"These lawyers have a name?"

"Levitch and Bertram."

"Really? What do you think they've done?"

"Not sure they've done anything," he said. "But my friend would like to know for sure. And if you can do this quietly without revealing names, it would be best."

"So your friend. He or she?"

"He." Chris squirmed as if contemplating how much more he should reveal. "He has gone to work for them and wants to be sure they are totally honest."

At that, Astrid couldn't check a burst of laughter.

"Totally honest, huh? Now that would be refreshing in any lawyer."

Chris guffawed, too.

"You're probably right. But, you see, my friend is a lawyer, too."

"Ah. Well. He must have a good reason for wanting to look into the record of Levitch and Bertram. I sat at dinner the other night with Mr. Bertram. He seemed like an easy-going, quiet man. And I met Mr. Levitch, too. He wanted to know if I had anything new about the militia in Greenboro. He didn't say why he was interested, but he acted as if he had a good reason."

Although Chris tried to appear disinterested in that information, Astrid saw the twitch and sudden attention he gave to adjusting the bread on his sandwich. He knew something beyond what he had revealed.

"I guess, if I'm to gather background on the lawyers, I should have the name of the man who wants it."

He changed position in his chair again, and took a few seconds more to find his answer.

"My friend is Drew Godfrey."

"And he can't look up this information for himself?"

"He's concerned for his job, of course, being new at it. He wouldn't want his bosses to find out that he was checking up on them."

Astrid reached back in memory for that name Godfrey. When the mist cleared, she knew.

"I seem to remember the name Godfrey in connection with one of the men at The Kingdom. Let me think. Ya. It was Lester Godfrey."

She began to put the pieces together.

"Is it possible that Drew is related to Lester? Is that why Mr. Levitch questioned me about what I know concerning that group? Maybe the shoe is on the other foot, so to speak. Maybe he's checking up on Drew. Is that it?"

If ever a face reflected being caught with his hand in the cookie jar, she was looking at it now. If the two men were brothers, of course there would be concern over hiring one for their firm. Drew could be one of them. They weren't a rag tag outfit with ignorant men and women angry over their lot in life. They were intelligent, middle and upper class people, obviously with wealth, angry with the system, intent on changing it even if that meant revolution.

The question was why did Drew send Chris on this mission of digging up dirt on the lawyers? Was he spying for the militia?

"Or is Drew on a more sinister mission himself?" she said. "Because if he is, I won't be part of it."

"No. I understand what you're thinking. He has nothing to do with his brother. I hesitate to tell you more, but maybe I should. This is complicated, but it's innocent."

She looked at her watch.

"Do you have time to hear me out?" Chris asked.

"I'll take a few more minutes, but we're short a reporter today and I do need to get back soon."

"Okay. But I need a promise that this will go no further. Please keep this between us."

"I don't usually make promises like that. I am a reporter, and if the need should arise to reveal something said to me in confidence, I'd be jeopardizing my job by not doing the right thing."

"I see. Then let me re-word it. Will you not spread the word just for the sake of telling someone? You know what I mean. If a legal issue should arise, I expect you to follow your own conscience. But if…"

"Ya, ya. I get it. No, I won't gossip. In that respect I promise you to guard your privacy."

"Good." Chris pushed back in his chair and pulled a leg over his knee. "The fact is he and I were prisoners in New York State. We were both paroled after we served our minimum sentences and we came here. Les offered housing for the two of us. When we found out what they were all about out there, we both left and took housing here in Fairchance. We had studied in prison. I became a computer technician and Drew studied law and passed the bar exam. We both worked hard to have a good position when we became free men again."

"Why here?" Astrid said. "Why was Fairchance your choice?"

"For Drew, it was his brother's urging to come. Drew didn't know what Les had gotten into or he would have gone somewhere else. For me…well, I had another reason."

"Which was?"

"My daughter. She lives here."

"Your daughter?"

Chris didn't answer, but Astrid had begun to piece it together. She recalled his attention to Holly and his deep concern when she heard that her parents had been killed.

"Are you Holly's father?"

He pleaded with his eyes.

"I don't want her to know that. I shouldn't have told this much. She had a good home, and as far as I know, good parents. I don't want to turn her life upside down any more than it is right now. Understand?"

"I understand that, but for some reason you came here where she is. Did you know that? Did you know that Holly was here?"

He nodded. "Yes, I knew. I just wanted to see her. I didn't think I'd see her so soon. I figured if I ran into the judge some day, I could go away quietly. My only desire was to see how my daughter had turned out, how she looked now. She was only a toddler when I last saw her."

Astrid looked away, studied the wall calendar, open to last month. If Chris hadn't been with Holly in her office at the time of the murder, he would surely be a prime suspect. But he was there and so was she. What about this Drew? And did the men know Judge Rutherford? If so, how well.

"You knew the judge, did you?" she said.

"As much as anyone being sentenced by him did. Drew and I both faced him in court. He sentenced us both. I know everyone who goes to prison says he's innocent, but I tell you honestly, I was innocent."

She looked at her watch again. It was time to go back to work.

"I know you need to leave," he said. "And I have only my word for it, but I did not murder my wife.

"Your wife!"

"That's right. She was killed in our apartment and I was in the bedroom asleep. I didn't kill her. I just couldn't prove it. Drew wasn't completely innocent of killing a man, but it was a barroom brawl that he tried to stay out of. He was attacked and the man was accidentally shot with his own weapon. It should have been ruled self-defense. The judge showed no mercy to either of us. We both served 20 years."

"I see. It wouldn't exactly inspire respect for the judge."

"No. It didn't. We were both angry at first, but we got into study programs. That made all the difference. Neither one of us would take revenge. Not now."

Astrid didn't want to sound critical of Chris or Drew, but this whole thing came as a complete surprise, nothing like what she might have guessed Chris would talk about with her. She had expected he might be inquisitive about Holly and whether he should go back to her office to continue the computer lesson so soon. But never this confession, as it were.

"Drew has a good position" he said, "and I have a good job. Why would we do something stupid like killing someone? We don't want to screw up what we worked so hard for. What Drew needs to know is whether his bosses had anything to do with the judge's murder. He can't work for anyone involved in a felony act, any more than I can."

"You think they might have had something to do with Judge Rutherford's death?"

"Drew's brother told him he should investigate the lawyers, and that he might be surprised at what he'd find. But that was all he said."

"And you think I can find that out for you. It's a tall order. And this is a lot to digest, Chris. I've given you my word not to mention this conversation unless I find something incriminating that has to come out. But I'm going to have to decide whether to get involved as you ask. Let me think it over. I'll let you know. Where can I reach you?"

CHAPTER 24

Chris sat at his table in the back room. Unlike most other times, today he didn't think about being a computer technician without even a desk, relegated to a storage room for empty boxes, modems, screens, keyboards and other parts. Instead, he thought about his weakness in giving Astrid so much information. What had he done? A reporter, of all people, now knew about both Drew and himself. If he told Drew about their conversation, what would he say or do? Drew was nervous enough as it was. And would Astrid think it over and decide that Holly should know about her father? Oh God. He hoped not.

"Damned idiot."

He pounded his fist on the table and sent his thermos bottle over the edge.

"Oh hell. Now that's broken."

He picked it up and shook it. Sure enough, the shattered glass shushed about like ice in a bartender's shaker. He threw it in the wastebasket.

How did I get trapped into telling her all that? She seemed to press just the right buttons, Of course, I never could keep much to myself. I'm stuck here in a way, without having a job or a place to move to. But I could ask the parole officer if I could leave. But then, she'd ask too many questions. I've spilled enough already. I'll just have to wait it out and see what Astrid does.

He'd have to avoid Dew for a while unless he wanted to tell what he said to Astrid. This was a damned mess. Telling Drew that he betrayed him, that he'd revealed his prison record to a reporter, that she could decide to print the information in the newspaper, he'd lose his only real friend, to say the least.

"No. Can't do that. What, then? How can I keep away from him?"

When he heard Chip call his name, Chris rattled the paper bag with his sandwich to make him think he'd been having lunch. The door opened.

"How about going over to Greenboro?" Chip said. "They've got a man out and need help."

"Sure. Good. I'll do that."

Speak of a godsend. This was the answer to his problem. If Drew called he'd be out of town.

"I don't have anything urgent here," he said. "My friend Drew might call. Will you tell him I'm out of town and that I'll be in touch when I get back?"

"Yeah. Take the company van. They have a couple of installations on the docket. You'll need to transport the computers."

Chip tossed the keys to the table. He looked toward the front door when it opened.

"I can handle the customers for the rest of the day. You may be needed over there more than just this afternoon. Better stop by your place and pack a bag. You know they have a back room with a cot in case you need to stay over."

"Yeah. I know. Fine. I'll get my things now. Oh, and Astrid Lincoln might call, too. You can give her the number in Greenboro. I hope you don't mind."

"O'course not."

As soon as he was out the door, Chris looked to the sky. "Thank God."

It may just be putting off the inevitable, but at least it will give me time to see what Astrid will do.

. . . .

By mid-afternoon Astrid had finished all her work and most of Will's sports pages, using some canned stories from the AP wire, when Will came in.

"How's Julia?" were the first words from Charlie.

Astrid stood up, both to greet Will and to stretch her leg. Since cutting it Saturday night, it had stiffened up to her knee.

"You look worn out, Will," she said. "You aren't going to try to work, are you?"

"Julia will be all right, the doctor says, but she's a very sick little girl. I thought I could get a start on things in the couple of hours that're left this afternoon."

"I agree with Astrid," Charlie said. "You shouldn't be in here. She's got most of your pages made up. What's left, Astrid?"

"Not much. You really should try to get some sleep, Will. Things are okay here. I'm glad to hear that Julia will be all right. How are the others holding up?"

"Everyone's relieved. The nurse shooed us all out and told us to come back tomorrow. If you think I'm not needed for the rest of the day, I guess I will go home and hit the couch. I feel like a bus rolled over me. I plan to be here by nine, if there isn't too much left to do. I'll stop first at the hospital."

He started to leave, but turned back.

"Did you get the college women's game, Astrid?"

"Ya, of course. They want me to play donkey basketball Friday night. You ever seen that, Will?"

"No. I know they play it and I've heard that it can be a riot. A friend told me some of the donkeys are trained to buck players off their backs. So be careful."

"Thanks for the warning."

"He's a good father," Charlie said after Will left. "I'd hate to see anyone hurt one of those kids. He'd kill 'em. Nice to be loved like that when you're growing up."

Charlie said no more, but Astrid thought she detected pain in those words. She sat down and puttered with her notebook, flipping pages but not reading them. After Chris left this noon, she gave thought to what he asked. It made sense for him to want to help his friend Drew. If Levitch and Bertram had been involved in illegal activity, a parolee working with them could be in trouble. She didn't know that for certain, but it reasoned that former prisoners had to walk a tightrope and couldn't have even the appearance of wrongdoing. They might be judged guilty even if only by association.

Besides that, if she should find something, she might get a good story out of it. Not that she mistrusted attorneys, or anything like that.

Well, maybe I do. Ya, I'll do it. I'll see if I find anything suspicious in their past dealings.

And she knew where to start. The talkative woman at the party, Daniella Caton. She said she was a neighbor of the Levitches, seemed to know a great deal about her neighbors, and wasn't shy about telling what she knew.

. . . .

The more Chris thought about what he had done, how he had revealed not just his own background but also Drew's, the worse he felt. Here he was on a thin, hard mattress, with his back breaking, and telling himself that he was happy to be hidden.

What could he do now? Call Astrid and plead with her not to speak of their prison records? She said she'd keep it confidential, but he didn't trust that she would.

Can't trust anyone these days.

He should pick up the phone and call Drew. He should confess that he went too far in seeking help from Astrid. He wanted to get it off his chest. He'd like to think that he was man enough to do that.

But was he?

Oh, goddam it, no, I'm not. I never was or I'd never have been in prison in the first place. It was my own damned fault that I got hooked on booze and drugs. Had a wonderful woman, a beautiful little girl, and what did I do? Got my wife killed by a drug dealer and lost my child to the judge, of all people in the world. Some man I am. I'm no kind of a friend.

CHAPTER 25

Daniella Caton raised her voice a pitch in enthusiasm at the prospect of talking with a reporter, and yes, of course, she remembered Astrid. Certainly, come over now, she had said on the phone.

"What can I do for you?" she asked now that Astrid was here.

"After our talk at the party, I felt that I'd like to get to know you better, if you have the time. I'd also like to know a bit about your neighbor's handyman."

"I have all the time in the world, my dear. Take that chair. It was my husband's favorite. He sat there every evening, reading."

She indicated a big chair with a faded rose stretch jersey cover.

Astrid dropped into the chair. "Oh," she said when she found herself sunk nearly to the floor in the well-worn formation of Mr. Caton.

Daniella laughed. She looked different today, disheveled as if she'd been cleaning in the attic.

"He was a heavy man. I guess he pretty much wore the chair out, but I can't find the heart to replace it with something new. I sit here at night and sometimes I talk to the chair just as if he were here. Oh dear."

Astrid reflected that the poor man might like a new one, even in absentia. The chair wasn't the only piece of furniture that was old. Daniella's chair was an old wood rocker with high back and scroll design at top as well as a flattened cushion in the seat. Her side table held a basket with broken handle and balls of various color yarn. A round oak table with claw feet, in the center of the room. held so much that Astrid stopped looking beyond the books, newspapers, letters, and tray of silverware. Some of the side chairs and stands could be antique.

Laying her tape recorder on the folding TV stand next to her, Astrid said, "I hope you won't mind being recorded. I do that with everyone. I never trust my memory, you see. I won't lie to you, Mrs. Caton, I'm interested in what's going on at The Kingdom in Greenboro. I believe the militia members are returning, and I want to know if there's a hint of their presence here in Fairchance. Has Mrs. Levitch said much about the man who works for her? I recall that you said he's one of those at The Kingdom."

"Oh my. I don't know that I've heard much about them. I look over and see him shoveling after it snows. He goes into the house and doesn't leave for sometimes as much as two hours. Now that you question it, seems rather odd, doesn't it? But I don't know that you can read anything into it. She's a quiet woman. Says very little about her family."

She leaned forward and, in a confidential tone, said, "Once she let slip that this is her second marriage, you know. When I asked her what happened to her first husband, she just turned away and changed the subject. So I really don't know anything about that. Seems odd, though, don't you think? Why wouldn't anyone talk about their past? I don't know."

"Is she from this area, do you know?"

"Mr. Levitch is, but she isn't. He was away for a couple of months one time, oh, about six years ago now, I'd say. And when he came back, here he had a woman with him. He told everyone she was his wife. No one thought he'd ever marry. He is a bit... well...you know, effeminate. Before he moved next door to me about ten years ago, he was in his family home on the other side of town. Let's see, the street is called Cottage Lane. I think his partner lives there now. Abe never had company. Even now they don't. I have never been invited in, but I see her outside or at a supermarket now and again. We talk a mite. The weather, how are you, and like that. I think they go out together once in a while. I see them drive away just before supper time, and they come in quite late. Probably go to a movie, wouldn't you think? So I just don't know much about them. Never heard the name of the handyman. Well, let me see now. Yes, I think I did hear her call him something one day. In the fall. I was hanging out clothes and she called to him when he was raking up leaves. Now what was it? Oh, where's my head? Sometimes it takes me hours to think of just one word. Wait, I know. She called him Press. Probably short for something else."

"Press."

"That's it. Press. Well, I don't think I've been much help to you. I'd say go see her, but she's so offish that she might not let you in, you know. That Press comes to the house when Mr. Levitch is gone, I noticed. Like I said, it might look odd except that she's a good 20 years older than he is. Can't be any attraction there, I wouldn't think. Would you? Of course, she's a good-looking woman. Doesn't look her age. Still..."

Astrid was anxious to leave, but she wanted to hear all she could about the people next door.

"So you've lived here for many years?" she asked.

"Oh my, yes. My husband and I bought this house when we'd been married only two years, and I've lived here ever since. When he died, I thought of moving to an apartment, but at my age it's not easy to pack up and leave your home. Trouble is this place needs a lot of work now. He was a good handyman, but I have no one now to do things. I do get a boy down the street to shovel me out and to mow the lawn in the summer. He'll be going off to college next fall, though. Then I don't know what I'll do."

She laughed.

"Maybe I could get that Press to do my work, too. Suppose? But I don't think I'd want one of them around my house."

"Have you thought of getting a high school student? They always need money."

"They won't come and work any more. No, the work ethic is different today than when I went to school. Parents hand out money like water and the kids think it should always be that way. We never expected parents to pay for everything. You didn't, did you, Astrid?"

Astrid could join Daniella in decrying the lack of work ethic among the young today, but she couldn't very well say she had to work her way through college.

"My grandfather saw to it that I learned to earn my keep," she said truthfully. "I grew up on a farm and worked alongside the farmhands."

"Well, you really did learn the value of a dollar."

"Ya. I did." Astrid did not elaborate on the wealth that her grandfather left to her. "You have always lived in Fairchance, Daniella?"

"I have. Went to the University of Maine, and came back to teach here. Taught fifth grade English literature for 40 years before I retired. That was in the old schoolhouse before they built the new one with all the bells and whistles. My. If children only knew how well-off they are. Oh well. My day is past. I like to think I helped students learn to appreciate good literature."

"I'm sure you did."

Astrid looked at her watch.

"I'm sorry to have to leave, but it is getting late and I need to go home. Thank you for talking with me. I've enjoyed it."

"I wish I could be of more help, my dear."

"You were very helpful. And besides that, I've enjoyed chatting with you."

Daniella brightened.

"Do come again. Any time. I don't get a lot of company, so when I do it's a treat. Oh dear. I didn't offer you refreshment."

"I didn't need it, believe me. Thank you again for talking with me."

As she drove toward home, Astrid thought about that name, Press. Could it be Preston? Preston Norman? If so, why did Mrs. Levitch befriend him? Daniella said he spent time with her alone, but apparently only when Mr. Levitch was not there. What was Geraldine getting into? She must find out before it was too late.

She could go out to The Kingdom and ask Geraldine what she knew about Preston. Probably she'd just laugh and say it didn't matter what he did. She was going to marry him.

Just 5:15. Maybe Larry Knight was still in his office. Beth had said he didn't get home very early. He should know something about the lawyer and his wife.

Turning at the first convenient driveway, Astrid was soon at the sheriff's office. He had not left.

"Come in, Astrid. What can I do for you?"

"I came over to see what you can tell me about a couple of things that aren't related to much of anything but my own curiosity."

She thought it best not to elaborate on why.

"You know the attorney, Mr. Levitch."

Larry nodded. "Yes."

"Do you know Mrs. Levitch, as well?"

A puzzled look crossed his face.

"Not well. I have met her. She's a very quiet, private woman. Why are you asking?"

"I don't know for sure. She has a man from The Kingdom working for her as a handyman. There is some speculation by her neighbor about that. I don't want to get anyone in trouble, so I won't say too much about it. I just wonder if you've checked out everyone over there. I'm especially interested in Preston Norman. He was there when the general led the militia."

"We did check on everyone there. We couldn't find anything out of the way. I'm not too happy to see all the weapons they have, but it's not against the law to have the ones I saw. They probably have more powerful ones in an armory on the property, but we didn't find them. I can't tell you about any one person in particular. I will say this, though, they all seem crazed to me and if Mrs. Levitch has befriended one of them, I don't think it shows the best judgment."

He reached in a desk drawer and took out a sheet of paper.

"This is a list of the men and women out there now." He ran a finger down the list. "Yes. Here it is. Preston Norman, confirming what you already know, I guess."

She looked away, studied the four wall pictures of antique automobiles.

"May I have a copy of the list?" she asked.

"Sure. Funny thing. When I asked for a list, it was as if they wanted me to know just who they are, and I can only guess why. I expect they are planning something, though I don't have a clue what, and want to be sure names are spelled correctly in our reports."

He held it out to her.

"Have the desk clerk run off a copy of this on your way out, Astrid. Tell him to put the original back on my desk. Any reason in particular why you are so interested? I hope we don't have another general taking over."

"Nothing like that. At least I don't think so. Do you know if the militia groups are gaining strength in this country? Is there any way the law can thwart the anti-government movements?"

"You're writing another piece about them, are you?"

"No. Not yet, anyway. I ask out of my own concern only."

"If you're not quoting me, then I can tell you this. If government or law enforcement officers press too hard to identify them state-by-state, or county-by-county, it's almost certain they'll react violently. Law agencies don't share enough information, though, so they have virtually no way to be sure a mass uprising isn't brewing. What we do here is visit The Kingdom once in a while, unannounced, and check on their activity. Of course, this place is more sophisticated than many in the U.S. It has an amazing array of communications equipment, for instance, as you know, and it's an organized township. It worries me."

Astrid knew he had just said more than he intended. If it weren't for the fact that she had already told him she wasn't writing another story, she would be tempted to do it now, mainly to alert the public to watch for suspicious activity by strangers.

"Having said that, Astrid, what *are* you up to?"

"To tell the truth, my niece plans to marry Preston Norman on Saturday. I don't know how she got tangled up in that group, but she is headstrong and seems not to care much about reputation. Naturally, I'm concerned. I haven't been close to her, ever, but still she is family. I'd like to know more about him and whether she would be in danger. I'm thinking I should have a talk with her, at least, before she ties the knot."

While she talked, Larry was busy organizing his desk and readying to leave. Now, he stopped and leaned over the desk.

"Don't go out there alone, Astrid, please. Even though the camp is calm at the moment doesn't mean that they aren't capable of just about anything, especially against someone who divulged as much as you did about them and probably had a good deal to do with the death of their leader."

"I didn't…"

"I know," he said, holding up his hand for her to stop. "You didn't really cause his death, but maybe the general went further than he might have if you hadn't written about the uprising that was planned. I don't know. I just say that to be safe you should go with Abram or somebody else. It's harder to excuse the death or injury to two than to one."

"Well. That's being a little extreme, don't you think?"

"No, I don't. And you, of all people, should know that."

He was testy, and Astrid didn't want to rile him more.

"Okay," she said. "I'll not do anything risky."

She got to her feet.

"And thanks. Give my love to Beth."

She left, full of remorse that she had told him anything about Geraldine.

Why? I have no reason at all to be concerned about her. She is making her own bed, and she can sleep in it. There's nothing I can do to stop her, anyway.

But she knew she would try. Maybe she could talk some sense into the girl.

CHAPTER 26

By the time Abram arrived home from work, she had fallen asleep in front of the fire. She started at the touch on her arm.

"Sleepy are you?" he said.

"Ya. I guess so. What time is it?"

"Ten-fifteen. I guess all that chatting with Larry tired you right out."

Oh-oh. She hadn't stopped to say hi to Abram.

"You heard about that? I just didn't think to stop and see you. Anyway, it wasn't a big deal. I just asked what he knew about the militia these days."

"And what did you find out?"

"Nothing new. Whatever they're up to, if anything, hasn't been discovered. Larry said they check the camp every so often, but can't find anything to worry about."

"I see."

For some reason Abram appeared to be suspicious. His left eyebrow was raised and that always meant trouble.

"Now, let me get this straight. You were asking about the militia?"

"Ya."

What's he getting to?

"So you found it necessary to inquire about a prominent attorney."

"How…? Ya, I did inquire about Mrs. Levitch, not Mr. Levitch."

"And have you uncovered a deep, dark secret about her? Something that needs to be discussed with my boss?"

"Oh. I hope it didn't get you in trouble, Abram."

"Hell, no. Other than I felt like an idiot when Larry came in and asked me if I knew anything about Mr. Levitch that he should know. I stuttered like a grade schooler. I had to say that I didn't understand the question, but no, I didn't know anything at all about him. Then he said you had just paid him a visit. He said somehow you linked the wife of our most prominent lawyer in town with someone from the militia and then said your niece was marrying that same man. Now that really floored me, given that I knew nothing about any of it."

"I told you about Geraldine getting married and that we were invited."

"When was that?"

"Late one night, in bed."

"Oh? And were my eyes open?"

"Damned if I know," she said. "You had turned to your right side. I couldn't see your eyes."

"Well my guess is that you were talking to a dead tired man on the verge of sleep, and I don't remember hearing you. So we're going to her wedding? When?"

"Saturday. Unless…"

"Unless?"

"Oh, nothing. But being Geraldine, anything can happen before then."

"No, no. You said unless. You're up to something. What is it?"

Astrid clamped her lips together. Why did he always pry things out of her?

"I want to talk with Geraldine before she goes through with the wedding. The man she's marrying is one of those militia guys. And he works for Mrs. Levitch. There are some odd circumstances there, and it doesn't all sound above board to me. So I thought I should have Geraldine ask him about that before leaping into a lifetime of misery with him."

"And you know this guy better than she does?"

"No, but I know the outfit he's in, and that's no good. If she gets married to him, she could be in great danger."

"Thought you didn't like her."

"Oh, Abram. I don't. But she's family, after all. I'd like to see her straighten out her life, not throw it away at her young age."

"So you plan to invite her to talk with you here?"

You're a cagey one. You know I don't want her in my house.

"Not exactly."

"Well, exactly where will you talk with her then?"

"I don't know. I'll think of some place."

When he got up, came to her chair and fell to his knees in front of her, took her hands, and looked her straight in the eyes, Astrid stiffened in surprise.

"Look, honey," he said. "I don't care where you talk with her. But promise me you won't go out to The Kingdom by yourself to do it. I love you, and I don't want you to get into any more trouble."

This humble plea tore at her defenses.

"I don't intend to get into trouble, Abram. Why does everyone think I'm so incapable of showing good judgment?"

She hoped he wouldn't answer that.

"I don't think I need to point out the several times you've stepped--no, jumped--into trouble in the past, nor the most recent episode of being shot at for trespassing at a junk yard, of all places. So I'll just repeat it. Please don't go to the militia camp again by yourself."

Almost what Larry said.

"Larry said the same thing to me. You can rest assured I won't be reckless."

"And?"

"And nothing. You and Larry just don't want me to get into trouble, and I promise that I won't."

"Oh what's the use. Okay. Have it your way. If you do get into trouble, you can be sure I'll remind you of this."

Oh ya. I'm sure you will. But I'll get to the bottom of this thing and come out the winner of the argument. I can take care of myself without this aggravation from you and Larry.

. . . .

Tuesday

Astrid checked the newspaper for possible errors. When she could find nothing significant, no more than a typo buried in a story that didn't change meaning or clarity, she felt a sense of pride that she had been able to substitute for Will when he, too, became ill with bronchitis. Not just that, but she and Charlie had managed to get almost all of the newspaper out by deadline.

She folded the paper, and prepared to leave.

"I have an appointment late this afternoon, Charlie," she said. "Everything looks okay, I think. No glaring mistakes in headlines and only a couple of typos in the town news. Did you find anything?"

"No, same as you. Considering our limitation without Will, the sports pages look excellent. You do good work Astrid."

Charlie seldom handed out compliments,

"Thanks," she said. "Front page is great, too. So I guess we're not only the players, but also the cheering squad."

He leaned back, folded his hands behind him and rested his head on them.

"Well, it's done for this week. Tomorrow we'll go over what's on the docket for next week so far. No doubt something will come up for page one before Monday. I hope Will can come in."

"Ya. So do I. Did he say how long he thought he'd be out?"

"Well, he thinks it will be only this week. But we'll see. He was pretty weak last night when I visited."

Anxious to get out to The Kingdom, Astrid mentally reviewed her noontime conversation with Geraldine when she had lunch in the conference room to have privacy for the phone call.

When she answered, Geraldine sounded hoarse.

"Hi," Astrid said. "Are you okay, Geraldine?"

"I'm okay. Just a little cold. Are you coming to the wedding?"

"Everyone has a cold it seems. I'd like to see you before that. Can you come over here?"

"No. I'm in bed, actually. Sick all night. Come here."

"Ya. I'll do that. Can I bring you anything? Do you have cold medicine?"

"Just some cough drops would be fine."

Astrid heard a door close.

In a whisper, Geraldine said, "Please, Aunt Astrid, get me out of here."

"What? You're in trouble?"

"Yes."

She hung up the phone, and Astrid stood looking at the one in her hand.

What the hell is that all about? In trouble. What's happening?

She must act, and apparently no later than today. There was never a question in her mind that Geraldine would have big problems with that man, but she thought it would come after the wedding.

Now it was 3:15, and Astrid went to the coat closet, put on her boots, heavy jacket, and gloves.

"Okay. I'm leaving now, Charlie."

He didn't look up from the computer when he said, "Yuh. Have a good one."

Sure, with a sick niece, and apparently a sicker bunch of whackos calling themselves militia, I'm sure I'll have a good one.

Before driving away, Astrid sat in her Jeep and thought, *Should I let someone know where I'm going? Both Abram and Larry would object. Probably Abram would demand that I go home and forget Geraldine. Charlie's so occupied with that research he's been doing that he wouldn't know what I told him. Maybe I should tell Dee. It would take only a few more minutes to run upstairs and tell her. On the other hand, Geraldine sounded genuinely scared. No, I'd better just go on over and find out what it's all about. I can always get back in the Jeep and drive away.*

CHAPTER 27

All day Chris had thought about what was basically his cowardice. He knew he should give Drew a call and confess to his slip up in asking Astrid for help in uncovering any illegal activity of the attorneys. Not only did he tell her he and Drew were ex-convicts, but he told her that Holly was his own daughter. He felt guilty of betrayal, and that was the last thing he meant to do. Drew would likely tell him to get lost as a friend, but he'd have to confess to all that sometime, so it might as well be now.

He looked at his work log while the phone rang at Drew's desk and found that there was only one more job to be done here. Phil could take care of that. He had enough training for the job.

"Levitch and Bertram. Drew Godfrey speaking."

"Drew, I want to tell you about my meeting with Astrid Lincoln. Can you and I meet somewhere for supper? Or have you made plans?"

"No, I don't have plans. How about the Lakepont? I'd like a real meal for a change."

"Yeah. Me too. I'll be there about 5:30."

Chris was finally on the road at 3:40, heading for Fairchance, a half hour drive without hurrying. On a section of road that was straight for a quarter of a mile, he saw a Jeep heading his way. As it passed he recognized Astrid, but she apparently did not notice him. His first thought was, *I wonder if she's going to The Kingdom.* He didn't know why he would think of that, considering that it was a large county and *The Bugle* covered all the towns in it. Well, it wasn't his business, anyway, but seemed like a reporter wouldn't be welcome at that camp.

He arrived home in time to make a quick change of clothing and to tell Mrs. Oswald that he was back, and then to the Lakepoint Restaurant, where he found Drew waiting at a window table.

"Am I late?" he asked.

"No, I'm early. Just studying the menu. Looks like we have some good choices."

Chris reached for his menu as he sat down. The lake view looked like a snow-covered field. Two men sat by a hole in the ice, dangling fishing lines.

"They look cold. I'd have to want fish real bad to do that," he said.

"Not my thing, either, but I do like fish. Think I'll have the poached salmon."

Drew laid his menu at the edge of the table.

"Have you decided already?" he asked when Chris put his there, also.

"Yeah. Sirloin steak for me."

A young waitress took their orders, and said, "While you're waiting, can I interest you in an appetizer?"

Both men said no, and she left after saying the orders would take 20 minutes.

"In that case," Chris said. "Will you bring bread now, please?"

"Oh, yes. Bread and salads will be right up."

They both put their forearms on the table and leaned forward.

"They get younger every year," Drew said.

"Probably a college student."

Chris tried to think how he could explain his discussion with Astrid in a way that Drew would understand he hadn't meant to reveal so much.

"You talked with Astrid Lincoln, then."

"I'm afraid I did," Chris said. "Sorry about this. I kinda screwed up, I guess."

"How'd you do that?"

"Well, you see, she got so interested in what I was telling her, and then she wanted a name before she'd agree to do any background search. One thing led to another and the first thing I knew I couldn't stop telling her about myself and that Holly's my daughter. She said she'd keep it between us. I believed her."

"But you're worried that she won't?"

"Oh, I am and I'm not. I believe she has what-do-you-call-it? Integrity. Yeah. I think she has integrity and won't let it get back to Holly. I guess that's not the worst of my worry, though."

Drew questioned with a sideways look.

"I never intended to say it, Drew, and I wish I hadn't. But the truth is that I told her we're both ex-convicts."

He waited for Drew's reaction.

"I've been thinking lately," Drew said, "that there's no way it won't get out no matter how cautious we are. Do you think she'll publicize it in the paper?

"No. I asked her not to, and she promised she wouldn't."

"Then that's all you could do, under the circumstances. I know how it is. I didn't hold back about the time I served when Mr. Bertram interviewed me. He passed right over it. Maybe we are more worried about people knowing than we need to be. After all, we did pay for the crimes we committed. In your case, I know it was an injustice. But we've done the time, and the law says we can join society now. It's bound to be rough, if the general public hears about it, because some will call us names and some may even think we don't deserve to return to a normal life. So all we can do is sit back and wait."

"Yeah, you're right."

"Chris. I mean it. Don't worry. You agonize over everything. Stop it. Enjoy your dinner."

"Yes."

"You are such a poor liar. You'll just go over it and over it. I know. But don't do that. You know, I said you should tell your church secretary all about yourself. You may be surprised."

Chris laughed.

"Possibly. She'll say 'Thanks for telling me. Now be off. I'm busy. And, oh, don't bother to call again.'"

"There's no way I can get to you. Well, then, if it helps you, just go on and worry. Try to hide, and quiver when anyone goes by. But me? I'm going to enjoy things as long as I can. And if it all goes to hell, then I'll go find something else, someplace else. But one thing for damned sure, friend. I'm not going to sit around and mentally rehash every word that I've said and every move I've made. I'm going to let life go on, one way or the other."

But Chris doubted his own patience. He looked again at the fishermen, now packing up their gear.

They've had all the waiting they can take. I guess when you get nothing but coldness that's the way it is. You pack up and leave.

. . . .

The first thing Astrid noticed when she walked into The Kingdom from the parking lot was shabbiness. Winter snow, ice and winds, coupled with neglect, had taken their toll on the homes. On one brick duplex a white shutter had gaping holes and hanging slats. At another, a trash barrel lay on its side and rocked when wind gusts blew. The sidewalk was impassable with unplowed snow. She walked in the street to the number Geraldine had scribbled for her when she and Preston Norman were at her house. She rang the bell.

From the other side of the door, Geraldine's husky voice said, "Who is it?"

"It's me, Astrid."

The door opened. As soon as Astrid was in the room, Geraldine shut and locked it. One glance at her told the story. She bore bruises on her cheek and around the mouth.

"What's going on, Geraldine?"

"Thank God you came, Aunt Astrid."

Her use of the word *aunt* was something new since she left the farm. At first Astrid knew she said it in a mocking way. But now, she wasn't quite sure if it was from a genuine feeling of family, or if Geraldine used it to garner sympathy. From past experience with her, Astrid knew that she was capable of being cagey. However, it didn't really matter. She was a victim of violence.

"You've been beaten. Did your boyfriend do it?"

Geraldine nodded. Tears rolled down her cheeks.

"I didn't want you to know." She gulped for air. "But when you called, I knew you were the only one who could help me. I need to get away from here. I'm so afraid. He hurts me. I'm afraid he'll kill me."

"He won't kill you, and he won't hurt you any more. Come on, get dressed. Don't bother to pack anything. We need to go quickly. Is there a back way to get out of here and to the parking lot?"

"We'll have to go through a patch of woods, but I know how."

"Hurry, then."

Astrid went to the front window to watch that Norman didn't come in.

"Where's Preston?" she called.

Geraldine answered, "He went to Greenboro for some things."

"When did he go?"

"An hour ago."

We'll just have time to get out.

"Hurry up."

Geraldine came into the room carrying a small bag.

"Okay," Astrid said, avoiding criticism for packing and taking up time. "Let's go."

They were at the back door when Geraldine stopped and started back.

"Where are you going?"

"I forgot my wallet. I'll need that."

She's so slow.

"Hurry, Geraldine."

It seemed like minutes before she finally came back.

"I'm ready."

Astrid pushed her out the door.

"Go as fast as you can. He could be back any minute now, if he's been gone an hour. Takes what? Half an hour to get to Greenboro?"

"More like 15 or 20 minutes."

"All right. Move it and be quiet now. We don't want to alert anyone."

They ran past two duplexes and the huge auditorium before they reached woods.

"This way," Geraldine said.

She took Astrid's hand and steered her along.

"Why are you holding my hand, Geraldine?"

"I don't want us to get separated. Here's the little path. Watch for the trap."

At that same moment, Astrid heard the click and fell to her knees from the hard force of an animal trap clamping onto her leg just above the ankle.

"Owww. What the hell? A bear trap out here? Why didn't you tell me?"

"That's why I wanted to steer you away from it. Guess I didn't, though."

Astrid thought Geraldine sounded a little too flip. Surely she wouldn't do something like this deliberately.

"You planned this? You did this on purpose?"

"Why Aunt Astrid. What an evil mind you have."

"Well, then, come over here and pull this thing apart."

Trying not to move much, Astrid studied the trap.

"All you need do is step down on the side bars. It will spring open. I can't do it alone."

"I'm afraid I don't know how to do that. No, I can't. If you'll give me your keys, I'll drive to the nearest house and get help. I can't go back to the camp. Preston is apt to see me."

She has a point. Going back is a bad idea. On the other hand, so is staying here helpless and freezing to death. It must be nearly zero now.

"Okay. Here." She took the keys from her pocket and tossed them to Geraldine. "Get back as soon as you can, please. It's too cold to stay here like this very long."

"Sure. I'll get help."

Almost as soon as the blue coat disappeared through the fir trees ahead, Astrid regretted letting her take the Jeep. The cold was more dangerous to her than the trap, although if she had to wait too long like this, with circulation to her foot cut off, she'd be in danger of losing it. She recalled when they used this type of trap on the farm. It was more humane, they said, than the sharp-tooth trap that cut into the animal's leg. This one merely clamped hard on the leg and the animal couldn't get loose. Usually no flesh was cut. But a bear trap--she feared her leg might be broken.

If only she could turn and drag the trap toward her, maybe she could pull the bars apart. But she couldn't do that without doing damage to her leg, and the chain holding the trap was short anyway. These traps held the leg in an iron grip. Any movement an animal made, the more its flesh was torn.

How did they have this trap hidden? I never saw it. Damn. Another good pair of pants ruined. How will I survive? It's getting dark. I must get out of it. Somehow there's a way. But how? If I move too much it will tear my skin.

She had fallen on her hands and knees, with the trapped left leg out straight behind her. The cold had penetrated her fleece lined gloves. The right knee, too, was cold. Wool pants protected, but not much in this position. She could probably lie down without too much damage.

In the old days when they used these traps on the farm, she recalled that if the traps weren't checked often, a fox or other animal might gnaw off its own leg to get free. Poor things. She could well understand it.

I don't think I'll do that, though. Might as well have a surgeon do it, if necessary. If help doesn't come, I'll have to get into a different position, no matter how much damage it does.

She heard a car stop in the parking lot and a door slam.

I could call out. But if I do, it might be Preston Norman. I don't want him to come. He might shoot me out of compassion, like shooting an animal that he catches.

Footsteps crunched on the snow, coming toward her. She prayed it wasn't Preston. From what Geraldine said, he was a dangerous man.

Where the blue coat had disappeared, a camouflage army jacket now came into sight.

Oh, no.

Coming toward her was Preston Norman, looking as angry as she remembered him at her house.

CHAPTER 28

Drew drove into the garage after supper. Although he felt as uneasy as his friend did that a reporter now knew about the two of them, it would do no good to dwell on it. What would be would be, and worrying beforehand wouldn't change it.

He entered the back door and started to walk toward his room, when he stopped to listen. He heard crying. It couldn't be Mr. Bertram. No, it sounded like a woman's cry. Should he investigate? He'd better not. It was probably that woman that his boss had here before. Whatever it was, it was no business of his.

He got to his door when a high-pitched wail pierced the air. Now he was concerned. No matter what Mr. Bertram would say, he needed to find out if the woman was in trouble. To cry out like that she must be. He ran down the hallway, making as much noise as he could on the wood floor, got to the kitchen door and knocked.

"Mr. Bertram? Is everything all right? I heard crying. Are you okay?"

What a stupid thing to say. Bertram wouldn't appreciate being accused of crying like a woman.

"I'm okay, Drew. No need for concern. Go back to your room. Everything's okay here."

Drew listened at the door for a few seconds. When he heard the two voices talking low, he left. He closed his own door behind him, but stood with his ear to it, trying to hear words. No sound penetrated his door.

Might as well settle down and read for a while. But if he heard another cry, he'd go down there and open the door to see what was going on. It wasn't sex, he was sure of that. This woman's cries were of sadness, not pleasure.

I should have gone in when I was there. Why didn't I? Because I could be out of a job if I saw something I shouldn't, that's why. Well, I won't hesitate next time.

．．．．

Astrid hadn't moved. Now she waited while Preston walked toward her.

"Well, well, what have we here?" he said.

Shaking from cold, Astrid said, "As you can see, I'm trapped. Get me out of this torture trap."

"What? I didn't hear the rest of that. What did you say?"

"I said get me out of this." He was going to wait until she said it, though it was the last thing she wanted to say to him. "Please."

"That's better."

He set his shopping bag down. At first she was afraid he'd do something disgusting like maybe pee on her. He had that smug, self-satisfied look that said he'd like to do that or to kick her. Instead, he walked away.

"Where are you going?" she said.

"I need a stick."

A blow on the head should do it. Just as good as a shot.

"Here's one."

He came back with part of a broken branch in hand.

"Okay now. When I say go, you pull your leg out. Can you do that?"

"I think so. Be careful. You could get hurt, too."

"Don't worry. I know."

With a gloved hand on the top bar and his foot on the other one, he pulled. His face turned red, but the trap didn't open.

"Sorry. This will hurt. You okay?" he said.

"Ya. Do what you have to do."

He moved his hand to a new position, pulled the top half again, and stuck the branch between the bars to hold them open. He went around to Astrid and put his arms under her armpits.

"Now. Pull together."

She clamped her teeth hard together to keep from yelling out as she pushed with her right foot and he pulled. The release hurt almost as much as when the trap clamped together on her leg above the ankle.

"I...oh...I feel woozy," she said when she tried to stand up. "Is that blood I see?"

"I'm afraid so."

He knelt down and pulled up her wool pant leg.

"Yup, that's just what happened. It's bleeding. It may be broken. These old bear traps haven't been used for years. I didn't know we had any left. It will hurt while the circulation returns. I'll help you up to the auditorium."

"I just injured my right leg the other day. At least it will be a matched pair now."

She attempted a laugh.

"That's rough. Well, I'll go get our nurse. She's home this time of day. She can take care of it."

"You have a nurse here?"

"Uh-huh. A good one, too. Sometimes a doctor comes on weekends."

She tried not to shake but couldn't control it.

"Try to hold together," Preston said. "You'll get out of this okay."

He pulled her arm over his shoulders.

"Okay. Can you walk at all?"

Astrid put her weight on the foot. Though it hurt, she didn't think it was broken.

"Ya. I can do it."

"Lean your weight on me. We'll walk in sync."

She did as he said, though the movement sent pain to the top of her head. She fought the dizziness.

"Step on your left foot when I step with my right one. Like a three-legged race."

"Okay."

She held her breath when they took the first step together. She let it out with what sounded like a growl.

"I know it hurts. But you need to get attention as soon as possible, and it's too cold to leave you out here until I can bring someone to help me with a stretcher."

"I know. It's okay. I can do it."

"Just don't bite your tongue."

"No." she said. "You left your bag."

"I'll come back and get it. We don't have far to go. Just to the auditorium."

They stepped together again. The pathway went between more fir trees, and Astrid wanted to say something other than how much she was hurting.

"It's pretty, the snow on the green branches."

"I've always enjoyed the woods in winter," he said. "I sometimes go snowshoeing. You ever do that, Astrid?"

"Ya. I was brought up on a farm, and I learned to walk on snowshoes at a young age."

Her words were coming easier now, even though she was sure she'd lose her foot, the pain was so strong. At least she had her nerves under control. Preston was a mystery to her. He seemed downright friendly and concerned. Maybe she'd been wrong to judge him harshly.

"How come you found me, Preston?" she asked.

"I saw the tracks in the new snow. This path doesn't get used in the winter, so I backtracked. Who was with you? Geraldine?"

"Ya. I talked with her on the phone this noon."

"I know. Did she say I hurt her?"

"Well…"

"Sure she did. But if she said I did it, she was lying. She was with someone else at a bar in Greenboro last night. He beat her up pretty good. I don't know why. But when I saw her condition this morning, we got into an argument, and I left."

"But you were there when I called her?"

"Yes. I had gone back to tell her she'd better pack her things and leave. There would be no wedding."

"That's not what she told me."

"I can imagine. For your information, she told me you were a monster, and I believed her just like you believed her about me. She's good at making up tales."

"Ya. I knew that, but still I did a stupid thing. I let her take my Jeep to go get help."

"Consider the Jeep on its way out of state."

"Oh God. I hope not. I'll call the sheriff as soon as I can get to a phone."

"There's a phone at the auditorium. You can use that."

"Thanks, Preston. I appreciate all this."

"Sure."

"Sheriff Knight can also tell my husband that I'll be home when I can get there."

Preston said nothing for a few more steps, then, "Your husband a friend of the sheriff, is he?"

"Oh, not just that. He's a dispatcher in the sheriff's office building."

"I see."

Astrid felt breathless.

"Can we stop for just a minute? I'm out of breath."

"Sure. Take as long as you need. Lean against me. You don't weigh much considering your height."

"No. I work out."

She did as he said, leaned against his chest and put her head on his shoulder. When she regained strength, she said they could go on, and they soon reached the auditorium.

Preston said. "I'll take you to Fairchance, Astrid. I have to see someone there, anyway."

They went to the back door, and Preston took out a key to open it. Inside, Astrid recognized the huge auditorium where she was taken by General Metcalf when she came out to interview him. Preston guided her to one of the side rooms where she could lie down on a bed.

After he called the nurse, he said, "She'll be right over. In the meantime, do you know the sheriff's number?"

"Ya."

He took the phone to her, and she sat up to dial. She sighed in relief when she was patched through to Larry.

"It's Astrid, Larry. I've had a slight mishap…"

He interrupted, "Huh! What else is new?"

She pouted at his insolence.

"Well, you see, my Jeep has been stolen."

"How did that happen? Never mind. You can tell me later. I should get out an APB at once. License number?"

After she gave him details of the Jeep and the driver, she said, "When you speak with Abram, will you just say that I'll be home before he is? I'll tell him the details later, too. And tell him I'm okay, not to worry."

She handed the phone back to Preston, and lay back on the pillows. She struggled with a feeling of guilt, now that she had a better perspective of this whole situation between Geraldine and Preston. He didn't deserve her contempt.

"Preston, I'm sorry that I misjudged you. It wasn't just because Geraldine pictured you as a woman beater, but I have to tell you that I heard you are a handyman for Mrs. Levitch. That gave me cause to wonder about what, if anything, you were up to. I'm afraid I thought the worst."

He was standing with his back to her, silent, still holding the telephone. When he turned around, his scowl was a question mark.

"I answered her ad and she hired me. That's all."

"A neighbor said you spend a lot of time with her when Mr. Levitch is out of town."

"Yeah, that's true."

He went to a chest of drawers and brought out a blanket which he pulled over her.

"And you want to know why."

"Ya. She implied the worst, of course. I'd like to understand what you and she have in common."

"So you think we have something in common. Well, we do. We're related."

Related. Astrid's surprise must have shown, because Preston bellowed.

"You're surprised. Probably want to know how a woman who is married to a Jewish man could be related to a rebellious son-of-a-bitch who plays war games with a home-grown militia."

He laughed again, and Astrid wondered what he thought was so amusing. He had stated it quite accurately. That's just what she thought.

From the front door came a woman's voice.

"Where are you Preston?"

He got up, went to the door and stepped into the main auditorium.

"In here. She got a pretty bad puncture in that bear trap. I don't know who the hell set it, but I'm going back and take it out."

He turned to Astrid.

"I'll be back by the time Mrs. Hall finishes. Then we'll go to Fairchance."

"Okay. And thanks again."

True to his word, Mrs. Hall had just put the tape around the sterile pad on her leg when he returned.

"I brought the car up to the front door," he said. To Mrs. Hall, "The trap is in the storage room and I locked it."

"That's a good place for it," she said. "Whoever put it out there doesn't belong here. One of the children could have been caught in it. Well, I don't think Astrid is injured too badly. I gave her a tetanus shot and cleaned the wound well. Unless it should show signs of infection, I don't think she'll need to see a doctor."

To Astrid, she said, "Now, that's my opinion, dear. If you want to see your doctor just to be sure, then please do so."

"Thanks, Mrs. Hall. I'm glad you were here."

Standing, Astrid quickly plunked back down on the bed.

"Whew. Guess I got up too quickly."

"Get your breath," Preston said. "I'll help you up and out to the car."

Once she was ready, she got up slowly, leaning against Preston once again, and they walked out to the car.

"Why doesn't everyone park here on the plaza? It's spacious enough," she said.

"We want it free of vehicles for just such emergencies as this one," Preston said. "And we hold dress parades out here just like any army, and other events, too."

"Of course."

They were soon on the Fairchance Road, and Astrid felt better just to be on her way home. The Cadillac didn't hurt, either.

"This is some automobile," she said, without stating the obvious that it cost way more than she would have thought a handyman could afford.

They rode in silence for a few more miles before Astrid decided to bring up the discussion that they were having at the auditorium.

"You said Mrs. Levitch is a relative, Preston. A close relative?"

"You could say that."

"So you don't care to tell me how close?"

"No."

What a revolting development this is. I wonder why he wants to keep it secret. I guess I'll just have to go on wondering.

Neither one said more until they came to the outskirts of Fairchance.

"You know how to get to my house?" Astrid asked.

"I remember. You want me to leave you there?"

"Ya. Please."

He looked over at her and grinned.

"That's more like it."

She felt that she now had a friend in Preston Norman. But experience told her not to jump to conclusions about another person's character. Just the same, she would rather call him friend than fear him as the enemy that she thought he was on first meeting him. That Geraldine. How she made everyone and everything look bad.

"I just hope they find Geraldine and my Jeep."

Preston drove into her driveway.

"Can you make it by yourself?" he asked when she opened the door to go.

"I think so. And again, thank you. I could have died out there if you hadn't come along. Do you think Geraldine could have set that trap?"

He stared straight ahead through the windshield before answering.

"I don't want to think that, but it wouldn't surprise me. When I met her, she seemed like an angel. She's pretty and quite bright. But slowly, this other side of her began to come out. My brother was like that. A nice, gentle person, it would appear, and then one day he'd attack me and beat me up, for no reason at all, until I had enough of it and gave it back to him. He didn't attack me again, but he did other things until..."

Astrid gave him a quick look and saw that he was struggling to go on.

"Until?"

"Ah, it was just plain perversity. When I recognized Geraldine's symptoms, I knew enough not to marry her, especially after last night's fiasco. I couldn't live with a woman like that."

"You did the right thing," Astrid said. "I don't know what will become of her. Maybe she'll go back to California, to her father."

Astrid had her hand on the door handle, when she said, "Thank you, Preston. You saved my life. I'll never forget that."

"I could say it's what I'd do for any animal that I found in one of those traps, but that would be insulting. I do have compassion for others, regardless of the prevailing sentiment of murder and mayhem circulating around that camp."

"So you don't agree with overthrowing the government?"

"Not now. I did when General Metcalf was our leader and talking about long-range plans, but since seeing how he ended up in his rush to make a name for himself, I've changed my views. If changes are going to be made, they'll have to be made by infiltration, not by bombs and guns."

Astrid thought about that, recalling that Preston was one of the general's aides.

"That's good to hear."

She felt sleepy, though her leg still throbbed.

"Good luck to you," she said.

"I hope you get your Jeep back in one piece."

"Thanks a heap."

CHAPTER 29

Astrid had just enough energy to make a peanut butter sandwich and carry it to the den, but not enough to start a fire. She turned up the thermostat instead. Without a fire, the room reflected her own dismal mood. She ate half the sandwich, covered herself with an afghan, and lay back on the sofa. In what seemed like minutes, she heard the back door slam.

Here it comes. Another confession time. Oh well.

She looked at the mantel clock. Five past ten. How could that be? It was 8:15 when she came in here.

Abram strode into the room and stood, feet apart, slightly bent toward her.

"So someone stole the Jeep?"

He wasted no time getting to it, and she sensed his mood immediately.

"Hi, sweetheart. Have a good day?" she said.

"Don't sweetheart me. You've been at it again, haven't you."

"I can't imagine what you mean. My Jeep was stolen, ya. But I haven't been at it, as you say."

"Okay then. Tell me how come Larry got a call from you that the Jeep was stolen and he came to me to put out an alert for it?

This was at quarter to seven. Don't tell me you were still at the office, because I tried to reach you there, and there was no answer."

"Okay, I won't tell you that."

He still stood at the end of the sofa, his eyes bright with heightened emotion, his jaw tight. He pointed a finger at her, like a parent with a naughty child.

"Don't play cute with me, Astrid. While I listened to the phone ringing and no one answering, can you even imagine the thoughts that went through my head? 'Has she had an accident?' 'Was she mugged and injured before the Jeep was stolen?' 'Was she calling from the hospital?' So you know what? I called the hospital, and they said you were not admitted. Now, after the agony you put me through, I want to know what happened? Where were you?"

She'd never seen Abram this upset, and she didn't like it. After all, she had a right to be where she wanted to be.

"Where was I? At The Kingdom, trying to rescue my niece. She begged me to get her out of there, and I wasn't about to leave her for more beatings."

Abram bent his head, apparently re-thinking his outrage.

"Then how did your Jeep get stolen by Geraldine? Or did you just give her the keys and tell her to save herself?"

He got that right, damn it.

"I did give her the keys, but at the time it wasn't to save herself but to save me. I told her to get help."

Now Abram dropped to the edge of a chair by the fireplace where he could still see Astrid. A look of confusion crossed his face, and he shook his head.

"You told her to get help for you. I'm afraid to ask. Why did you need help?"

At least, his voice had come down a decibel.

"Because I was caught in a leg trap and couldn't get out of it without help."

"Caught in a leg trap. I heard it, but I don't believe it. Only you. How did you get into that predicament?"

"We were going through the woods to the parking lot so we wouldn't be seen, when I stepped into the trap. Geraldine said she couldn't open the trap to get me out, so I gave her the keys to the Jeep and she said she would get help. But she didn't. Luckily Preston Norman came up the path and found me. He got the trap open and I pulled my foot out. They have a nurse there and she came and patched me up. Then Preston drove me home. And that's all there is to it."

"I see."

He got up and started toward the kitchen.

"I'm hungry."

"Well, you don't have to take that attitude, Abram."

"What attitude would you like me to take? Should I kiss you? Slap you around? What? I knew you'd get into trouble, but you did it sooner than I expected. So now, I guess you're right. That's all there is to it. I can't tell you not to jump in with two feet because you'll go off and do just that. Or you'll jump into a trap with one foot. I'm hungry and I'm going to get myself something to eat."

Astrid threw off the afghan, and stood up to follow him.

"O-o-o," she moaned.

"What?" Abram called from the kitchen.

"Nothing. I'll be right out. I'm hungry, too."

Her stomach was doing flip-flops. She stepped on the injured leg, careful not to bear her full weight on it.

Well. That worked okay. I guess I can do this.

After a few wobbly steps, she limped to the kitchen and sat in a chair.

"What are you fixing?" she asked.

"Scrambled eggs and ham."

"Would you make enough for two?"

"Looks like I'll have to. The way you're walking, I'd say you're hardly able to do much for yourself. Maybe that's a blessing. Maybe you'll stay put and not go running around to a dangerous camp where you could get shot or caught in a trap. Maybe you won't rummage around in a scrap yard and dodge bullets. Just maybe, if I'm lucky, I won't get partial information that leaves me worried that I may have lost my wife. Do you get that? I don't want to lose my wife, Astrid."

He stood still and looked at her with pleading eyes.

"Can you possibly understand that?"

His modulation from roaring anger to a murmured plea nearly broke her heart. Her leg felt like a heavy boat anchor, more painful by the minute. Before she realized it, her belly muscles twitched. Salty tears slipped into the corners of her mouth. Trying to be quiet, she put a hand over her eyes, hoping Abram wouldn't notice. But he did.

"Oh, honey," he said.

Setting the frying pan aside, he came to her, dropped to a knee, placed his hand behind her head, and held it to his shoulder.

"Let it go. I know you've had a terrible experience. I'm sorry I came down on you so hard, my love."

He could be so aggravatingly nice, Astrid thought as the tears flowed over his neck and shoulder.

When she finally pulled away and wiped her face on her napkin, she said, "I'm sorry, too. Especially about losing the Jeep."

Abram cleared his throat.

"Sure. I understand. Well, I guess I forgot to tell you something."

He left her side and went to the stove where he put the pan back on the burner.

"What? What did you forget to tell me, Abram?"

"I forgot to tell you that they picked up Geraldine at a diner on Route One."

"Why you…" Then she thought, *why didn't he say that they have the Jeep?*

"And the Jeep? Did they get that, too?" she said.

"Oh yes. It's back at the station now. Larry wants me to take you over in the morning to get it. He wants to know if you intend to file charges."

"I guess…" She had to think about that. She didn't want to have a story in the newspaper about it, and since she willingly gave the keys to Geraldine, she didn't really have grounds to charge her.

"No. I won't file charges. I don't want to wait until morning to get it. Will you drive me over there so I can get it tonight and have it in the morning?"

"I don't think you should be walking around on that foot."

"I have to, Abram. I have to help at the office. Will is out sick and there are only the two of us. We have work to do. I don't need to be there a full day, but Charlie and I need to work out the news menu for the coming week."

He looked as if he would put up more of an argument. Instead, he cracked the eggs into the pan and said, "If you must. I insist you eat before we go, though."

"Ya. I will. Thanks."

• • • •

Wednesday morning Astrid lay awake, as she had most of the night, thinking about the pain in her leg. When she drove the Jeep home, the only good thing about the pain was that it was not in the right leg. Now she had to get out of bed and off to work, no matter how much it hurt. She quietly moved to her feet. And not so quietly, fell back onto the bed.

Abram sat straight up.

"What? What happened?"

She moved to a sitting position so that she could pull her leg up and remove the bandage. Swelling and redness alarmed her.

Abram saw it also.

"Oh no. You're not going to work this morning. I don't care about the damned paper. You're going to the hospital. Don't bother to dress. Here, put your robe on. It's all you need. I'll get your coat when we get downstairs. Let me help you put those fuzzy slippers on to keep your feet warm."

The sight convinced her that Abram was right. She needed help.

"Why has it become so inflamed?" she said. "I thought the nurse did a good job of fixing it."

"Obviously she didn't."

He sounded like he could strangle the woman with his bare hands.

"I guess not."

While he talked, he was dressing as if he were going to a fire.

"There. I'm ready. Be careful. I'll help."

Slowly, they reached the bottom of the stairs, and Abram helped her to the hall chair.

"I'll call ahead and alert the doctor that you're coming in."

"You think they'll get me in a bed so soon?"

"They will, you can be sure of it."

• • • •

He was right. Attendants wheeled her to X-ray first, and then to a room to await the doctor's arrival. When he came in, his news was not good.

"Well, young lady, you've been walking around on a broken leg."

"You're kidding!"

"Am I laughing? No, I'm not kidding. The good news is that you won't need surgery. We'll keep you here today. I'm quite sure there's no nerve damage. For now, a nurse will apply cold to the area and give you something to bring down the swelling and ease the pain. Basically, for a while, you'll need to rest, and stay off it."

"So how long should she stay off it?" Abram asked.

"It's not a long-term complication. The direct sideways blow, like she got in the trap, fractured the fibula. It's the bone that runs parallel to the tibia, the larger leg bone. And it's much less a problem than as if the tibia were fractured."

He turned his attention to Astrid.

"Stay off the leg and do what the nurse shows you today--apply ice and take Motrin or another kind of NSAID. Do that, with plenty of rest, for a couple of weeks. Then come see me. We'll give you complete instructions and the appointment time before you leave. And we'll provide crutches. If you have to walk anywhere at all, even to the bathroom, use them for a few days. I'll apply a walking cast once the swelling goes down."

"Thanks, doc," Abram said. "I'll try to keep her tied down."

"I understand, Abram."

When the two of them were alone, Astrid said, "Keep me tied down?"

"Am I going to have to get some heavy rope and tape?" he said. "Not today."

Finally Astrid was settled in a bed, where she would remain for the rest of the day. The woman in the next bed appeared to be asleep until a nurse came in and pulled the curtain around her bed. Then two doctors arrived. Astrid heard a conversation that sounded like a psychiatrist might be talking with her. Everyone was a stranger to Astrid until a neatly dressed man went by her bed, and she saw that it was the attorney, Mr. Levitch. She remembered him from the party. He didn't look her way, so she said nothing.

What's he doing here? Is that his wife in the other bed?

Levitch spoke so softly that Astrid couldn't make out a word. The woman said nothing. He came by again, this time with shoulders sagging. He looked tired.

Astrid glanced at the wall clock.

Oh damn. I should be helping Charlie right now and here I am, helpless.

When a nurse walked by to go to the next bed Astrid recognized her as one of the nurses who tended Abram when he was here.

"Lynn. How are you?"

"Oh, Mrs. Lincoln. I read that you and Abram were married. Congratulations. What are you doing here?"

She picked up the chart at the end of the bed.

"A hairline fibula fracture."

"Ya. I'll only be here today."

"It should heal fairly quickly. And how's Abram doing these days?"

"Just fine. Better than me, I'm afraid. Would you mind pulling my table closer so I can call my office?"

"Not at all. Are you comfortable? Do you need anything?"

Lynn was closer now and Astrid whispered, "What's the woman next to me here for?"

In equally hushed voice, the nurse said, "Please don't print or repeat this. She tried to commit suicide. Cut her wrists, but I never told you that."

"Is it Mrs. Levitch?"

She nodded, made a zipping motion across her lips, and went behind the curtain to tend her patient.

Why did she do that, I wonder. Suicide. And slashing her wrists? Must be an easier way to do away with yourself.

She dialed the office, and was surprised to hear Dee's voice.

"You're helping Charlie, Dee?" Astrid said.

"Yes, just this morning. We're coming along fine. How are you doing, Astrid?"

"Oh, it's a long story. Nothing too serious, just a leg wound. I should be back to work in no time."

"That doesn't sound good. Is there a news story in it?

"No, I'm afraid not."

"Well, don't come back until you're really ready. We can handle this here."

"Do you have any word from Will?"

"He and his family are home, and he says they are all getting better each day. He expects to be back by the end of the week. Well, someone has just come in, so I'd better go, Astrid. You take it easy and get well."

"I will."

After hanging up, she lay back on the pillows. This whole episode with Geraldine seemed almost unreal to her. To think that her niece could be so cruel and heartless as to injure anyone in that manner was more than she ever believed of the girl, and she had some really bad thoughts about her previously. Where did that streak come from? Others in the family didn't have it. Of course, she didn't know her older brother at all. She closed her eyes, expecting she might be able to sleep a bit.

"Oh don't tell me," the voice said, and she opened her eyes.

"Preston. How did you hear…oh, I guess you're not here to see me."

"No. I came to see how my…to see how Mrs. Levitch is doing."

"I'm sorry to hear about her. Was she here when you left me?"

"No. As a matter of fact, I found her."

"I heard what happened." Astrid made a slashing motion over her wrist. "That must have been terrible. Will she be all right?"

"The doctor said she will, but I'm not sure."

Astrid realized she had been whispering again.

"I'll stop to talk a bit before I leave, Astrid. Gotta see her now."

"Ya, of course."

He went behind the curtain and spoke softly to the woman, but there was no response. Then he yelled, "Come on, Mum. Look up. It's Press."

Maybe Mrs. Levitch wasn't awake, but Astrid was wide awake. *Mum. She's his mother. Well, well. How strange. Why all the secrecy?*

She jumped when her phone rang.

"Astrid. It's Holly. How are you?"

"Holly? Are you all right?"

"I'm okay. Your editor said you were in the hospital and I got concerned. So what happened?"

"Oh, I had a little accident. Nothing too serious. Just a small fracture in my leg. I'll be okay. I've meant to call you, but we've been busy at the newspaper."

"I understand. They still won't let me go home. I'm so anxious to get back."

"You still want to live there?"

"I don't have any other place to go, and I'm tired of sponging off friends. I think they're getting tired of me, too. You know what they say about guests and fish."

"Ya, I know."

They laughed together.

"Did you get your new computer figured out yet?" Astrid asked.

"Not quite, but I'm learning. Oh I want to tell you that the funeral service will be held on Friday. Sergeant Lenfest thinks I can go back home after that. I sure hope so."

"I do, too. I'll speak to Sheriff Knight, if you'd like, and get confirmation of that."

"Thank you, yes. Will you be able to come to the funeral?"

"I will. Friday when?"

"At ten."

Friday. Oh dear. I said I'd play donkey basketball Friday night. I guess that's off.

Astrid thought they were finished.

"All right, Holly" she said. "It's nice of you to call me."

"Astrid, wait. There's something I want to talk with you about."

"What?"

"I think I'm getting paranoid. I keep seeing a man just wandering around out back of the Sillers' house, in the evening. I've caught him looking at my window a couple of times. It worries me and I don't know whether to call the police."

"Did you speak to the Sillers about it?"

"No. I really don't want to get him in trouble. You see, it's Chris Benning. He seems like such a nice man. I can't understand it. It's always after dark, so it could be someone else, I suppose."

Chris is watching out for you.

"Tell you what, Holly. Get him to come to your office for whatever you need help with on the computer, and while he's there just ask if he is the man you've seen near the Sillers' house. If he says yes, then ask him why. He'll most likely have a good reason, if he is the man."

"I know I should do that, but it scares me a bit."

"Don't be scared. I'm sure he's harmless. He and I have talked a bit, and he really is a good man. So be bold and, in a nice way, ask him if he is the man, and will he please explain himself."

"Do you know something you're not telling me, Astrid?"

Oh boy, now what do I say?

"I do. But I have a good reason not to say more. Okay?"

"Okay. And I will get to the bottom of this."

"Good. The nurse has just come in, so I have to go. Call me with what you find out."

"I will. Get well."

And I hope Chris will tell you everything.

It wasn't the nurse, but Astrid couldn't very well tell her it was Preston Norman, and that he was about to leave.

"Wait Preston," she said.

CHAPTER 30

He returned, but instead of looking at her, kept his eyes riveted on the curtain partition between Astrid and his mother.

"Thanks for stopping," Astrid said. "Can you stop a minute? I've seen people coming and going by me, but no one stops to talk with me."

"Sure, glad to."

Though she hadn't judged him to be overly emotional or expressive, she thought he appeared exhausted today. Either that or he'd been crying, and that seemed even more remote than any other emotion in him.

He pushed the chair back near the foot of the bed, so he could face her.

"Your leg was hurt worse than we thought?" he asked.

"Seems I have a hairline fracture. The doctor wasn't too concerned but said I should wait the day out here, for whatever reason."

He rubbed his right-hand fingers together.

"A full day in the hospital, a full day's charge."

"Ha. You're right there. Did you hear that they caught up with Geraldine? Not long after the alert went out, I understand. And my Jeep is all in one piece, thankfully. I got it back last night."

"That's a break. What will happen with her?"

"They asked me if I wanted to file charges, but I said no. After all, Preston, I handed the keys over to her. I wouldn't have much to charge her with."

"No."

A cough and whimper sounded behind the curtain. Preston started to rise, but sat back.

"Do you want me to ring for the nurse?" Astrid said.

"No. They have her pretty well sedated. She'll go back to sleep."

He kept his eyes on the curtain, obviously listening for any more sounds.

"So you came to see your mother, did you Preston?"

"Oh, you heard that, did you? Okay. Now you know. Any chance you'll keep it to yourself?"

"If you want me to, I will. You mean to say that it's a secret?"

He looked down at his hands where they rested on his knees. What was going through his mind? Did he want to tell her more? After a few deep breaths, he relaxed and pushed back on the chair.

"It is and it isn't a secret. Of course, her husband knows, but the community doesn't. That's the way they both wanted it, and I stay away except when she needs me. I did go there last night because she hasn't been herself lately. When I got there, Abe had left, and I found her in a pool of blood in the bathroom. Why she did that, I don't know. Not for sure, anyway."

Astrid guessed that he knew very well, and if she were to bet on it she'd say the woman was unhappy with Abe Levitch. No woman that she knew could be happy when her husband was out of town so much. At least, the neighbor said he was and that was when Preston came to do work for her. Strangely, though, even that inquisitive neighbor didn't know about the mother and son relationship. She would have revealed it if she had known, judging from all the rest of the gossip she was willing to share.

"She hasn't told you why?"

"No."

"You mentioned that you have a brother."

"I did have a brother. My twin. He's dead now."

"And he didn't live here?" Astrid said.

"No."

Brief answers, so he just didn't want to divulge too much of his family history. The reporter in her wanted desperately to ask more questions and try to get at the real reason for his mother's death wish. Astrid had met Mr. Levitch, and could almost figure it out. On the other hand, judging people of late had proved to be off mark, so best not to go there without real knowledge.

"Astrid, you know Geraldine led me down the wrong path in describing you, and I was less than courteous to you at your home the day we were there. I apologize for that. You're very different than I believed you were."

"Oh," she waved it aside, "please don't worry about that. I did my share of judging because of Geraldine, too. You and I cleared the air on that yesterday. I'm quite impressed with you, Preston. I don't want to offend you, but I do hope you will leave that militia group and go into work that will be more worthwhile to you and to society."

"You're something else. Outspoken and direct. My father left me well off and I think I needed to feel that I was useful and could best serve society by joining the militia. I was wrong, of course. Now, I think I'll finish my studies in medicine. Yeah, I was studying to be a surgeon. Rather lofty, but I still think I'll go for it. So I'll be leaving this area very soon."

He assumed a devilish expression.

"If you weren't married, Astrid, I'd ask you to join me. And coming from me, that's a compliment. Your husband is a lucky man. I hope someday I can find a woman like you, but I doubt that any have been cloned."

Floored by this admission, Astrid laughed. The very thought of being with any man other than Abram never crossed her mind. How strange for Preston to express himself like that.

"I see that I've embarrassed you," he said. "Sorry. I just had to say it."

"Ya, I am embarrassed, but I couldn't have heard such flattery from a better person than you, I'm sure. Geraldine should have cleaned up her act and stayed with you. I wish you great success."

"Hmm. Now I'm just as happy that she didn't."

He rose, held out his hand, and they shook.

"I hope you'll soon be on your feet," he said.

• • • •

Lunchtime couldn't come too soon for Astrid. Whatever they sent up to her would do fine. If it would only arrive. She watched the clock and had just about decided that they wouldn't feed her, when she heard the cart outside the door.

"Oh good," she said when the aide brought a tray and set it on her movable table. "I'm starved."

"We wouldn't want that to happen," he said. "The cook made lasagna today, and it is very good. I can vouch for that."

"One of my favorite dishes," Astrid said.

"Is the lady in the other bed having lunch?" he asked.

"I don't know. You can ask her."

He went behind the curtain, and came back shaking his head.

"No can do there," he said.

"How about me?" It was Abram, all ready for his afternoon classes. "If no one wants a serving, I'll take it."

He pulled the chair to her bedside, and the aide set down another tray on Astrid's table.

"He said it was good, and it is," Astrid said, after sampling. "Thanks for having lunch with me."

Abram kissed her before sitting down and starting to eat.

"How are you feeling?" he asked.

"A little dopey. I didn't sleep much last night, and this is no place to try to take a nap. I can't believe all the traffic. Nurses, doctors, and visitors going past my bed all morning. It's like Grand Central Station."

"Maybe it will be quieter this afternoon."

"Do you know when they will discharge me?"

"No. Sorry. I expect the nurse can tell you when she comes in. I'll return after classes, before work. Maybe you'll be ready to go home then."

"I'm ready to go home now."

She checked the clock to see how much time they had for discussion. He could be here another 15 minutes.

"Abram, has any progress been made on the murders? Holly called and is anxious to go home. I didn't think she'd want to go back into that house, but she plans to."

"No one is saying much, but I think the sheriff has new information. He was standing outside my open door yesterday afternoon, and I heard him tell a couple of deputies to go out to The Kingdom again and fingerprint everyone. Maybe they found a full print on that car somewhere, but I don't know that."

"Let's hope they can wind this up," Astrid said. "It will be good to have peace and quiet again in Fairchance."

"That would be unique. Well, I have to go now," Abram said.

"You're finished?"

"Uh-huh. I need to ask Professor Vinton a question before class. His explanations tend to run on. Hate to leave so early, honey. You're right. The lasagna was very good. I'll see you later. In the meantime, take it easy. Relax."

"Not much else I can do," she said.

She watched him go down the hallway, as far as she could see. She no sooner heard the elevator doors open and shut, than she had a cold feeling of being alone and somehow vulnerable.

I wish he'd brought me a book to read.

Though she wanted to have a quiet mind and relax like Abram advised, her brain kept going over everything that had happened since the day Holly got the news that her father and mother had been murdered. Early on, Astrid dismissed Danny as the possible murderer, even though he was bad news, according to the animal shelter owner. After their confrontation at the real estate office, and then when gunshots were fired at her as she tried to leave the junk yard, she pretty much placed him at the top of her private list of suspects. He'd bullied Holly and obviously had little regard for a life, animal or human.

Even though Danny's anger at Holly's parents would provide the simplest motive for murder, it just didn't feel right. No matter how she tried, Astrid couldn't believe the young man would then have the gall to marry Holly if he were the killer. He would have to know that she'd find out some day, and then what? Would he then do away with his wife? Not a likely scenario.

It did appear that Judge Rutherford was not a particularly popular man in town or at the college. Professor Vinton told her that much. There again, he mentioned the man's anti-Semitic views, and spoke of a lawyer who filed a lawsuit against the college for hiring him to teach. Too bad Vinton didn't give her the lawyer's name.

At the birthday party, Astrid met three attorneys. One handled the interests of *The Bugle* and the other two were partners, Levitch and Bertram. Mr. Bertram, who sat at their table, spoke with the reserved manner of one who might be burdened by deep secrets. Mr. Levitch approached her to ask if she had any updated information about the encampment at The Kingdom. Now she understood. His step-son was Preston Norman. Could it be that he mistrusted Preston? Perhaps so, since he avoided talking with the sheriff that night.

Daniella Caton made up her own mind about the relationship between Mrs. Levitch and Preston. Astrid almost laughed when she thought about that. But it was a shame that Daniella spread malicious gossip about her neighbor.

Then there was Holly's blood father, Chris. His revelation that he and his friend Drew were parolees nearly floored her. Could Chris have devised a plan for having the Rutherfords killed while he was with Holly in order to have a perfect alibi?

"No," Astrid said aloud.

Maybe she didn't always get it right regarding characters, but she felt certain that Chris was not a murderer. He declared that he was innocent of the murder that got him sentenced to prison, and she couldn't decide whether she believed that or not. But she did know that he wasn't faking his concern over Holly that fateful day of the murder. He nearly cried when he saw her emotional distress.

I just hope he'll tell her everything when she questions him about being outside her friend's house.

The room had become quiet, and apparently the nurse had pulled the blinds shut next to Mrs. Levitch, because everything was dark. Astrid felt sleepy and closed her eyes. The thoughts continued to swirl going from one person to another, asking questions, answering them, and asking again.

"So you're the one."

Astrid blinked away sleep and surprise. She had no idea how long she'd slept.

"Who are you?" she asked of the woman whose wan face nearly touched her own. Oily strands of brownish hair clung to her forehead and cheeks.

"You know who I am. I heard you talking to Preston. Why are you talking to my family? What did he tell you?"

Astrid pushed the woman's face aside and attempted to sit up. When she saw the eyes, like an animal's in headlights, she knew this was not a good situation.

"Mrs. Levitch? Everything's all right, now. Nothing to get excited about."

A knife! Oh my God. She wants to kill me.

"Put the knife down, Mrs. Levitch. Your wrists must hurt. You shouldn't be using them. Don't you want to go back to your own bed and rest?"

Where had she hidden the knife?

"What did he tell you? Did he say what I did?"

Astrid tried to move to the other side of the bed, but Mrs. Levitch got atop the sheet, held the knife above Astrid's neck ready to stab.

"I don't know what you're talking about. No one has told me anything about you."

"Don't lie to me."

She was a slender woman and obviously very spry as well as strong. There was no time to ponder on where the switchblade had been hidden.

"I'd tell you if I knew anything. What do you think I know? Can I help?"

Mrs. Levitch shrieked like an overly excited monkey.

"Help? No one can help. I got justice. I did what needed to be done. Now I want to die, but they won't let me."

She raised the knife.

"Wait! Put it down. You don't want to…"

As the knife descended, Astrid yanked the sheet, forcing Mrs. Levitch to reach out and keep herself from falling off the side of the bed, while Astrid rolled off the other side. Keeping her eye on the knife as she pushed the button for help, Astrid put a hand up to ward off her attacker. Again the knife came at her. Astrid pulled her arm away, but not soon enough. She felt the sharp blade penetrate the fleshy part of the lower left arm.

"Stop it Mrs. Levitch. Stop it. Whatever is wrong, it can be fixed. Just settle down."

Like a mad woman raving unintelligible words, Mrs. Levitch moved with lightning speed. Astrid knew she couldn't overcome her. If her bandaged wrists hurt, she didn't seem to feel the pain, and she wasn't about to stop her attack.

As the knife came toward her again, Astrid did the only one thing she could do. In her loudest voice, she yelled, "Help! I need help now!"

CHAPTER 31

Each time she related the horror of that scene, Astrid had to stop and look to Abram to finish it for her. Even though she was in the warmth and comfort of her own den, the fireplace roaring on this cold Saturday afternoon, she got to that life-threatening part when she screamed for help, and stopped, as Gunnar and Charlotte listened and waited for more.

"I'll take it from there, honey," Abram said. "As you can imagine, Astrid's shout for help was heard all the way to the first floor."

"Don't exaggerate, Abram."

"I'm not. I heard it just before the elevator doors opened. I made a beeline for her room, but I couldn't see her. I went to the other side of her bed, and there she was, on the floor trying to fend off this tiny woman."

"She wasn't all that tiny, Abram. And she was strong. I wish you'd stop exaggerating."

"Whatever you say, dear."

She knew he was teasing, but the thought of that knife striking her still sent chills down her spine.

"He enjoys doing that, you know, Charlotte. And if I didn't say so before, I must say now that you look great. I'm so glad you came. Thank you both."

"When we heard," Charlotte said, "we had to be sure you were okay. I'm so sorry you had such a horrible experience."

"It was horrible. I thought I would die right there. Once Abram got there and got her off me, I saw that I was hurt worse than I thought."

Abram came to the couch and bent over her to smooth strands of hair away from her face.

"Am I telling this or are you?" he said with that sparkle in his eyes that told her how grateful he was he arrived in time to save her life.

"Go on, then."

He returned to the fireplace and stood with an arm on the mantelpiece.

"The two of them were covered in blood. Looked as if they'd bathed in it, and I didn't know whose it was. I got a strangle hold on Mrs. Levitch so that she dropped the knife. By then, nurses and attendants came in and struggled to get her through the door. All that blood was Astrid's. As you see by the patches, her arms were the worst. Her face has a couple of cuts that won't leave a scar, the doctor said. They're all fairly minor cuts."

"I must be a sight," Astrid said.

"Yeah. But everyone knows I'm not the Frankenstein monster."

"Abram! Are you saying I look like the wife of Frankenstein?"

Gunnar joined Abram in laughter, while Charlotte simply smiled and said, "Oh, no. Of course not. Stop it, you two."

"So what happened to Mrs. Levitch?" Gunnar said, "Why did she attack you like that? Just plain crazy or what?"

"Well, as you know we had a double murder recently," Astrid said. "Judge and Mrs. Rutherford were shot in their own home, and the police couldn't find any clues to lead them to the killer. I stumbled onto the fact that Mrs. Levitch had a handyman from the militia group."

"I thought they were disbanded," Gunnar said.

"Ya. But many have returned and picked up where they left off. After all, they did build a town there, you know, and really nice homes. Anyway, I went out to The Kingdom--you probably remember that's what that mountain area is called--to see Geraldine. She had said she was going to marry Preston Norman, and when I called her, she sounded all secretive and begged me to come get her out of there. So that's why I went there, to take her away. But as we were following a path through the woods to the parking lot, I stepped into a bear trap."

"Oh my God, no," Gunnar said.

"Exactly," Abram said.

"If you two will shut up, I'll tell you what happened next. Geraldine couldn't open the trap, so I gave her my keys and told her to go get help."

Gunnar had his hand in the air.

"What is it, Gunnar?"

"Well, call me simple, but why didn't she just go back to the camp and get someone to help?"

Astrid sighed.

"Because she didn't want to run into Preston. At least, that's what she said. So, to make a long story short, she left and I just knew I'd made mistake."

"Huh," Abram grunted.

"Ya, well. I didn't know what I would do until Preston came up the path. He helped me out of the trap and got me to the camp where a nurse dressed the wound."

Abram said to Gunnar in a confidential tone, "And she walked on a broken leg."

"What? Did you, Astrid?" Gunnar said.

"Well, it's only a hairline fracture and not too serious. So, anyway, Preston brought me to Fairchance and left me here. The next day, it hurt pretty bad, so I saw the doctor, who put me in the hospital, just for the day. Now, in the next bed to mine was Mrs. Levitch. She had slashed her wrists in a suicide attempt. Preston came in to see her, and stopped to talk with me. He had gone to her home and found her bleeding after he left me. So we didn't talk much, but Mrs. Levitch thought he told me everything, and that's what set her off against me."

Gunnar and Charlotte said at the same time, "Why?"

"Oh, because she murdered the judge and his wife."

Again, Gunnar said, "Why?"

Astrid looked over at Abram.

"You can do this part better than I can," he said.

"Well," she said, "it seems that Preston is her son. Levitch is her second marriage. However, Preston had a twin brother, Peter. He was a hot head, and got into trouble in New York. They said he was bullied a lot because he was gay. He went to a gay bar there and saw a friend being pushed around, so he jumped into the fight and killed a man. And guess who the judge was at the trial."

"Rutherford."

"That's right. He sent Peter to prison for life, even though he had a good defense lawyer by the name of Levitch."

"His step-father?"

"Right. Well she and he weren't married then, but because of the trial they did get married. Just by coincidence, the judge moved his family to Fairchance. The judge and Levitch would see each other socially once in a while. Mrs. Levitch and Mrs. Rutherford volunteered at the same day care center for children. One day, other volunteers recall now that it's all over, that she went to the center and yelled at Mrs. Rutherford that she and her husband should be satisfied now that justice had been done. She never explained herself, but she was mad because Peter was killed in prison."

"Ah. Now I see. So she shot the couple in revenge," Gunnar said.

Abram said, "Partly. She thought she was exacting justice since the judge was known to have sent many others to their deaths in prison."

"But she couldn't live with the guilt," Charlotte said. "I know that feeling."

Gunnar reached across the chair arm and patted her hand. No words were exchanged.

"That's right," Astrid said. "And when she failed in taking her own life, she simply went out of her mind. I don't know how she got that switchblade into the hospital, but I think it was in her purse and no one bothered to look through it. At any rate, when she heard Preston and me talking, she thought he had told me about her guilt, and tried to kill me so I couldn't say anything."

"Did Preston know that she was the killer?" Gunnar asked.

"I don't really know," Astrid said. "He was the one who provided the car, though he didn't know why his mother wanted it. And she had him meet her at night out of town where she abandoned it. Sheriff Knight claims that the partner to Levitch, Mr. Bertram, knew. If all this hadn't happened, he was ready to turn her in. She had confided in him the most, I guess. No one really knows about Mr. Levitch. He will not be under indictment."

"What will they do to her?" Charlotte asked.

"She'll spend time in the Psych Center," Abram said. "The sheriff said they found the gun, a nine millimeter Luger, when they searched the Levitch house. It had belonged to her first husband."

Astrid laid back on the pillow, exhausted from going over it all again. She closed her eyes and listened to the conversation that followed among the three. Her thoughts turned to Preston, and she wondered if he would become a surgeon. The first time she met him, when he came to her house with Geraldine, she thought he was the wrong man for her niece. Why was that? She thought about his eyes. They appeared to her dopey, in a way. In fact, his attitude had been surly enough that she thought he'd been drinking. Had she been right? Was he a split personality like his brother? And would she ever know one way or the other?

"Honey? Are you asleep?" Abram said.

"No. Just resting my eyes."

"We're going to the kitchen for a snack. Can I bring you something?"

Astrid looked into her husband's eyes and sighed with contentment, as painful as it was.

"Ya. You can serve me up a plateful of justice, dear."

"Huh?"

"Oh nothing. Just wondering if there ever is such a thing as justice. I wonder how many of those Judge Rutherford pronounced guilty were innocent. I wonder how he could justify sending so many offenders to the death penalty, like we heard. I wonder if..."

"Ah, wherever all this is leading, I wonder if you'll just give me an answer. Do you want a snack? An answer today would be appreciated."

"Not now, thanks. I have a lot of thinking to do."

"Maybe you could try not thinking so much? It has a way of getting you into trouble. In the meantime, I'll just go to the kitchen and scare up some sandwiches. You know, like the monster I am."

As he walked, he made the motions of the Frankenstein monster, his arms outstretched, legs wide apart, and his mouth incanting, "Food. Take me to food. Drink and women can come later, master."

"Abram, you can be so aggravating." *But so funny.*

It hurt too much to laugh, and now she wondered if she really did look like the wife of the monster man.

EPILOGUE

Once again Fairchance residents watched TV news to learn more about the conclusion of a murder, this time a double murder, that of Judge and Mrs. Rutherford. Like Daniella Caton, several who watched said, "Just goes to show that even the wealthy elite have skeletons in their closets."

For Holly Rutherford, everything changed. She would never forget the happy years she lived with her adoptive parents. At the same time, she adjusted quickly to the knowledge that Chris Benning was her biological father. In searching through legal papers left behind in the Rutherford house, she discovered her original birth certificate as well as the document of adoption. The last lingering doubt about Chris faded then, and she determined that she would do all she could to make up for the years he paid for the crime he did not commit. When he told her how much he loved her mother, Holly had to believe that he would never have killed her.

The first thing Holly did was to sell the stately old house she inherited and buy the vacant lot which Astrid owned. In another year, she had two homes built on that two-acre empty lot, one for herself and one for Chris and his new wife Sandra. Further, she bought the real estate agency from Letitia Udall and hired

Sandra as her secretary. Chris happily continued to work for Chip's Computers.

Drew Godfrey became full partner with Mr. Bertram when Abe Levitch moved to Florida where he took up residence in a gated senior citizen community. The name of the law firm was changed to Bertram and Godfrey, though Drew became the more sought-after attorney as years went by.

The militia activities at The Kingdom began to diminish, while the men and women living there sought ways other than revolution to improve society. One very wealthy militia member was elected to the U.S. House of Representatives where he became a leader in the neo conservative movement that began to disrupt government in its own obstructionist way.

As for the Lincolns, Abram became a deputy sheriff. He continued to caution Astrid not to get involved in dangerous investigations, but she never could avoid tackling a good challenge when it came along.